THE
LINE

A WITCHING SAVANNAH NOVEL

D0089550

THE
LINE

A WITCHING SAVANNAH NOVEL

J.D. HORN

Text copyright © 2014 by J.D. Horn

Published by 47North, Seattle
www.apub.com

Cover illustrated by Patrick Arrasmith

ISBN-13: 9781477809730
ISBN-10: 1477809732
Library of Congress Control Number: 2013939891

For Rich, who brings magic into every life he touches

ONE

"All right, you handsome devils, if y'all are here for this evening's Liar's Tour of Savannah, then you are at the right place," I said, surveying the group of men who had found their way to the Waving Girl statue. Four middle-aged corporate types, young enough not to have gone completely soft from life behind a desk, old enough that moving them around too quickly in the Savannah heat would be a little risky.

"Now the bad news is that it is hot," I said while slipping off my backpack and fishing out four Liar's Tour souvenir plastic cups. A trickle of sweat rolled down my back as I handed them out. Anyone who truly thought ladies didn't sweat never spent the summer in Georgia. "The good news is that it is legal in Savannah's historic district to imbibe on the streets as long as you are over twenty-one." I hesitated before the last member of my pack, who had a full head of silver hair. "You are twenty-one, aren't you?" I smiled and winked at him.

"At least twice over," his buddy said and laughed. I handed the cup over.

I pulled a large thermos of gin and tonic from my backpack. "Sorry, the ice cubes may have watered this down a bit, but we'll hit River Street next and you can pick your own poison." I looked

1

around to make sure the coast was clear before filling their cups. My twenty-first birthday was still a couple of weeks away, and I didn't have a license to serve liquor. I'd never had any problems before, but I didn't want to press my luck by snubbing the law right under an officer's nose. I dropped the empty thermos back into my bag and swung it over my shoulder. Its weight pulled the front of my shirt tighter, and I noticed that the men were appreciating the view. As long as they didn't touch, they could look for a bit. I counted down to myself: Five-four-three-two-one. Enough. I waved a finger in front of my face to direct their gaze upward.

"I am very pleased to meet you all. My name is Mercy Taylor, and I am a native Savannahian. I'm going to take you fine upstanding gentlemen around town, get you a little buzzed, and tell you some black and wicked lies about the people of my dear home. Now you might ask why I would make up lies about a city with so many interesting true stories to tell." I looked directly at the roundest one and paused. "Go on, ask . . ."

He smiled. "Well, why would you?"

"Let me tell you why. First of all, most of the 'truths'"—I stretched out the word to the point of irony—"you are going to hear about Savannah have been so embellished as to be unrecognizable to those who lived through the circumstances. And frankly, by the time I turned twelve, I was already sick to death of hearing the same old stories over and over again. One fine summer day I was complaining to my dear Uncle Oliver about this fact, so he filled up a traveler cup very much like the ones you hold in your hands and let me lead him around, paying me a dollar for every colorful lie I could come up with on the spot." I paused again and gave them a very serious look. "Now, when it comes time to tip your guide, please do remember that Oliver is family, and that my cost of living has greatly increased since I was twelve."

The guys laughed, and I smiled. "But honestly, I think the real reason I do it is 'cause my Aunt Iris volunteers for the historical society, and it pisses her off to no end when she hears one of my tales being repeated as gospel. Take, for example, my story about this fine lady here." I motioned to the statue of Florence Martus. "Florence here was known as Savannah's Waving Girl. What everyone else in town is going to tell you is that young Florence got her heart broken by some sailor, who left promising to return and marry her. Between 1887 and 1931, she came out to meet every single ship pulling into Savannah, hoping that her man might be on board. Tragic story of an innocent girl done wrong, right?"

"Sounds like it," one of my group chimed in. He was a pleasant looking guy with glasses and thinning hair.

"Okay," I snorted, "you expect me to believe that any woman is going to come out and wave at ships for forty-four years just because she was waiting on some man? You boys sure know how to flatter yourselves." I rolled my eyes, and my fellows all laughed on cue.

"So what was really going on here, I found myself asking, and I came to the following conclusion: Florence Martus, Savannah's own Waving Girl, was involved in the transport of contraband goods, and all this waving she was doing was actually her way of signaling information to the smugglers. Think about it. A code based upon what color apron she was waving and different signaling patterns would be complex enough to tell them everything they needed to know about where, when, and with whom they should be transacting their business. This woman was the center of one of the world's greatest and longest-lasting black market rings, importing everything from slaves to opium, you name it. Heck, during Prohibition half the rum in this country was welcomed into port by our Florence. Broken heart? Maybe. Fat bank account, for sure." I pointed at the dog by her side. "I bet even her collie there wore diamonds at home.

"Now if you will all bid adieu to Miss Florence and follow me, we will head up River Street, where I am going to introduce you to some of the deadliest frozen concoctions you will ever taste." I turned and began to lead the way to where King Cotton had abdicated in favor of the tourist bars and restaurants that now fueled the city's economy.

"Mind the cobblestones," I warned as we approached the old ballast-lined roadway. "They've been the death of more than a few people, and not just from tripping over them. Back in Savannah's dueling days the men who were too poor for pistols used these stones as weapons. Many an argument were ended by a well-aimed shot-put or slingshot."

The River Street regulars—the shopkeepers, the homeless, and the waiters—waved when they saw me and called out my name as we passed. I hadn't been lying to the guys when I'd told them I was a native. My family had been in Savannah since shortly after the Civil War. We were a part of its weft and weave, even if we weren't to be counted among its founding families.

I led the group to the frozen drink bar and waited outside, mentally plotting out our route and spinning through my standard list of lies. I would lead the guys counterclockwise through the city, stopping upstairs at Factors Walk where I'd point out the ironwork from the old Wetter mansion. Then I'd share my malicious theory that the missing body of Alberta Wetter's relative, Mrs. Haig, had been served to the family as their Christmas Eve dinner by a kitchen slave whom Mrs. Haig had mistreated. Next, I'd take them down Bull Street, not only because it was the oldest street in Georgia, but also because it was a fittingly named path for the Liar's Tour. We'd work our way over and stop at the Juliette Gordon Low house, where I'd talk about how the CIA once used Girl Scout cookies to test the effects of LSD on a wide population. Outbreak of UFO sightings, anybody?

I'd spin a few tall tales along the way about anything that caught the guys' attention, until we had made our way over to Colonial Park Cemetery. There, I would relate how the Nobel Jones family came to change their name to De Renne. Of course my story didn't play out well on any conventional timeline, but making the apocryphal Rene Rondolier, historic Savannah's answer to Boo Radley, the progenitor of the surviving branch of the Jones line made for great storytelling. Forbidden love, two murdered children, trumped up charges. It was the kind of tall tale people wanted to believe, even when I kept repeating with every other breath that I was lying through my teeth. It had also very nearly sent Aunt Iris into a fit of apoplexy, so I tried to use it only a few times a year. I'd pick out a few stones on Colonial's back wall to talk about and then I'd drop the group off at the Pirate's House, where they could have dinner or carry on with their drinking, whichever they chose.

I put on my best smile to welcome the guys as they spilled out of the bar and back onto the street. "Room for one more?" a newcomer asked. It was Tucker Perry, a middle-aged lawyer and real-estate developer. His blond curls were carefully coiffed to appear carelessly tousled, and they framed soulless pale blue eyes. He glowed with a golfer's tan and the easy insincerity of a man who has always believed he's at the top of the food chain. "I've been wanting to come with you for quite a while, and there's no time like the present."

"We're already under way, maybe some other time," I said, using my best poker face to hide my distaste for the man.

"Oh come on now, Mercy." He smiled, narrowing his eyes in a way I am sure he thought was seductive. "Let me tag along, I promise I won't be any trouble." The guys shifted a little, waiting for a cue from me. I held my ground, and Tucker took it as a challenge. "Has she told you any of the spooky stuff yet?" he questioned the others. "I'm not talking the ghost stuff. You know our girl Mercy here is a witch, right? She and her whole family."

Everyone knew the Taylors, and ever since our arrival, Savannah's tribal knowledge has allowed that we were witches, even though most of the tribe didn't really understand what the word "witch" meant. My family had always had enough money to ensure a welcome into polite society, but in most situations, that welcome never extended beyond the most superficial of levels. Truth was, we'd always been held at a respectful arm's length, sensed to be useful but dangerous—kind of like a nuclear power plant. People liked to benefit from our presence, but they didn't want to think about us too often or in too much detail.

But while my family tree was electric with power, I had none of it. As fate would have it, I was the first total dud in a line of witches that could be traced back at least six hundred years. Although no one other than my Aunt Iris's husband would ever say so openly, my family viewed my lack of power as an unfortunate if not entirely debilitating birth defect. Well, maybe that's too strong. Maybe they saw it as being on par with my ginger coloring—not ideal, but nothing to be ashamed of.

"Mr. Perry, if I had any magic powers, I assure you that I would use them to make you disappear," I said, provoking a laugh from my group.

Perry didn't like being refused, and he liked being laughed at even less. "No seriously, Mercy. Tell them," he said. Then, turning toward the men, "Trust me, her aunt Ellen and I have shared some very unusual pillow talk."

"I think we should continue on with our tour," I said, ignoring Tucker's comment. "Maybe another time, Mr. Perry."

"Oh, I do hope so, Miss Taylor," he said, reaching out to touch me. I stepped back quickly, and my guys stepped in between us, forming a protective wall. Over their shoulders I could see Perry lifting his hands in surrender, an oily smile on his face. He turned and started walking south on River Street, but then stopped and called back to me.

"Mercy, remind Ellen that I will be picking her up tonight for Tillandsia. As soon as you and Maisie turn twenty-one, you'll both be very welcome. I'd love to be your sponsor. After all, it was your mama who brought me into the fold." Tucker's mention of my mother made my stomach turn. It was bad enough to know my aunt was involved with him. I certainly didn't want to consider the possibility that my mother had once had a connection to him. The thought was enough to make me lose my game face, and my guys noticed it.

"Are you okay?" the tall one asked. He probably had a daughter my age, I realized. "Do we need to worry about him for you?"

"Why no, not at all," I said and managed a not-too-fake sounding laugh. I was getting too good at this lying game. "You just witnessed a bit of our local color."

"What was this Tillandsia thing he was talking about?" the round one asked.

The Tillandsia Club was a dinosaur, a throwback to the days when Savannah society was still comprised of iron magnates and wannabe railroad barons. Its ranks have included senators, congressmen, governors, bankers, judges, and other such white collar thieves. Social democratization had passed Tillandsia by entirely. Even today, the only way in was to be sponsored by a member in good standing. The members of the club wanted to be able to get their good times on without word of their behavior getting out and tarnishing their public image. Tillandsia was one of the few groups to which my family's wealth had opened the door, and since Ellen could drink a man twice her size under the table, it seemed like a natural fit for her.

"Tillandsia is the genus of Spanish moss," I said, gesturing widely at a cluster of trees that were visible from where we stood on River Street. "It's also the name of my aunt's gardening club." I lied about the club if not the classification of the plant, knowing that it would help move the guys off the subject. "Onward and upward, gentlemen!"

Our route would take us over some large cobblestones and up some uneven steps, and I knew it would be best to get the guys past these hurdles before their drinks kicked in. I hustled them over to the trees between the Old Savannah Cotton Exchange and Bay Street, releasing any thoughts of Tucker Perry as I breathed in the dappled golden light, letting Savannah possess me. One of the ghost tours passed by, and the guide raised his hand to me in greeting as he carried on talking about Moon River Brewing and the ghosts that bump around on the building's upper floors. The only hauntings I ever mentioned on my tour were the ones I knew to be false, particularly if they could be twisted into stories that were funnier than they were creepy. After all, I advertised as the Liar's Tour.

Truth was, there was magic in Savannah, magic that was beyond that of the Taylors. Sometimes I wondered if my family had come here in an attempt to tame this raw energy or maybe even harness it and make it their own. Savannah had the power to hold people long after their final sell-by date had been carved into marble. You didn't need to be a witch, or even a psychic, to see spirits in Savannah—you just had to pay attention.

I let the tour proceed on automatic. The guys were happy just to be outside in the warm evening air, momentarily free from the pressures of work and family, with a more than adequate, but still legal, blood alcohol content. My stories flowed without interruption until Drayton Street, when one of the guys asked, "So this cemetery we're going to, is it the one from that *Garden at Midnight* movie?"

"No, that is Bonaventure," I said, moving swiftly past the thought that my own mama was buried in Bonaventure. Death and life, death in life. The two weren't just joined at the hip in Savannah, they were downright symbiotic. Witches, even powerful ones like my mama had been, aren't immortal. Their lives are just as fragile as anyone else's. "We are going to visit Colonial. Bonaventure is still an active cemetery," I said. "There haven't been any burials in Colonial since the 1850s. Everyone who loved anyone who's buried there has long since passed themselves."

I forced a smile onto my face and began my tale about Rene Rondolier, arriving beneath the Daughters of the American Revolution eagle just as I got to the part about the illicit love affair between the giant and the Savannah belle. Sunset was still over an hour away, but the keepers of Colonial kept to a fixed calendar regardless of the sun's opinion. "The gates are going to be locked soon, so let's duck in real fast and head toward the back wall," I said and began to guide them toward the tombstone-lined wall. I was still talking when I realized that the guys had fallen back; their attention had shifted from me to some fracas that was going on near the center of the cemetery.

An elderly but still sturdy woman with skin as dark as coffee was trundling along in a line as straight as the few remaining monuments would allow toward the gate we had entered moments before. I recognized her instantly. Known as Mother Jilo, she was a worker of Hoodoo, Savannah's response to New Orleans's Voodoo. The main difference between the two was that Hoodoo had at some point become decoupled from the African gods, leaving behind only the practice of sympathetic magic, a conjuring method that uses like to affect like. "Sympathetic" had always struck me as a rather warm and fuzzy term for a brand of magic that was most often used to seduce away otherwise faithful spouses and bring about the death of enemies. Over time, Hoodoo had even taken on a decidedly Protestant flavor, coming to be known as "root magic," meaning that its power was rooted in the Bible itself. Those who practiced it, or at least practiced it well, were known as "root doctors."

Jilo was the undisputed queen of Savannah's root doctors, the large brim of her yellow sun hat shading cruel and mercenary eyes, her folding chair serving as the throne from where she ruled her empire. Only a local fool or an outsider ignorant of Savannah's ways would ever mistake Jilo as anything other than the powerful tyrant that she was.

A much younger woman followed in Jilo's wake, scurrying to catch up to her. When she got in front of Jilo, she collapsed onto her hands and knees. "Mother! I beg of you! I want to take it back," she half moaned, half screamed as she reached out, trying to catch the older woman by the ankle.

Even in the failing light, my eyes were dazzled by the colors of Jilo's ensemble—a large daffodil yellow sun hat and a violently purple dress that probably once fit her but now hung loosely from her bones. Her outfit was jarring against the vibrant green of the folded lawn chair she was half carrying, half using as a cane and the small red cooler she was clutching in her other hand. I shuddered as I considered the likely contents of the cooler.

"What do you think is going on there?" one of my guys asked as I approached them.

"I think that is something we best stay out of," I responded.

Jilo managed to avoid the woman's frantic grasp, stopping to swat at her with the chair. "Jilo done told you it too late to take back."

"But I was wrong," the woman cried, ducking her head beneath her raised arms. "He never cheated on me."

"Well that between you and yo' man." Jilo wheezed and took another lumbering step toward the gate of the cemetery.

"But he's going to die, Mother!" The desperation in the woman's voice was heartbreaking. The tall, paternal member of my group stepped in front of me, placing himself as a protective barrier between me and the unpleasant goings-on. Lord knows, growing up in Savannah, I'd seen much worse skirmishes than this little drama. I poked my head out around him.

"That right, he is," Jilo responded, her voice as cold as ice water. "That what you done paid Jilo for." The old woman straightened her back and coughed repeatedly, then bent and spat on the ground.

"But I was wrong! I'm sorry." The woman fell facedown into the turf, sobbing.

"That ain't Jilo's fault. Now, if you want Jilo's help getting a new man, you let her know. That she can help you with, but yo' old man, he as good as gone, and the quicker you get used to it, the better." Jilo continued on her way as though nothing untoward had happened, passing beneath the eagle as we silently watched her.

"That was really quite extraordinary," the tall guy said in an undertone. "This 'mother' arranges murders for hire?"

"Isn't that a police station on the other side of the wall there? Should we maybe go report this?" my round fellow asked. Beads of sweat had popped up on top of his bald head.

"That would be a waste of time," I responded. "The police know exactly what she's up to."

"And they don't do anything about it?"

"Honestly, there isn't much they could do. You see, Mother Jilo isn't any kind of hit man, she's a magic worker."

"A witch?" the tall one asked, laughing. The sobbing woman had pulled herself up off the ground and was weaving toward the exit as falteringly as a drunk.

"No, definitely not a witch," I said, "but as close as you can get to one without being the genuine article. She works spells for revenge, for money, for *love* . . ." I was suddenly struck with an idea that I wasn't comfortable entertaining. It was the kind of idea that could lead me down a path I knew better than to tread.

"For gullible people, like that poor soul," the quietest member of my crew chimed in.

For a few moments the guys stood around, staring wordlessly at me. "Ah, I get it," the round one blurted out with a snort. "You're still lying to us aren't you?"

I laughed along with him. "You got me," I lied. "I don't have the slightest idea what any of that was about." I heard the bells from St. John's begin to ring the hour. It was 8 P.M., and I knew the city workers would show up at any moment to lock Colonial up for the night. "Come on, y'all," I said, moving toward the gate. "I am going to introduce you to the ghost of Billy Bones."

TWO

"Mercy!" Sam's gravelly whisper carried across the field like the call of a cicada. Even at this distance and in the dark, I recognized the old man. The moon reinforced the silver in his hair and his pronounced limp as he hurried toward me. "Mercy, you know you should not be here. Not even during the day, but specially not at night," he said as he reached me.

"It's okay, Sam . . ." I tried to protest, but he interrupted me.

"No, it is not okay. There are men out here—hell, even *women*—who'd rape you or kill you just for the fun of it."

"Sam, I'm just a couple of miles from home," I said.

"And you are a world away. Normandy Street ain't your Savannah. Trust me on this," he said, reaching out in an attempt to place a wrinkled hand on my shoulder. "I know you think you safe 'cause you a Taylor, but they some people out here, they no better than animals. They might decide killing you a smart way to make they mark." He paused. "Let me accompany you home. I've known you since you were a tiny little thing. It'd kill this old man to let him think he let something happen to you." I didn't have the heart to tell him that he was already dead, that his body had been turned over to the medical school three months ago. Now Sam was just another spirit caught in Savannah's web.

"I'm here on business, Sam," I told him, easily moving through his grip. The smell of sweat and booze nearly brought tears to my eyes. Even in the afterlife, the homeless man was best loved from upwind.

"Now what kind of business could you possibly have out here?" he asked. "Just who do you need to see here at this time of night?"

"I'm here to see Mother Jilo," I replied.

His bright eyes bulged out of his thin face. His mouth fell open to reveal gums that were pocked here and there with a few remaining teeth. "Girl, you ain't got no kind of business with Jilo. Your Aunt Ginny would skin you alive if she knew you out here in the middle of the night to talk with a juju doctor."

My great-aunt Ginny Taylor was the true seat of the family power in more ways than one, and an insufferable tyrant to boot. "It was Ginny who sent me." I hated lying to Sam, but if I didn't, he might take it into his head to inform Ginny, which would be disastrous. If there was one person Ginny held more deeply in contempt than me, it was Jilo. I couldn't risk that he would take it upon himself to look after what he thought were my best interests by going to Ginny.

"You telling me the truth now?" he asked, eyes narrowed. I nodded my head yes, and he let out a deep sigh. Who knew that a ghost could sigh? "Your Aunt Ginny, she gotta understand. It's a different world than it used to be. When I was young, your people were respected. Everybody knew not to lay a finger on one of y'all. The young ones these days, they don't respect nothing and they don't fear much."

"They fear Jilo," I said.

"That's because Jilo deals with them on their own terms. A gangbanger cross her and a gangbanger gets killed—or worse.

Frankly, it has been a long time since y'all have given them anything to fear. Everybody think your family is toothless."

"Well, they are soon to find out otherwise," I bluffed. "That's the reason Ginny sent me here to talk in secret with Jilo." I paused for a moment then added, "She'd be angry if she knew how much I've told you."

"You swear to me that Ginny know you here, and you under her protection?"

"I swear," I assured him.

"Then I'll let you get on with your business, but you mind yourself," he said. He turned and headed back the way I'd just come. I watched as he moved noiselessly across the empty field then dissipated beneath one of the street lights on Randolph. I settled my bike down into the tall grass, praying that it wouldn't catch the attention of anyone who might have a mind to steal it.

Before me lay the beginning of Normandy Street, which wasn't really a street at all, at least not anymore. Time had taken its toll, and now it was more like the memory of a street. Choked in parts with barbed greenery, it intersected the old railroad tracks but not much else.

Sam had tried to warn me off with good reason. It was one of Savannah's well-known secrets that there was a homeless encampment not far from here, north of the cemetery and west of the golf course. But that wasn't where I was headed. A little way down, Normandy Street was intersected by a narrow lane that had long ago lost its name, assuming it had ever had one. Jilo ran the commercial end of her practice out of Colonial Park Cemetery, but it was at this crossroads where she performed her art.

I took a deep breath and dove into the thickets that formed the gateway between the Baptist church's parking lot and no-man's-land. It felt like every living green thing was clawing at my ankles and begging me to have the good sense to turn back. If they were, I ignored them, heading farther down the path instead. I stumbled over a beer bottle and thought about turning on the flashlight I had brought in my backpack. But then I remembered that anything that made it easier for me to see would make it easier for me to be seen. The moonlight would have to be enough of a guide.

One thing was for sure: This was a place for those who had nothing left to lose. Remembering how very much I had to lose, I walked slowly and carefully, listening for movement. As I drew nearer to the spot where I hoped to find Mother Jilo, I sensed, more than heard, a presence. It moved with me, stopping when I stopped. It seemed both intelligent and feral. Suddenly an empty glass bottle was thrown out of nowhere, splintering into shards at my feet. It took everything I had not to scream like a little girl and run, but I held my ground.

"Everybody know this here crossroad belong to Mother Jilo." A voice spoke from the darkness. "A precious little white girl like you should think twice before she go digging around here. She might not like what she turn up."

I scanned the bushes, sensing menace but seeing nothing. "Is that you, Mother? I've come to see you," I called out in the direction of the voice. "I need your help."

Her brittle laughter preceded her footfalls. "Jilo thought her help was beneath you Taylors. That right," she said stepping out from the trees and onto the moonlit road. "Jilo recognize you. She know who you are. You Mercy Taylor."

Mother Jilo herself stood there before me, dressed mostly in black now, with a scarf of a dark but indeterminate color tied around her head. An aged leather satchel, kind of like an old doctor's bag, was clutched in one gnarled hand, and the other held a squirming burlap sack. She sat the satchel on the ground, but held tight to the sack. "Jus' what kind of 'help' you wantin' from Jilo?" she asked, circling me counterclockwise, keeping her eyes tightly on me. "'Cause, girl, only thing Jilo inclined to help a Taylor to is an early grave."

I turned in time with her movements, determined to keep her in front of me. "I need you to work a spell for me, Mother. I can pay," I said, but she started shaking and waving her free hand at me.

Laughter tore through her, and her chest started to heave and rattle until she coughed up phlegm. "A high and mighty Taylor witch wanting to hire Mother Jilo to work juju?" She gasped out the words, punctuating them with more mucus. She coughed again then caught her wind. "So tell Jilo now," she said, her eyes burning bright with the desire to do harm, "who is you wanting to curse?"

"I-I," I stammered, "I'm not wanting to curse anyone."

"Well what is it you-you-you is wanting to do then?" She mocked me. She looked up at the sky. "The moon be headin' to dark. You got your red head here nosin' around lookin' for Jilo. And it after midnight. If you ain't come for cursin', you must not know what the hell you doin'." She paused. "So you tell Jilo. What you doin' here at her crossroad?"

"I came to see you. I want you to work a spell for me. I can pay," I repeated myself. Here, in the middle of the night, in the middle of nowhere, standing before Savannah's busiest root doctor, I felt my cheeks heat with embarrassment. I couldn't look the woman in her eyes. Instead, my focus fell to the grimy ground near her feet. "There's a boy," I began.

"Of course they a boy," she said. "They always a boy when a girl your age come to Jilo. I seen him. That pretty young man your sister been leading around by the nose lately. You in love with him, ain't you? You want Mother to help you steal him from your sister. You want Mother to work you a love spell," she said, stretching the word "love" out until it was something dirty. "Little miss got an itch she need scratched." With her free hand, Jilo rubbed her crotch and laughed again, the croaking sound scaring an owl from a nearby limb.

The old woman was right. I loved Jackson, my sister's boyfriend, more than I could find the words to say . . . and had since the moment she'd brought him home six months ago. A mere glance from him made my pulse race and fire rush through me, and I envied my sister his touch. God, how I envied her. But I loved her too.

"No. Yes. I mean," I stammered, but she interrupted me before I could explain.

"Now Jilo ask herself, why don't pretty little miss just work it for herself? Just don't want to get those dainty little hands dirty? Or don't you want the magic to be trailed back to you? But then again," Jilo continued, "you ain't like the rest of your people, are you? That sister of yours. What her name?" she asked.

"Maisie," I responded.

She acknowledged the name with a slight nod of her head. "Between you two, she got all the power, ain't she? That mean you gotta do the work just like Mother herself."

It was true, Maisie, my fraternal twin, was capable of performing just about any miracle she set her mind to. I couldn't even move a pen without using my fingers. Between the two of us, Maisie had won the genetic lottery, there was no use denying it. Along with her blond hair and bottomless blue eyes, she had gotten all of the power. "It's true," I said. "I don't have any power. I'm not a natural born witch."

She moved in close to me, so close I could smell her sour breath. "Jilo ain't no natural born witch, but you think she ain't got no power?" she asked, her eyes fixing on me. They were black,

I noticed now—the irises and pupils merged together into bottomless, burning pits. "You need her to show you what she can do?"

"No," I responded quickly. The fear in my voice placated her, and she smiled. "It's just that you know how to tap into the power. I don't."

"Girl, ain't your family never taught you nothing?"

"They taught me that the power isn't something you can simply draw into yourself. It's the other way around. A true witch springs from the power. The people who borrow the power, they aren't real witches. They can steal it from time to time, but the power escapes quickly when it's clenched in a fist."

"Oh, that is old Ginny Taylor talkin' there. No doubt about it," she said. Her gnarled hand clenched and released as if it were aching to strike out.

"You saying it isn't true?" I asked, taking a step back.

"No, no. It true enough. That old auntie of yours, she ain't been lyin' to you. But it ain't the whole picture. Just 'cause you don't own something, don't mean you gotta steal it. Nothin' stopping you from borrowing it from time to time. And 'sides, Jilo ain't never claimed to be any kind of witch."

"But you can work magic . . ." I started.

"Of course Mother know how to work the magic. You ain't gotta be no witch to work the magic. It just take a bit longer. And you gotta be willing to make a few sacrifices." She shook the burlap sack at me and laughed again as the creature inside began to gyrate frantically. "For a girl like you, it simple enough to learn a trick or two, so why then your family not teach you like Jilo done taught herself?" She didn't wait for a response. "Jilo tell you why. They look down on Jilo 'cause she has to borrow the power. They'd rather you be ignorant than you be like Jilo."

I said nothing, as I knew she was right. My family, especially my great-aunt Ginny, did look down on the old woman of the crossroads. Jilo stayed silent too, coiled up as if she were waiting for me to argue with her.

The silence grew too much for me. "Ginny says your kind of magic is dangerous. That it weakens the line."

"Oh, Jilo heard your Ginny going on about her precious line," she said, her tension fading. "How it's what keeps the monsters from crawling up out from under Jilo's bed and eating her." She chuckled. "But Jilo ain't no little girl to scare with talk of demons."

"They're real—you know that, right?" I asked, modulating my voice so that she wouldn't think I was talking down to her.

"Course they real," Jilo shot back at me. "Jilo know that. But keeping them out of our world, that yo' people's problem, not Jilo's."

I wondered how much the old woman knew about what the line was, or how it was created. Probably not a whole lot more than I did. The details about the creation of the line were a tightly kept secret from those of us who weren't born of the power. We only got the story in broad strokes, if we ever learned about it at all. All I knew was that it was the witches, people like my family, who saved our reality from the monsters who had once ruled it. Religion calls these beings "demons"; science might call them "interdimensional entities." But whatever you call them, they came to our world. They made us their slaves. They fed on us like cattle. They meddled in the evolution of humans, and even more so in the evolution of witches. But they underestimated their own creations. Eventually we rebelled.

Witches used their magic to change the frequency we live on. Kind of like when you switch the station on the radio to tune out a song you don't want to hear, they swung our world just out of the demons' reach. They modulated the energy of our world just enough so that the scary things don't get picked up. Of course the witches who moved us out of harm's way couldn't pick and choose which magical beings to allow into our reality. In order to get rid of the demons, we lost the unicorn. Most magical creatures didn't make it through the great energy shift with us. Given the demons' taste for human newborns, though, I figured it was a fair trade-off.

Once our world was out of harm's way, the witches raised the line, a safety net of energy that prevented our former masters from burrowing their way back in. The witches who maintained the line were called anchors, and only these anchors know how the line was created or how it might be destroyed. Originally there were thirteen anchors at a time, one from each of the witch families, but three of the families came to regret their part in the rebellion. Now the line was maintained by anchors from the remaining ten united families.

Ginny was the only anchor I had ever met. I didn't really know what being an anchor entailed, but I knew that it had left Ginny bitter and alone, even though she was surrounded by family.

"The world lost a lot of its magic when they shifted us," Jilo said. "The witches, like yo' family. They try and act like they did some noble thing for the rest of us. But all they did was take every last bit of the magic left in this world for themselves. They built a kingdom where they the kings, and they can do whatever the hell they want with the rest of us. And Jilo s'posed to act like they doin' her a favor."

I disagreed with her interpretation, but Jilo didn't give me the chance to respond. She had already shifted gears anyway. "Jilo sure love to see that Ginny's face right now. The look she get when she see you standing here before Mother Jilo asking her for help to steal yo' sister's man." She cackled and spat on the ground.

"You don't understand. I don't want to take Jackson from Maisie," I said. "There's another boy. His name is Peter. He's my . . . I'm not sure what he is. Outside of Maisie he's the best friend I ever had. He's wonderful. He's perfect. He should be my boyfriend. He loves me, and I want you to make me fall in love with him."

Jilo tore the night apart with her amused screech. The night birds stopped their calls, and even the insects fell silent in wonder. Although we stood in the moon's low light, I could still see the tears streaming from her eyes. It took some moments for her to pull herself back together. I felt the blood rush to my face, the heat of embarrassment changing into anger. "You want Mother to work a love spell on you?" She shook her head incredulously. "You ain't got no idea how magic work, do you?" she asked, but the sharpness in her tone had given way to something like sympathy.

Her softness got to me in a way her derision had not. "I'm sorry," I said backing away hastily. "I shouldn't have wasted your time. I didn't realize you couldn't work the spell."

"Not so fast, missy. Jilo never said she couldn't work this spell you wantin'. She just say you don't understand what it would take."

"I said I can pay you," I replied tersely.

"Lord help, girl. Jilo ain't talkin' about money. She talking about mojo." She looked at me as if she were being asked to explain green to grass. "When people come to Jilo for a love spell, they come with a fire inside them. They burnin' for the person they want, and Jilo use they fire to work the spell. You come to Jilo lovin' the one man and wanting her to make you love another. They nothing but guilt in you. Guilt for lovin' the one. Guilt for not lovin' t'other. Jilo, she can use guilt for laying down revenge, but she sure can't use it for love."

"Then what would it take for you to work the spell for me?"

"Blood," she spat at me. "It take blood!"

"I couldn't let you hurt an animal for me," I eyed the burlap guiltily.

"It take a lot more blood than the hen Jilo got in this croaker sack," she responded.

"You could use my blood." I just couldn't carry on feeling the way I felt for Jackson, knowing how much Maisie loved him, and how devoted Peter was to me. Even if my feelings weren't wrong, they were dangerous and destructive, and they were burning me up inside. I had to find a way to control them, not let them control me. If I could have found the strength in myself to do so, I wouldn't be standing here offering my blood to Jilo, but I had no strength when it came to Jackson.

She shook her head again. "It take all the blood you got. And then the spell do you no good anyway."

"I can't hurt anyone," I said, realizing my case was hopeless.

"Mercy. Folk like us, like you and Jilo. We want power, we got to be willing to sacrifice for it. You love your sister, right?"

"Yes, of course I do. That's why I'm here," I responded.

"Well Jilo loved her sister too. Jilo loved her more than anything in the whole wide world. And this crossroad where we standin'. This here where Jilo done buried her. Jilo cut her and buried her right here, right beneath your pretty little feet. Jilo buried her while she still breathing, so that her blood and spirit would spill into the ground. That why this crossroad and the power in it belong to Jilo."

"I can't do this. I can't be here," I said, my head starting to spin. My stomach lurched at the thought of being near this woman for even a moment longer.

"People like us, we gotta make a wound to draw from. If you ain't willing to sacrifice, you ain't never gonna know the power. Jilo get this much mojo from her sister, imagine what you could do with yo' Maisie in the ground beneath yo' feet." She stopped and leered at me, licking the spittle from around her lips. "My sister, she about dry now. But that Maisie. You could draw off her forever."

"I'm leaving now," I said, more for my own benefit than hers. I was not like her, and I never would be. I started to walk away.

"Jilo gonna work that spell for you."

I stopped and turned back toward her. "I changed my mind. I don't want your help. Forget I came."

"Too late," she replied. "You done asked."

"I won't give you anything. I won't pay you."

"Jilo don' care, little girl. She gonna do it, just 'cause she lookin' forward to see how it gonna play out."

I started walking again, forcing myself not to run. I prayed to God and all my ancestors that she was bluffing. Getting what I wanted, what I came to this crossroads for, would be a curse now, knowing now its source was rooted in murder.

"You give my best to Ginny," she called out behind me, squawks of laughter mixing again with hacks of phlegm.

THREE

Great-Aunt Ginny summoned me shortly after sunrise, the message being passed on to me by Aunt Iris. Ginny dealt with me directly as little as possible, so I knew it spelled trouble. Sam mustn't have fallen for my story. Or maybe he had believed me, but had gone to see Ginny anyway.

"I have no idea what this is about," Iris said to me as she poured her husband Connor another cup of coffee. "But I suspect that you do."

"Just what have you been up to, girl?" Connor asked, shifting his massive bulk on his chair. He gave me a steely glare from behind his towering stack of pancakes.

"I haven't been up to anything," I replied, pouring myself some juice. I did my best to look innocent and not think of Jilo.

"You might as well come clean now, darlin'," Iris said, taking the pitcher from my hand. "Maybe then I can plead with Ginny on your behalf."

"I don't need you to plead for me," I said, suddenly angry. "I am tired of Ginny and the way she thinks she can boss everyone in this family around. It's about time someone stood up to her."

Connor laughed and leaned back in his chair. "Well, we all wish you luck with that. But when she hands you your ass in a brown paper bag, don't you come crying to me."

"She wants you there by nine," Iris said, shaking her head. "Do not be late."

I wasn't about to give them the satisfaction of hearing me slam the door, so I went out quietly. Ginny wanted to see me by 9:00. Fine. She'd obviously caught wind of my visit with Mother Jilo, even if she didn't know the specifics of why I went. I had no doubt that she was furious, and that I was going to catch all seven shades of hell from her.

I had plenty of time, so I figured I would at least take the scenic path to my execution. I grabbed my bike from the garage and headed toward the river, in the exact opposite direction of Ginny's house. I spun up to Columbia Square and stopped in front of the Davenport place. The house was one of Savannah's many officially haunted locations, with one unique twist—the resident ghost was a cat. Ever since I was little, I had used this place as a barometer when I was worried about something. If things were going to turn out okay, I would always spot the spectral old tomcat staring out the window. If I didn't see him . . . well, things were generally not going to go my way. I waited in the square for ten minutes watching the windows. "Here, kitty, kitty," I called softly then decided to hell with it. Let Ginny bring on her worst. She had been trying to run my life for twenty years. Enough was enough. Today was going to be my independence day.

St. John's bells carried over the sound of Savannah's "rush hour," and I counted eight peals. Out of nowhere the thought came to me that Peter would shortly be arriving at a site a little off Chatham Square, where he and his crew were renovating an apartment building. I had to see him. I had to know if Jilo had held true to her promise, a promise that had felt more like a threat. I hated myself for having gone to her, and my one consolation about the chewing out that Ginny undoubtedly had in store for me was that she'd be able to heavily curtail, if not completely disable, any magic Jilo had sent my way.

Before I even registered what I was doing, I was back on my bike, heading toward Peter's work site, which was just past Aunt Ginny's house. I zigzagged to Taylor Street, passing Calhoun Square and then Monterey Square, where a group of retirees were busy snapping photos of Mercer House. I made a wide berth of Ginny's house, because I certainly didn't want the old biddy to spot me on my bike if she was out on her morning walk. I didn't want to be berated out in the open for any and all to see. And more important, I didn't want anything to keep me from seeing Peter. I *had* to know if Jilo had worked her spell.

I recognized him from blocks away; his bright red hair was hard to miss. Already shirtless in the growing heat of the day, he was walking with a couple of bags of concrete slung over his square, lightly freckled shoulders. I dismounted and watched him. He was facing away from me. His worn jeans hugged his lower half in a way that would without doubt stop traffic, if there were any.

I compared my mental image of Jackson to the man who stood before me. They were about the same height and close to the same build; I wasn't sure who could take the other in a fight. Other than that, they didn't look much alike. While Jackson had blond curls and classic features—the kind of face you'd find carved into marble in a museum—Peter was a fiery redhead, and his Celtic features were anchored by a strong chin. Like the rest of him, Jackson's eyes were perfect, a piercing blue the color of a bachelor's button; Peter had mismatched eyes, one royal blue and one nearly emerald.

Jackson was as close as I had ever seen to the physical ideal, but the truth was that Peter's quirky imperfections were closer to my physical ideal. He was a fine sight. And I loved him, really I did.

Just not in the way I loved Jackson. I felt no new passion for him tugging at my heart. I was relieved and disappointed at the same time.

Peter seemed to sense that he was being watched, and he turned to face me. There was no way I could take off without being seen, so I raised my hand and waved. "Didn't want to distract you," I called. He lowered the cement to the ground and walked toward me, the sunlight glistening on his skin.

I had known Peter my whole life. Jackson was a newcomer to Savannah. But when I looked at Peter, I saw a dear and beloved friend, and when I looked at Jackson, I saw a piece of myself that had been missing since birth. I had no idea why, and it frustrated me to no end. I wanted to want Peter. I just didn't.

"You can distract me anytime you want," he said with a big smile.

"No, I don't want to get you in trouble with the foreman," I responded, unconsciously maneuvering my bike between us.

"He isn't here yet. He's off bidding on another project in Isle of Hope," Peter responded, leaning across my bicycle to plant a quick kiss on my lips.

"I was in the neighborhood," I said, pulling back. "Ginny has summoned me to the royal court."

"Uh-oh," Peter smiled. "What have you done now?"

I started to protest my innocence, but decided it was best not to get into details. "That's for me to know . . ." I began.

"And for Ginny to bitch about," Peter finished.

I laughed, and he placed his large, rough hand on mine. I told myself that I wasn't doing anything wrong by being with Peter. Then my conscience kicked in, and I wondered if I would have already broken up with Peter if I had met Jackson first, if he had looked at me the same way he looked at Maisie. Should I cut Peter loose so that he could find the love he truly deserved?

"Mom and Dad were hoping we would come by the bar tonight," he said, breaking into my moral quandary. His parents owned and operated Magh Meall tavern. It was not much more than a hole in the wall near the river, a few blocks away from the treacherous cobblestones of Factors Walk. The bar took its name from the Irish equivalent of the Elysian fields, but the Irish flag that jutted out proudly toward the river was its only sign. So like its fabled namesake, you had to make a valiant effort to find it, or be one of those lost on the sea for life, driven there by some providential wind. A honeyed dark wheat microbrew and a small stage where local talent performed made Magh Meall popular with both the tourists and the local crowd, and on some hot nights, it was standing room only from opening until the arrival of the fire marshal. "I've been asked to play with the guys who are performing tonight. I told them only if you were up for it." Peter was a natural musician. Guitar, violin, you name it. If an instrument had strings, he could make it sing.

I nodded my assent, and he kissed me once more. This time, I let him linger. When he pulled away, I hopped back onto my bicycle and began to pedal away. When I looked back over my shoulder, he was still watching me, his face glowing with the type of love I wished I could give him.

It only took me a few minutes to reach Ginny's place. She had lived alone all my life. She always lectured the rest of us about the importance of family, but she sure didn't want to spend much time with us—well, other than Maisie. My sister had spent as much of her childhood in her room at Ginny's house as she had at the home the rest of our family shared.

I leaned my bike against the live oak that wasn't yet big enough to completely shade Ginny's front porch. I was surprised to see that the door was cracked open, and that Ginny hadn't pulled the shades against heat. Ginny wouldn't allow air-conditioning in the house, preferring to keep things somewhat bearable, though gloomy, by blocking out the morning light. She had finally capitulated and accepted an oscillating fan into her house a few summers back, but that was only because Maisie had insisted.

I climbed the steps and knocked on the doorframe. "Aunt Ginny," I called out, but there was no reply. I opened the door fully and stepped inside. "Aunt Ginny, it's me, Mercy. I'm here. I even got here a little early," I called out from the narrow foyer.

I had spent a lot of time in this barren entryway. When Maisie and I were children, Ginny had insisted on taking advantage of the yearly break in our formal schooling to teach my sister a witch's ways. Other than a few family outings like our Fourth of July picnic, she had refused to let Maisie out of sight for very long from Memorial Day until Labor Day. When I'd come over to play with Maisie, Ginny would make me wait in a chair in the hallway until my sister's lessons were done. That same chair still sat sentinel in the hall, directly across from a blank spot on the wall. I swear Ginny kept that area undecorated with the sole intention of making my wait more painful.

I tried bringing books a few times, but Ginny would always take away the ones she didn't approve of, which was basically all of them. I tried bringing paper and pencils to draw. "You have no talent, don't waste the paper," Ginny would say, tearing my drawings in two. So I'd sit there in that straight-back, wicker bottomed chair with nothing but my imagination to keep me company. It was there that I started making up many of the outrageous stories I now shared on my tours.

I took a couple steps farther in. To the right was Ginny's rarely used dining room. To the left, a room whose furnishings were so antiquated I could only bring myself to think of it as a parlor. There was absolute silence in the house.

Except for the buzzing of a horsefly. And Great-Aunt Ginny's discount store clock striking off the seconds louder than a jackhammer striking concrete.

An unexpected odor enveloped my senses. Metallic and alkaline, it was unmistakable, yet impossibly out of place. I registered it as the smell of blood, and then everything slowed way down. I followed the coppery scent into the parlor. There were splatters on the wall. Still red, just turning brown.

Ginny's body was on the floor, her head cracked clean open. I didn't feel for a pulse. There was no need. Ginny was still and silent and horrible. I knew she was dead. The top of her skull was lying six inches away from the rest of her. God knows I hated the old biddy, but seeing her here like this . . . I obviously didn't know what the word "hate" meant. This here, this picture stretched out before me was hate. There are a lot of gentler ways to take someone out. Whoever did this enjoyed the doing.

The room began to move in and out in waves, and I wished the blackness would just suck me under. More than that, I wished—oh, how I wished—that Ginny's death would be sucked back into the sea of the things that *might* happen, but never would. Someone was screaming. I realized it was me, and I let myself continue.

The rational part of my mind told me to stop carrying on. To call for help. I told it to fuck off, and continued screaming until I was good and satisfied that the heavens had heard me. Then, and only then, did I reach for my phone.

FOUR

"You did the right thing calling us, sugar," Aunt Iris said pulling me into her overly perfumed bosom. "You did the right thing calling us before the police. We'd never been able to get a fix on the energy in this room if the sheriff and his bunch of dimwits had been traipsing all over the house, contaminating the scene with their thoughts."

"She's done messed up things here enough herself," Connor muttered. Iris released me and gave him a look that would wither concrete.

"What's done is done. Right now, we need to put up a concealment around this place to keep people from nosing around until we are done here." A concealment didn't make objects invisible or render sounds silent; it just made folks ignore whatever it was you wanted to hide from them. The two set about silently working the concealment spell, although to me their efforts just looked like they were trying to finger paint the air.

"Who could have done this?" I whispered. I couldn't imagine how anyone could have harmed Ginny. And I don't mean that in the "who could harm a defenseless old lady" kind of way. I mean it in the "who the hell could have busted through her defenses and slayed the dragon" kind of way. I felt the blood freeze in my veins. Could this be the sacrifice Jilo had promised to make on my behalf?

"That's what we're trying to figure out, my girl," Connor said. "But you aren't helping us any by hanging out here and projecting your thoughts so loudly. Now get the hell outta here while we work." His right hand adjusted the belt straining over his paunch while the pendulum in his left began to swing in spurts and stops.

"Connor!" Iris exclaimed. "The poor girl is already shaken up enough."

"And her vibrations are shaking this room apart. Go on, girl. Get out of here before you make it impossible for us to suss out what the hell happened," he said, returning his attention to the swinging arc of his pendulum. The pendulum was Connor's connection to power, even if it was a weak one. Most true witches have a few gifts in common—with focus, just about all of them can read the thoughts of non-witches, and most can move things without having to touch them. But witches tend to be particularly skilled in one or two specific areas. Connor was weak as water in most things, but he could use his pendulum to track down just about anything, from a missing pair of glasses to a missing child. I knew without asking that he was looking for the murder weapon.

"Come on, sweetheart. Your uncle's right. I think it would be best for you to get out into the fresh air. You shouldn't have had to see any of this."

I let myself be guided outside and deposited on the squeaky old glider that had been on Great-Aunt Ginny's porch longer than I'd been alive. Within moments the Savannah heat began to lick around my ankles and up my calves. It took me slowly, but confidently, with the experience of immemorial dawns.

The sun traced a finger up my thigh, the solstice morning in Savannah marking its passage across the sky and projecting the shadow of a weathervane from a nearby house onto me. Leaning back on the glider, I surrendered to the heat, the scent of blood, and the relentless ticking of Ginny's clock, which I could still hear from the porch. The seat groaned beneath me, the sound lost somewhere between protest and pleasure. A horrible thought occurred to me: The same heat that was warming my skin was beating in through the window and onto Ginny's body, hastening its decay. I shook the thought out of my head and tried to focus instead on the first tiny bead of sweat that was forming behind my knee. I tried not to imagine what had happened, tried not to corrupt the energies that would help Aunt Iris and Uncle Connor figure everything out.

Through the screen of the open window I heard Aunt Iris say, "She couldn't help it. She hasn't been trained." Her voice carried through the still air like a stage whisper.

"Nothing to train," Connor snorted in reply. I shot him a look through the window. He and Iris had raised Maisie and me. My mother, Emily, the youngest female in the Taylor tribe, had died giving birth to us, and she'd never seen fit to tell anyone who our daddy was. I would have turned to Connor like a flower toward the sun if he had shown me the slightest modicum of paternal affection. But that had never happened. Far from it; he saddled me with the nickname "The Disappointment" by the time I'd turned six. Our eyes locked as the name crossed through my mind, and for a moment I thought I sensed something like regret in his expression. Was it in the twitch of his mouth or just the way his eyes darted back to the pendulum he carried? The look was there, and then it was gone. He returned his focus to the pendulum, walking around in a seemingly random fashion as the pendulum turned or stopped. "Damned shame it weren't Maisie here first instead of her sister."

Maisie had been his darling since birth. She had come into this world with so much strength that the other witch families hadn't even needed a birth announcement—she'd simply registered on everyone's radar. Me, I had come in a weak second, kind of like the universe's afterthought. Most were as shocked to learn of my arrival as they were saddened by my mother's passing.

"You need to have some consideration for the poor girl. This has been a shock. She knows this goes beyond what happened to Ginny. She knows that the line may have been damaged."

"Darlin', I ain't blaming her. I blame myself. If I'd acted like a real father and taken her in hand, explained things to her . . ." Connor repented. "Mercy's a good girl," he said. "She did the best she could by calling us." I was surprised to hear a break in his voice. It was the first time he'd betrayed any tenderness for me. "But right now, we only got a few minutes left to figure out who did this to Ginny. Mercy's panic when she found Ginny was almost fierce enough to overwrite what happened here. We have to try to catch whatever imprint is left, and then we gotta make sure that the line is holding. I need you to focus too. When we're done, I'll call Oliver and tell him to get his sweet ass home, and you can start rounding up the rest of the family."

Connor disappeared from my view, but I could still hear his heavy steps as he shuffled around the ground floor of the house. Then the squeak of a loose stair told me he was heading to the second floor. I focused on Aunt Iris as she knelt over the body and began to sway silently, reaching out for whatever energies might still be lingering. Silence gave way to sobbing as Iris surrendered to her grief. Strange, growing up, I'd often wished Ginny dead. Granted my wish, seeing what her death looked like, my blood called out to hers and screamed for justice. Guess she really was family after all.

"The weapon ain't here," a defeated Connor said, returning to the room. I heard him fall noisily into one of the armchairs.

Aunt Iris didn't respond. She didn't even seem to register that Connor had spoken. Her sobbing stopped, but she continued to sway over Ginny's body.

Psychometry was Aunt Iris's specialty. She could hold any object and tell you about its owner or anyone who had a tangential relationship with it. Not necessarily the most amazing of powers, but much appreciated in a city full of antiques with questionable provenance. If Connor had succeeded in finding the weapon, Iris would have had a good chance of finding out who had used it against Ginny. Holding the murder weapon would have left her open to some pretty fierce energy, but without it, she would have no choice but to lay hands on Ginny herself, which would be exponentially worse. Opening herself up to that degree of dark energy was mighty dangerous. Even when it's just a regular Joe who's died, a door gets opened and things that should be kept on the far side of that door sometimes make their way through. Murder compounds the problem, inviting in even darker things. The murder of someone like Great-Aunt Ginny could rip the door right off its hinges. And I realized I hadn't helped matters any.

"The energy is receding," Aunt Iris said, opening her eyes and standing stiffly. "It's now or never."

"Girl," Connor called out to me, making me jump. "You try calling your sister. See if she's on her way yet. And try Ellen again."

"Maisie's phone went straight to voice mail when we called," Aunt Iris replied. "That means she's out with that boy, and she isn't going to be picking up. And I don't begin to guess where Ellen spent the night, but she's probably still passed out or too hungover to be of any service. We need to do this now." She paused, as if weighing her options and then called out to me. "Mercy, honey, you come on back in."

"Ah, hell no," Connor began to object.

"It's now or never!" Iris cut him short. "We don't have time to hunt anyone down, and I have even less time for nonsense from you." She took a breath and composed herself. "Come on Mercy, I'm gonna walk you through this." The porch swing sang out like a Greek chorus as I stood. Iris sensed my hesitation. "Don't be afraid."

I went back in, averting my eyes from the body on the floor. The perspiration that had formed between my shoulder blades turned cold and trickled down my spine.

"Now I know you have never been shown any of this before, sugar, but you are gonna do just fine."

"All right," I replied, but my knees felt like they were going to buckle at any moment, and the scent of decay in the room was making me light-headed. "What do I do?"

"Remember when you girls were little, and you'd play Red Rover with Peter and his friends?" She smiled a little, her own recollection of watching us momentarily taking her away from the horror at her feet. "What we're gonna do is very much like that. I'm going to call out for a certain energy, but once I open myself up, there may be other forces that try to beat their way in. I just need you to stand here and hold hands with me and Connor. Your strength, your inner light, it'll help keep anything bad from breaking through." I stood next to her and took her small, cold hand. Connor stepped forward and swiped up my other hand into his meaty paw. "Okay. Good." She smiled reassuringly at me and then closed her eyes. "You may see some things. Don't let them frighten you. They're only shadows. Keep your mind focused on something real. Something you love. Something that makes you feel safe."

My mind began to reel like a roulette wheel, clicking past people, places, and things, but not settling on anything that gave me the level of comfort I suspected I would need. My mama had died before I could know her. I had no idea who my daddy was. Aunt Iris had tried to raise us as best she could, but Connor had tainted our relationship. Uncle Oliver, he was great for swooping in with presents and recounting colorful stories, but he spent as little time in Savannah as possible, and he didn't spell home to me. Aunt Ellen shared what she could with me, but her beauty pageant makeup secrets and the stories of her old romantic conquests were always whispered through the whiskey on her breath. There was Peter, but I was too confused about our relationship to take any comfort from him, and Jackson just made me feel guilty. In the end, there was only Maisie. Despite our differences, and the jealousy I had always felt toward her, she was the one person in this world who made me feel safe and loved.

"Have you found what you need?" Aunt Iris asked.

"Yes'm," I replied breathlessly.

"Good. Now you focus on that. You keep it in the front of your mind and your heart. Let your heart and mind focus in equal measure." She knelt down, placing her free hand on Ginny's body. Her grip on my hand tightened, and suddenly it seemed like I was looking at the room through a strange fisheye lens, the objects closest to me looming largest in my vision while the rest of the room retreated to the edges. Shadows began to form and darken in my peripheral vision, inching menacingly toward us. "Focus, Mercy," Aunt Iris commanded, and I tried. I stared straight ahead and thought of Maisie. But as her face rose to my mind's eye, a flash of blue lightning hit the room and then everything went black.

FIVE

Part of me wanted to keep my eyes shut, as if everything that had happened might go away if I chose not to face it. I could feel something sticking into my arm, and I could tell that the bed I was lying in was not my own. These two things alone were enough to tell me that I was in a hospital. I lay still for a few moments, trying to put the pieces back together, but all I could come up with was blood, a blue flash, then blackness. I heard tapping near me. Not random tapping, but a sound that spoke of someone's well-honed skill of typing on a cell phone keypad. There was only one person on earth I knew who could work a phone like that.

"Uncle Oliver," I said. I noticed that my mouth was very dry.

"Hey there, my little Gingersnap," he said using his long-standing pet name for me. "You getting ready to join us again?" As I opened my eyes, he came forward and pressed the nurse call button.

I blinked against the light that was streaming in through the window. I guessed it was afternoon, but I couldn't be sure of the day. It would have taken Oliver about a day to get from San Francisco to Savannah. From the few words he had spoken, I could tell that his southern accent had started creeping back into his voice. When he was on the West Coast, he had no accent.

After a week in Savannah he went full-fledged Uncle Remus. He was early on in the process, so my guess was that I'd been out for a couple of days.

"Three days, as a matter of fact," he stated flatly, reading my mind. I hated that he could do that with me. It didn't work with the rest of my family, just with us non-witch types. The youngest of my mother's siblings, Oliver was strongest when it came to telepathy, but his real fortes were glamour and persuasion, getting a person to see what he wanted them to see, believe what he wanted them to believe, and feel what he wanted them to feel. No wonder he made such a killing working in public relations. No wonder he has broken so many hearts. "And I resent the tar baby reference," he said. "You could have said Ashley Wilkes."

"I didn't actually say a thing," I said. I tried to sit up, but gave up after realizing how weak I was.

"You take it easy there," he said. A nurse bounced in and out like a yo-yo, telling us she'd be right back with the doctor. "Bring us the young blond one who fills out those drawstring pants so nicely," Uncle Oliver called out after her. In spite of myself, in spite of a three-day coma, I blushed. My uncle squinted. "You are beet red," he said. At first he seemed concerned that there might be something medically wrong with me, but he must have scanned my thoughts because he laughed after a moment. "My dear, you are still a virgin. So much for the stories of your hard living Iris has been writing me about."

I felt myself rocket from embarrassment to anger. "Stop reading me and start explaining what happened."

He smiled at me and brushed his fingers through my hair. The anger evaporated, and I relaxed instantly. I knew he was charming me, but I was too tired to fight it. Too tired to even want to fight it.

I stared up at his smooth, serene face. I knew he was nearing forty, but the man standing next to me could not be over twenty-five, not really that much older than me. I wondered how much of what I was seeing was real, and how much was magic. What must it feel like to have a choice about whether to show the world the person time has made of you? Another wave of comfort hit me as Uncle Oliver tried to derail me from that train of thought.

"What happened?" he echoed my question thoughtfully. "Well, Gingersnap. You know how during a storm you sometimes get a power surge, and it causes one of the switches in your breaker box to switch off?"

I nodded.

"Well, you, my dear, were the switch that got flipped." Irritation—no, outright anger—washed across his face for a moment. "Iris and Connor are idiots. They should never have tried using you as a ground. It's like putting a child in a cockpit and telling her to land the plane. Not that you are a child," he added, searching my thoughts for any feelings of offense, ready to soothe them away if he found them.

Pieces of what had occurred at Ginny's abruptly flew back up and coalesced in my mind. "Did they get what they needed? Did Aunt Iris see who killed Ginny?"

"No, sweetheart. I'm afraid you collapsed like a card table at a Baptist potluck. They got nothing. And they were fools for putting your life at risk to try to find out who did it. They should have left things to the police. What were they going to do anyway? Send Connor after the killer with a rifle? Or were they planning on going all Macbeth and hexing the son of a bitch to death? Now they got nothing, and by the time the police were finally called, the crime scene was so compromised that an outright confession wouldn't land us a conviction."

"I'm sorry," I started, but I didn't complete my thought because the doctor had come in. He was in his fifties but still handsome. Not the young blond that Oliver had been hoping for, but I doubted he'd be too disappointed.

"Welcome back, Mercy," the doctor said, then glanced coldly at Uncle Oliver. "Oliver," he said and whisked out a pen flashlight to examine my eyes. From the way he said Oliver's name, I knew there was history there. Seems like Uncle Oliver had history pretty much everywhere.

"Good to see you, Michael. Or should I call you Doctor?" Oliver asked.

"I'd recommend not calling me at all." His face was an icy mask, displaying zero emotion. He must have been a hell of a poker player. I had a feeling that I liked this Doctor Michael, whoever he was. He took my pulse, looked at my chart, and then nodded, as though declaring himself done with me.

"Well the one thing I have learned in dealing with you Taylors is that I will never figure out what causes your ailments or what it is that cures them," he said. "I'm going to keep you here another night, but that's just to make sure the hospital doesn't get sued. I could run more tests and fluff up your bill, but you're a Taylor, and I know for a fact that if a Taylor wakes up, a Taylor is going to live. My condolences about Ginny. She was a good friend to my grandma." He hung my chart up at the foot of my bed and left, being careful not to make eye contact with Oliver.

"I guess that's that, then," Oliver chuckled. I wasn't sure if he was referring to the doctor's pronouncement on my health or to whatever had happened between the two of them in the past. "I should call your sister to let her know you're awake. She was here by your side up until about an hour ago. I finally made that pretty new beau of hers drag her out of here."

"Jackson," I said, providing Oliver with the name. "Jackson," I repeated, and the mere thought of him caused a pleasant warmth to flood me from head to toe.

"Mmm!" Oliver interjected loudly. "I can see we are bound to have some trouble over that boy. By the way, those flowers, the big bunch," he said and nodded in the direction of a towering arrangement of roses, "those are from Peter. Maisie said he dropped them off at lunch. Probably spent a week's wages on them."

I closed my eyes and pretended to sleep. Trying to fool a telepath is no easy feat, but Oliver let me get away with it. In a few minutes, pretense turned to reality, and I drifted off.

It must have been around midnight when I woke up. My first thought was that a nurse must have come into the room, but as my eyes focused, my heart skipped a beat before hiding its head in shame. It was no nurse. Jackson was standing over me. He ran his right index finger along my cheek, and held the other up to his lips to shush me.

"I didn't mean to scare you," he whispered, his voice husky. "I just wanted to see how you were doing." I marveled at how good he looked even under the dim fluorescent lighting—his blond curls gleamed and his eyes shone bright blue. It was as if he carried a patch of the summer sky with him wherever he went.

"How'd you get in here?" I asked. "It's way past visiting hours, isn't it?" The monitor I was connected to bore witness to the effect he had on me—my pulse was racing. I knew he belonged to my sister, and I knew it was wrong. But in the end, it was harmless. I could never compete with Maisie, and Jackson adored her. Eventually the two of them would marry and make beautiful cherub babies, and my little crush on him would never amount to anything. If I kept it to myself, no one needed to be the wiser. With time, I hoped that the feelings I had never invited would go away. I made a mental note to be more guarded around Uncle Oliver.

"I have my ways," he responded, a glint in his eye. "Oliver said you were doing okay, but I wanted to see for myself."

"What about Maisie?"

"Don't you worry about her. She's at home getting rested up. Your family has something big cooking, and Maisie is evidently going to be right in the thick of it. She spent most of the day with Iris and Connor, then they put her to bed early. They were all being real closed-mouthed about what was going on, and Connor invited me to leave right after dinner in his usual charming manner. Maisie told me she'd explain everything tomorrow. Something about a 'line' that's been disrupted by Ginny's death."

"Someone's going to need to take her place," I realized out loud, instantly regretting my words. I didn't know how much Maisie had already shared with him, but I did know that it wasn't my place to do any of that sharing. "Ignore me," I said, trying to sound more discombobulated than I was. "I think my brain still has some crossed wires."

He smiled at me and took my hand. "I expect that I'll get used to all of this spooky stuff your family's into sooner or later," he said, "but I've got to admit that I was feeling the need for a little bit of normal, and I started thinking about you."

I felt myself flinch and pulled my hand out of his grasp. Normal wasn't exactly a compliment in my family, and it unquestionably wasn't a word I wanted to hear Jackson use to describe me.

"I'm sorry," he said tenderly. "I shouldn't be bothering you. I just wanted to check on you. You close your eyes now, and get back to sleep," he said, and despite myself, I did as he asked. I felt his lips brush my forehead, the way a parent might kiss a sick child. And then quickly, tentatively his lips touched mine. My eyes popped back open, but he was already gone.

SIX

I spent another full day in bed after being released from the hospital, but at least it was my own bed. When I awoke early the following morning, I felt normal again, and was itching to get out. I made a point of abandoning my cell phone on the night table before making my escape, hoping to evade Iris's mothering. The years I'd spent sneaking out as a teenager served me well; I climbed out the window and down the trellis, and found myself free on a fine, if humid, morning.

I started wandering around Savannah more or less on automatic pilot, without thinking about where I'd end up. I found myself near Chippewa Square, so I grabbed a coffee to go at Gallery and went into the park. The city had recently cut back the overgrown azaleas that many homeless had been using as make-shift shelters. I recognized the necessity of the work, but it still seemed like a shame. I kind of liked Chippewa in its derelict state; there was something familiar and even comforting about it.

The benches were all occupied, either by tourists doing their best Forrest Gump impersonations for the camera or by the very homeless people that the city was hoping to shoo out of the square. I deposited myself on the ground in the shade of my favorite tree. I tried to avoid thinking of Ginny, and of the violence done to her, by eavesdropping on every conversation around me. I drank my coffee and let my eyes trace the outline of the steeple on the Presbyterian church.

An angelic little girl ran past me, laughing as her father caught her and swung her up into the air. The distraction was bittersweet. Lord help me, how I envied that little girl's relationship with her father, even now. If only my mama had revealed who our father was, maybe Maisie and I could have had days like that with him. Of course, I knew mama must have had a real good reason for not sharing, but I sure wish that she had.

"I knew you'd be here," Aunt Ellen called out from behind me. "When you were little, and you were nowhere to be found, I could always count on finding you here, sitting in the shadow of that old gentleman." For a second I thought she was saluting the statue of Oglethorpe, but I realized she was just shading her eyes. "That sun burns a whole lot hotter than it used to." She made as if to join me on the grass, but then seemed to think better of it. "My dear, I'm afraid that I'm beyond the age of rising gracefully from the ground under my own steam, but not yet at that age where my pride would allow me to accept your help. Come on, get up and walk a bit with me."

I smiled at her. Her eyes were clear, her voice was steady, and she seemed to be far more present than she had been in months. Her face was fresh. Her fair hair had new lowlights. Her nails were flawlessly manicured, and a slight tremor in her hands told me that she hadn't had her first cocktail of the day. Ginny's death had brought on an impromptu family reunion, and our house was packed to the rafters, buzzing not only with the extended Taylor family but with MacGregors, Ryans, and Duvals, known to us Savannah Taylors collectively, and somewhat derogatorily, as "the cousins." I wondered if Ellen were trying to put on her best front for the larger family group, or if the house was simply too crowded for her to be able to raid the liquor cabinet surreptitiously.

Despite the unforgiving light and a decade or more of heavy drinking, Aunt Ellen was still beautiful. More beautiful than any other of the Taylor women, except, of course, Maisie. I stood and brushed the grass, moss, and sandy earth from my jeans. She offered me her arm, and I took it. "You've missed the worst of the gathering, you know," she began as we moved our way along the McDonough Street edge of the park. "The part where the cousins all tried to act like they gave a damn about Ginny's . . . passing." She looked a bit guilty. "I shouldn't be talking like this."

"It's okay. She hated me. I must admit, her death isn't going to create any great void in my life," I said. I didn't really mean a word of it; I wasn't sure I'd ever be able to resolve my feelings toward Ginny and what had happened to her.

"It's terrible. I know I should care more, but Ginny wasn't just mean to you. She didn't have a kind word for anyone since something like 1984. She was old and bitter and angry to the end." Ellen stopped herself.

"But how did she get to be that way?" I asked. "I know she had too much responsibility to have a family of her own, but I don't think she really wanted one anyway. I don't understand what made her so hard."

"I've got a theory. Now it's only a theory, mind you, but I think I may be right," Ellen began. "Ginny was a handsome woman, but not what I'd call beautiful, and the men weren't exactly lining up for her. She was intelligent too, but *shrewdly* intelligent. Not a great intellect. She certainly lacked your amazing imagination. There was nothing that called her out into the larger world, so being chosen as an anchor gave her a tremendous sense of purpose and validation. But instead of using it as an opportunity to expand her horizons, she shut herself off, and as her world shrank she began to see herself as larger and more important than she had any right to. She saw herself as the sun, and expected us to spend our lives orbiting around her." Ellen stopped talking as a tourist trolley pulled up alongside us. Something about its arrival put an end to her candor. "What a fine pair we are, speaking so poorly of the dead," she concluded. Her forehead creased and she folded her arms around herself.

"Will the police be able to release the body in time for the memorial?" I asked, trying to bring her back out of her private thoughts.

"I don't know, dear. Oliver is working on getting the body released, but I'm afraid it might be a few more days or even weeks before we'll be able to lay Ginny to rest." She paused. "I have to apologize to you, Mercy. I couldn't help you when you were hurt."

"What happened wasn't your fault, Aunt Ellen."

"But it was, in a way," she began to tear up. "I wasn't reachable when Iris called me. After you found Ginny, that is. I'm sure you know why I wasn't home, why none of you knew where I was. Hell, I didn't even know where I was. If I hadn't been passed out, I would have answered my phone. I am going to quit drinking. I know, I've tried before . . . But this time I'm going to do it." She looked squarely at me. "For real, this time, sugar. Do you hear me?"

I desperately wanted to believe her. For her sake. I smiled and tried to pull her to me, but she pushed away.

"I'm not through," she said, determination putting lines on her forehead. Her knitted eyebrows exposed her cornflower blue eyes and made them seem somehow larger. "I couldn't help you. Do you understand? I tried to heal you. Iris and Connor brought you to me before taking you to the hospital. It should have been easy. You had a jolt, but you're young and strong and healthy, and

I should have been able to heal you. Instead, I could have let you die." The tears flowed heavily down her cheeks.

"I wasn't hurt that bad!" I exclaimed. "Just knocked for a loop."

"You were unconscious for days," Ellen said.

It was true, helping me should have been a no-brainer for her. Out of my mother's three siblings, I was most in awe of Ellen's talents. I'd seen her stop bleeding cold and regulate the beat of a heart. Once I witnessed her bring someone back from the brink of death. I was scared to go near her for days after that. And maybe she had caught death's attention by straddling the threshold between life and death for too long, because her own son and husband were killed in a traffic pileup a week later. I was certain that she blamed herself for what had happened. Nowadays she spent most of her time hiding from the sun with a cold glass of something strong in her hand.

"I don't know what's happened to me. I can barely patch up a scraped knee on my own these days," Ellen continued. "You were in the hospital for a full day before I could locate your essence. Even then, I needed Maisie's help to pull you back from your coma. But you wait and see; I'm going to get things back together. You have faith in me even if no one else will, okay, darlin'?"

"I do have faith in you." This time she didn't resist when I pulled her into my arms. I didn't think the alcohol could be the only thing interfering with her powers, but I knew now was not the time to kick out any of Ellen's supports.

"Will you walk me back into the house?" she asked. "I can't face that bunch of buzzards on my own." We took a few more steps, and she stopped again. "What do you think she wanted? Why did Ginny want to see you?"

"Honestly," I lied, "I haven't the darnedest." We turned down Perry and headed home.

Folk usually chose to cross the street rather than passing directly in front of our house, an almost embarrassingly large, but still graceful, Victorian that took up the better part of the block. Maybe they crossed out of respect or fear, or maybe a century and a half of people doing so had carved some kind of psychic groove into the walkway. Which is why it was an entirely new experience to see a stranger sitting on the front steps.

"Adam Cook! Although it's Detective Cook now, isn't it?" Ellen addressed the man. A policeman. I knew without asking that he was there to interview me. I'd been expecting this conversation, but I had hoped that the police would find Ginny's killer before I was forced to relive the morning I found her body. Unrealistic, I knew, but it would neither be the first nor last time I fell prey to foolish optimism.

"Yes, ma'am. That's correct," the officer said, standing and taking Ellen's hand. "Thank you for remembering. It's good to see you again." Even after stepping down onto the sidewalk, he towered over the both of us. Mixed African American, American Indian, and Caucasian blood played in his handsome features. A high forehead, straight nose, and nearly cinnamon skin came together in an extremely eye-pleasing way.

"Oliver is going to be so pleased to see you," Ellen said, then remembered herself. "Good heavens, don't tell me you were left out here on the doorstep! Did no one respond when you rang the bell?"

"Oh, no, ma'am. There was a response. I was kindly asked inside to wait, but honestly there was so much . . ." he searched for a word and settled on " 'activity' going on inside, I thought it would be better to wait out here and enjoy the morning air. I do hope to pay Oliver a visit before he heads back to California, but I'm afraid I'm here on official business." His intelligent, tea-colored eyes flashed over to me. "Miss Taylor," he said. "It's good to see you up and about. I saw you in the hospital while you were still out, and I have to admit that I'm amazed by your recovery."

"Well, we Taylors are a hardy stock," Ellen responded for me.

"Yes, ma'am, I know that for a fact from personal experience," he said, but his lips arced into an embarrassed smile, and he quickly changed the subject. "Miss Taylor, would you feel well enough to talk with me about the incident?"

I made the connection between his embarrassment and his history with my uncle. Detective Cook had obviously been another one of Oliver's conquests. I almost blushed myself at the thought of the two of them together.

"Sure," I responded. To my surprise, I was a bit relieved that the discussion I'd been dreading would soon be over. Maybe telling the detective my story would be enough to exorcise it from my dreams. "I can't say that I'll be able to help much, but I'll do my best."

"Fine," he said, smiling, his manner clearly intended to put me at ease.

"Then I must insist that you come inside," Ellen interjected brusquely, her furrowed brow betraying that she was offended. "We do not discuss such matters on the doorstep."

"Yes, ma'am. Of course. I apologize for my tactlessness," Cook responded.

As Ellen ushered us into the house, Maisie caught my eye. She wore an old white sundress, and her golden hair was knotted into a careless bun, but even so casually attired, my sister was one of the most breathtaking beauties Savannah had ever known. She pointed almost imperceptibly to the ceiling, and I knew she was telling me to meet her in our not-so-secret secret meeting place, a linen closet in the back corner of the house's uppermost floor.

Ellen guided Detective Cook and me into the library and shooed away the members of the extended family who had set up shop there. Cook stopped a moment and took the room in. Ceiling high shelves with ancient leather-bound books lined the length of the western wall; the eastern wall was taken up by two sets of French doors that opened out onto the house's side porch. The northern wall was devoted to an oversized fireplace that we rarely lit. A painting of my grandmother hung over its mantel. It was a beautiful room, but I spent so much time in it that I'd stopped noticing. Cook's admiration prompted me to see it through new eyes.

"I should get Iris and Connor," Ellen said. "They can fill in any blanks that Mercy might have."

"No, thank you," Cook replied with a little too much vehemence. "I would rather talk alone with Miss Taylor, if that is all right with you?" he said, looking at me for agreement. "If I understand correctly, you are shortly to turn twenty-one, and this is just a casual, informal discussion. You are certainly not suspected of having been involved in your aunt's, or great-aunt's that is, assault." He chose the most benign terms: incident, assault.

"I believe the phrase is 'cold-blooded murder.' And yes, I am fine with discussing what I saw without 'adult supervision,'" I responded. Ellen's eyes warned me not to reveal too much. Too much about what? I didn't know who killed Ginny. Hell, I wasn't even quite sure what had hit me and turned out the lights. "It's okay, Aunt Ellen. We'll be fine."

"At least let me fetch you something to drink, Detective. Some sweet tea, perhaps?"

"No, thank you, ma'am. I don't anticipate taking up too much more of y'all's time. I appreciate this is a trying time for the family, especially Miss Taylor here."

"All right then. You call out if you change your mind," Aunt Ellen said and quietly shut the door behind her.

"That's her way of saying that she'll have her ear pressed to the door," I joked and then realized that any number of my cousins could use their powers to listen in on our discussion. Many witches have the ability to project their consciousness to a place— even somewhere on the other side of the world—and witness the events happening there. Spying on our library would take no effort at all. I suspected that Aunt Ellen was even now rounding up someone with this ability.

Detective Cook smiled. "Do you mind if we sit? I really won't take up much of your time, but I've been training for the upcoming marathon, and frankly my middle-aged legs are beat and my dogs are barking."

"No, of course not." I sat down in the upholstered wingback and motioned toward the love seat that faced it.

Cook ignored my gesture and pulled an ottoman toward my chair instead, sitting directly in front of me. Up close I could make out a shadow of stubble that was reclaiming the territory it had lost when he shaved that morning. His appearance, his every move, demonstrated the easy type of masculinity that Uncle Oliver found so attractive. Cook leaned in toward me and began, "I grew up here in Savannah. Not two miles from this very house. I am loosely acquainted with your family. I even used to hang with your uncle from time to time when I was young. Now I know y'all have your own ways and such, but I do have to ask." He leaned back as if to take me fully in. "You walk in to your elderly aunt's home. You find her bludgeoned to death on the floor, and the first call you make is to your aunt"—he flipped open a small black notebook—"Iris? Didn't it occur to you to call the police first, or maybe an ambulance?"

"I didn't call for an ambulance, 'cause I could tell she was dead."

"Oh, so you're medically trained then? From what I have gathered from talking to your family, you are quite the student. A class or two at Savannah College of Art and Design qualifies you to determine if someone is beyond medical assistance?" His sudden aggressive turn took me by surprise, as he'd no doubt calculated it would.

"No," I shot back, suddenly angry. "Seeing the top of her skull lying across the room and her brain popping out the top of what was left qualified me."

Cook leaned back a bit further, attempting to look more relaxed. "I'm sorry. That came out harsher than I meant it to. I'm just incredibly frustrated with the tampering you all did at the crime scene."

"I never touched a thing," I replied.

"Maybe not with your hands, but you passed out on top of the body. You knocked it a good foot away from its original placement, and got your hair and clothing fibers all over."

"I'm sorry. I didn't realize," I mumbled, now understanding his consternation. I couldn't believe that no one had told me, but then again, I would have preferred never to have found out.

"Okay. Let's talk about the facts of life here, Miss Taylor. I really, really do not suspect that you had anything to do with your great-aunt's death." He bent back in and looked me squarely in the eye. "Really," he repeated. "But I am sure you are aware that in most cases someone is murdered by someone they know. And more often than not, by someone in their own family." He paused.

"Looks to me like whoever did the old lady in hated her," he said. "It took three blows to take her down. She was one tough old bird. But that last blow, as you witnessed, took the top off the roof, so to speak." He leaned back toward me and in a lowered voice, he asked, "You didn't like her much, did you?"

"No. But I sure didn't hate her. Not really. Certainly not enough to kill her."

"Why did you hate her?" he asked, completely ignoring my statement to the contrary.

"What does it matter? I sure would never have hurt her."

"I believe you, I do," he insisted. "But if she inspired hate in you, it is likely she did the same in other family members. Maybe someone else hated her for the same reasons you did. And maybe sharing those reasons with me will help me bring her killer to justice." He hesitated. "I know you Taylors have your own way of thinking about how things should work, but you do believe in justice, right?"

"Of course, I do. Ginny didn't deserve to be killed, especially like that."

"Then tell me why you hated her."

I stopped resisting and spoke a truth I had been waiting my entire life to share. "I hated Ginny," I replied, "because she made me feel like I was a mistake. Like I didn't have the right to exist."

"Go on."

"My mother died having me. You know I have a twin sister. Maisie," I informed him, sparing him another peek in his black book. "Ginny adored Maisie. Me, not so much. She thought my mother might have made it if there hadn't been two of us." Hot tears burst from my eyes, and I gasped with the pain as the words ripped out of me.

"And she made you believe that, didn't she?" he asked. He reached out and nearly touched my hand, but he must have thought better of it because he gently pulled his hand back.

"Yeah, I guess she did." And I realized it was true. I did believe it, and I always had. I swiped at my tears with my bare hands and tried to pull myself together.

"Well, she was wrong. I suspect Ginny Taylor was wrong about a whole lot of other things too," he said, pulling a tissue from a pack in his jacket pocket and handing it to me.

"Really, like what?"

"Like thinking it was a good idea to leave her doors and windows unlocked. The door was unlocked when you got there, right?"

Again, I felt myself tighten up. "Yes. Aunt Ginny never locked up. She didn't need . . ." I started, but then realized that if I explained how Ginny thought she could keep the bad guys out, I might be opening another whole can of worms. Cook smiled and let my faltering statement pass. He had known my family for years all right.

"So it was common knowledge among your family members that Ginny never locked her doors."

"Well, yeah, it was common knowledge to everyone. The dry cleaner, the grocery delivery guy. Everyone, not just family."

"I see," Cook said, briefly flipping his black book open and then closing it again just as quickly. "So tell me, Miss Taylor. Why did you call your Aunt Iris rather than the police? Were you maybe trying to protect someone? Someone like your Uncle Connor, that is? He's a big man, with a big temper. He's well known for it, right?"

"Uncle Connor"—I began almost choking on the "uncle" part—"had nothing to do with Ginny's death."

"You sure about that? You can give him an alibi?"

"I saw him at breakfast. I'm sure he was with Iris all morning. You can ask her if you haven't already, but I know he never would've done it."

"Not even for the inheritance he's going to get from Ginny?"

"He isn't getting anything from Ginny," I guffawed. "Ginny made no secret of the fact that she thought Maisie was the only one of us who was worth a spit and polish. It wouldn't be Thanksgiving dinner without her announcing that when she was gone, she planned on leaving everything to Maisie." I realized I had stepped in it.

"Well thank you for your time, Miss Taylor." He stood up abruptly, if a bit stiffly. "I can let myself out." He smiled and left the room, leaving me with the strong sense that I had just been had.

SEVEN

"Mercy! Mercy!" an excited squeal came from behind me. I almost jumped out of my skin, but then I turned to see Wren standing in the corner.

"Were you in here the entire time?" I asked.

"Yes," he responded, looking down. "I just wanted to show you this," he said as he held up another new toy, this time a blue pickup truck.

"You know you aren't supposed to come into a room without announcing yourself," I said, trying my best to sound stern. But how can you get angry with a little boy who has been a little boy forever, even before you were born? A child you once played with yourself? A child who isn't even really a child? When dealing with Wren it was easy to forget that he wasn't real, that he had started out as Uncle Oliver's imaginary friend. But when a young witch with as much power as Oliver has invents a playmate, that playmate can truly take on a life of its own. While Wren looked as real as could be, he was in actuality just a thought-form, a bit of imaginative energy so thoroughly well imagined that it had been able to separate itself from the one who originally envisioned it.

Wren dropped to his knees and began to push the truck up to me, running it over my feet as if they were speed bumps. After a moment, he stopped playing with it and looked up at me. "I don't like that man," he said, trying to change the subject just as a real child might.

"I don't think I like that man much either," I said. I put my hand on his head, and his warm, glossy curls felt so real to me. After all these years and too many games of ring-around-the-rosy to count, I don't know why it still surprised me, but it did. Even though he looked just like any other kid you might see riding his tricycle down the street or tagging along with his parents in a store—your average six-year-old—Wren was an uncanny creature, something unnatural to this world. And it didn't seem right that there weren't any outward signs of that.

Iris told me that Wren had faded away by the time Oliver hit puberty. The family had thought he was gone for good, but he had evidently been dormant, waiting for the arrival of another child to reawaken him. That child had been Ellen's son, Paul. By the time Maisie and I were born, Wren had already returned to being an accepted part of the family, never growing or aging past his initial incarnation.

"My truck is better than Peter's," Wren said.

"And how do you know that?" I asked, amused.

"I've seen his truck. His is old."

"Yeah, but his is real," I said, regretting it instantly. He stood and kicked the truck away, causing it to roll into the far corner.

The door opened, and Ellen stuck her head in.

"Ellen!" Wren squeaked and ran toward her, totally deserting the toy truck that had captivated him only seconds before. She came into the room and knelt down next to him, kissing his forehead and pulling him to her.

Ginny had often complained that "it" should be dissolved and laid to rest. The family's job was to maintain the line, not pluck at it like a guitar string. But after Ellen's son Paul died, she had latched onto Wren. No one, not even Ginny, had had the heart to rip another child from Ellen's arms, so in spite of Ginny's churlishness, a tacit agreement seemed to exist in the family that Wren would be kept "alive." I suspected it was the combination of booze and this need to hold onto an illusion that was siphoning off Ellen's power. He had to be getting his juice from somewhere; I doubted that he was pulling much from Maisie, who had no need for him anymore, and I had none to give him.

"I can't find my ball," he said, addressing Ellen. His lower lip poked out comically, causing Ellen to laugh and hug him even more tightly. I was concerned about what he was doing to my aunt, and I knew it wasn't natural for him to be here with us, but I couldn't help it. My heart went out to him like it would to a real child.

"Don't worry, baby," she said. "If we don't find it, I'll set Connor on the case with his pendulum." She looked up at me. "And you, young lady, don't you worry about Adam. He's going to realize he is barking up the wrong tree soon enough."

"He thinks one of us did it for Ginny's money," I said.

"Aunt Ginny didn't have any money of her own. She got her stipend from the trust just like the rest of the family does. Just like you and Maisie will, starting on your next birthday. Nobody's going to gain financially from poor Ginny's death. What she had to give wasn't money. It was knowledge."

She reached out and took my hand. "He's wrong, you know, this detective. It wasn't anyone from the family, close or extended, who hurt Ginny. If a witch with bad intentions had been approaching her, Ginny would've sensed the danger from a mile away." Ellen weighed her words. "Someone born of the power, we have a signature, something like a vibration. When we get near someone like us"—she looked away from me, maybe feeling a bit guilty for excluding me—"that vibration either falls in sync and kind of hums along with ours or is like nails scraping against a chalkboard." She let go of my hand and turned her attention back to Wren. "Ginny would have sensed it if a rage-filled witch was coming at her."

"But if she could know when a witch was coming at her, why couldn't she tell if a normal person was headed her way? Seems to be a hell of a blind spot," I said and then regretted having used the word "normal" for non-witches.

"I would say 'regular' instead of 'normal,'" Ellen corrected me, but I could tell she wasn't really upset. "Whoever hurt Ginny was regular. But they certainly weren't normal. My feeling is that the person was probably deranged. You know how disturbed people tend to get more excitable during a full moon?"

"Sure, it's why we have the term lunatic," I said.

"Precisely. It's kind of the same when a crazy person, pardon my lack of political correctness, approaches the line. The vibration causes them to become more unhinged than they might typically be. And Ginny was the focal point, the anchor for our portion of the line. So you end up taking crazy and turbocharging it." She paused. "As far as Ginny not picking up on a threat, I suspect she thought she could control the situation. That she underestimated the strength or craziness of whoever attacked her. All the same, the killer is not one of the family."

"Yeah, I know, but I don't think I helped convince Detective Cook of it."

"Don't worry. He will chase his tail a bit, but he is keeping an open mind. And by open, I mean open enough for me to poke around in a little." She placed her hand on Wren's head.

"What did you see?" I asked.

She began to stroke Wren's blond curls, the muscles in her forehead relaxing at the contact. She took a lot of comfort from him. "One of the neighbors spotted a young man in Ginny's yard, the morning she was killed. African American, I gather. I couldn't pick out the actual description, just Adam's impression of that description. It looked like no one I knew."

"My ball," Wren was growing impatient.

Ellen patted his head and stood. "All right, little man," she said, taking hold of his hand. "Let's go find it. Where do you remember playing with it last?"

"Outside," he replied.

"Then let's start there," Ellen said and led Wren from the room.

Seconds later, Teague Ryan, one of the cousins, popped his head into the room. "You done in here?" he commanded more than asked. Teague's square jaw and high forehead landed him somewhere on the looks spectrum between high school prom king and newscaster. His sense of entitlement positioned him somewhere between a spoiled six-year-old and Louis XIV, the Sun King of France.

"Yeah," I replied. "All yours." He stood stock still in the doorway, preventing my exit.

"Excuse me," I said, but he didn't budge. I managed to duck around him into the hall, but he reached out and grasped my arm before I could walk away. The pressure of his grip made me wince at first, but I managed to shake myself free.

"You Savannah Taylors think you got this all wrapped up," he said, his harsh northern accent making the words all the more abrasive. "But I don't think you should be so sure of the outcome this time." He circled in front of me, blocking my way again. "You Taylors are weak and spoiled, while others, myself for example, have been working on our discipline, building our strength. I think the line is going to pass your family over this time. The rest of us have been dancing to the Taylors' tune for generations now, but Ginny was the last one of you to lord it over us. It's our turn for the power now."

"As far as I am concerned, y'all are welcome to it," I said, pushing past him and doing my best to avoid the psychic feelers that I could feel directed at me from every corner of the house. I was an easy target for the cousins to read, and they all knew it. I concentrated on the mantra, "Mind your own damned business!" hoping it would blare out the rest of my thoughts.

I climbed the stairs and headed down the long hall toward the linen closet where I knew Maisie was waiting for me. We had been using the space as our clandestine rendezvous point since we were old enough to walk. The closet had a window and was actually large enough to serve as a small bedroom. It might have housed a servant at some point, back when it was still socially acceptable to have live-ins. Over the years it had become more to us than a place to whisper secrets. It had become a sanctuary, a holy of holies. And now, with the house crawling with the cousins, it was also the only place left to share even a nominally private conversation.

It was silly, I knew, but for tradition's sake, I softly tapped our secret knock. The door opened silently for me, revealing Maisie, whose face was softly lit by the glow of candles on the cake she was holding.

"Happy birthday to us," she said, smiling. I stepped into the room, and the door automatically swung closed behind me. Maisie was so powerful that she probably hadn't even needed to consciously direct it.

"But our birthday isn't for days yet," I said.

"Yeah, but if I get selected to replace Ginny, I won't be able to spend it with you. I'll be off training under another anchor. And I don't want to miss celebrating our twenty-first together," she said. "Now come here and help me blow out these candles. I've got a surprise for you."

I laughed. "I'm already surprised."

"This," she said, "is better."

I walked over to her, feeling the warmth that emanated from the candles.

"On the count of three," she said and counted, "one, two, three!" We drew in air together and blew on the candles. To my delight, the flames leaped right off the candles and danced into the air instead of flickering out. While most of them maintained their color, one was the bright blue of a gas flame. "These are twenty-one memories for you to relive," Maisie said. "Well, to be precise, they're twenty memories and one wish—my wish for the two of us."

I stood there in silent amazement, watching the flames bob up and down in the air.

"Go ahead!" Maisie encouraged me. "Touch one!" Her eyes shining blue flames of excitement.

I lifted my hand and gingerly poked at the nearest flame. A rush of warmth immediately enveloped me, and suddenly I was in Forsyth Park with Maisie, sharing an ice cream cone. Behind us, a group of boys were playing half rubber, Savannah's own brand of stickball. I knew instantly where—and when—we were. It was the Fourth of July, and Maisie and I were ten. Uncle Oliver was visiting, and that morning he had given us new bicycles, which we had taken to the park. I knew exactly what would happen next; we were about to meet Peter for the first time. He was one of the boys playing half rubber, and against the other boys' wishes, he would invite us to join in. We would, and we'd kick ass.

It had been the most perfect Fourth of July of my life, and I got to experience it all over again. After we won the game, the vision faded, and I was once again standing across from an adult Maisie in our little room. I felt tears form in my eyes. "That was incredible," I said. "How did you do it?"

"Just a little trick Ginny taught me," she responded. "Somehow it seemed appropriate to include a bit of her in your gift as well," Maisie said and smiled, though her eyes betrayed the loss she felt. The cake in her hands disappeared and was replaced by an old Ball jar. She ran her finger around its lip, and the remaining flames started to descend and fill the jar. All except the odd blue one. "You've got nineteen more to enjoy whenever you like. But I'd like it if you looked at my wish now." She tightened the lid on the jar and handed it to me. I gazed for a moment at the flames, which were bouncing around like so many trapped lightning bugs. I wasn't going to waste them; I would parcel them out and save them for the days when I really needed a happy memory. Still feeling giddy with wonder, I set the jar down on an old table that had been relegated to the closet.

I looked up and reached out for the hovering blue flame, this time feeling an intense spark, like a jolt of static electricity. Once again we were in Forsyth, and once again it was summer. But Maisie looked like she was in her late twenties or early thirties. Children were playing nearby—two perfect little blondes and a couple of rough and tumble redheads. My heart swelled at the site of the redheaded little ones. They looked so much like me, but each of them had mismatched eyes—one blue, one green. Maisie poured me a glass of cold wine, and I turned when I heard a voice. Jackson and Peter were standing by a smoking grill, beers sweating in their hands. Settling herself down next to me on the ground, Maisie called out something to our children and then kissed my cheek.

When the vision faded, Maisie was standing across the room from me, and the smile had left her lovely face. "It's very difficult for me," she said, "not to read your thoughts. We are so connected. I try to stay out of your head, but when you have an intense feeling, it just comes to me. I can't help it."

I stared at her like a deer caught in headlights.

"I know how you feel about Jackson . . ."

"I am so sorry," I interrupted her.

The smile returned to her lips, and she rushed forward and hugged me. "I know you are. Truly, I know you are. And I want you to know that I understand. Believe me, if anyone understands why you love Jackson, it's me." She released me from her embrace, but kept my forearms in her hands. "I know if you could change the way you feel, you would," she said. Then she asked me, "Is that why you went to Jilo?"

There was no use denying it, my thoughts evidently belonged to her almost as much as they did to me. "Yes," I said. "I wanted a spell that would make me feel for Peter . . ."

"The way you feel for Jackson," Maisie finished for me. "Did she work it?"

"I changed my mind. I told her not to," I said. "But she told me she was going to do it anyway."

"That is not good," Maisie responded. "Love spells almost always backfire. The feelings they create aren't real, they're counterfeit, and they can easily warp into passions that have nothing to do with real love. I'd never attempt something so foolish. Have you noticed any changes in the way you feel about Peter?"

"No," I responded, but then the thought I'd been suppressing since the moment I found Ginny's corpse mushroomed up before me. "She said the spell would take blood. Lots of it." My body began to tremble.

"Don't even go there," Maisie said. "The old bat was just pulling your leg. You don't use blood to work a love spell. Even if Jilo was involved with Ginny's murder, it had nothing to do with you or this spell. You hear me?" I nodded, feeling an enormous weight lift off my chest.

"I suspect that Jilo was totally bluffing about working the spell, but if you do notice anything out of the ordinary, you come to me." She paused for a second before continuing. "The sad thing is that if you ever do open your fool eyes, part of you will always wonder if your change of heart had something to do with Jilo. But let's not think too far ahead. For now, you stay clear of Jilo. She is dangerous. Don't ever go to her again. For anything." She released me and paced the room. After an eternity she finally stopped, and turned to look at me. "I've always envied you, you know?"

"You envied *me*?" The thought was too preposterous. I had spent my entire life in her shadow—less pretty, powerless, and probably less intelligent too.

"Yes. I've envied your freedom. While you were out wandering around Savannah and making friends, Ginny kept me close," she said. "She always thought I'd take over from her one day, and she spent my whole life training me for it. I was always okay with that, but I did think it would come much later in life, after I'd done a little living. I'd even hoped the two of us could travel the world together once we gained access to our share in the family trust."

"We still can," I said.

"Not if I become the anchor. Anchors hold the line in place, and I'll need to spend the rest of my life within a stone's throw of this city. But I am okay with that, since I will have Jackson here with me." She began to pace again. "It's only that your life has so many possibilities for happiness. For me there is only Jackson." She stopped and turned to look at me again. "I can't tell you whether Peter is the right man for you. All I know is that he adores you; he always has. But I can tell you that Jackson loves me. He does."

"I know he does," I assured her, but she ignored me.

"I sense, though, that it's in your power to confuse him about that. He's as drawn to you as you are to him."

"How could he ever want me when he has you?" I asked sincerely.

Maisie was momentarily at a loss for words. Finally she shook her head and rolled her eyes. "Mercy, your perception of yourself is way off. If you saw yourself the way Peter sees you, the way Jackson sees you, you wouldn't be asking that question. But please, don't make me stroke your ego at the same time I am begging you to leave Jackson to me."

"I'm sorry," I said, feeling both selfish and narcissistic. This time I approached her and put my arms around her.

She let me draw her close for a few moments, but then gently pushed me away. "We understand each other, then?"

"Yes, we do," I responded. "And please promise me that you know that I love you more than any other person on earth, and that I would never knowingly do anything to hurt you."

She smiled and shook her head. "I've got one more surprise, and I hope you'll be happy for me. It's been killing me not to say anything to you." Beaming, she pulled a chain out of her shirt collar and revealed a solitaire engagement ring. "Jackson and I are getting married! We've been waiting for the right time to start telling everyone, and I wanted to start by telling you. We were going to make an announcement the next time the family got together, but considering the circumstances of the current reunion . . ." her voice trailed off. I felt my attention, my entire being contract as I stared into the ring's gleaming stone. "Well, say something, Mercy! Are you happy for me?" Maisie's voice took on a keening quality. She stood there frozen, waiting for me to respond.

I shook myself back into my body. "Of course! Of course, I am happy for you!" I pulled her back into my arms. And by God, I *was* happy for her. I had to be. I simply had to be.

There was a loud rap on the door. I turned and opened it to find Connor standing on the opposite side, pendulum in hand. "Found you," he said, looking past me at Maisie. "Your aunts and I need to talk to you about the lot drawing."

"We'll need Mercy too," Maisie said. "She's going to be part of the draw." I noticed she had surreptitiously tucked the engagement ring back inside her shirt.

"All Mercy needs to know," Connor said, speaking as if I weren't even there, "is that she'll stick her hand into a bag and pull out a white chip of wood. You, on the other hand, stand a very good chance of being selected as Ginny's replacement. And that would mean a lot of changes in your life." Connor eyed her. "A lot of changes."

A shadow crossed Maisie's face. "Even if I am selected, I won't make the choices that Ginny did. I'm going to have a life of my own."

"Well, my girl, let's see how things shake out before you get your dander all up. And don't go judging Ginny too fast. You might find yourself wearing her shoes and then you can start making speeches about how you aren't going to be like her. Come on, now. Your aunts are waiting for us."

Maisie gave me one last smile. "Happy birthday, sis," she said and headed from the room.

"I love you," I called after her. Connor gave me a cool, dismissive look—his nickname for me flitted through my head, "The Disappointment"—then padded out of the room after Maisie. I returned my attention to the jar of memories Maisie had given me. It was cool to the touch, but bright as a nightlight. I took it to my room for safekeeping and hid it inside a box of toys and things from my childhood that I was saving for the day I would have my own children, perhaps the very same redheaded ruffians Maisie had envisioned for me.

EIGHT

I felt the cousins' prying minds swoop over me, so I extended the mental image of a "No Trespassing" sign and then a fist with a raised middle finger for those who wouldn't take the hint. The probes fell off en masse. I decided to get out. It would be lunch time soon, and I knew Peter's crew always took their break in Chatham Square, so I decided to swing by Parker's Market for provisions and surprise him with a picnic. The memory of what had happened after my last visit to his work site tried to surface, but I pushed it away. I grabbed my backpack, dumping the Liar's Tour souvenirs out onto my bed. There would be plenty of time to start doing tours again after Ginny's funeral.

I caught a glimpse of myself in the mirror, and briefly considered applying at least a little makeup, using the artistry Ellen had taught me. With the golden light playing on my cheekbones, I looked pretty, even beautiful. It helped that Maisie wasn't standing next to me. In comparison to her, I would always suffer. Realizing that any attempt at a pageant queen face would melt as soon as I stepped outside, I applied a little moisturizer with sunscreen and called it good. Makeup was the surest way to tell a tourist from a woman who lived in Savannah—only a tourist would be foolish enough to think her foundation could withstand ninety-eight degrees combined with 98 percent humidity. I pulled my hair back into a ponytail, knowing full well that anything else would be a waste of time. I changed into cutoffs and a snug tank top, hoping that the judicious showing of a little skin would make up for the sweaty mess I'd be by the time I arrived. I slung the backpack over my shoulder and went outside.

Stepping out into the Savannah day was like walking into a steam bath. Perspiration immediately began to build beneath the strap of my backpack. I found my bike and hopped onto it, the metal of its frame fiery against my thighs.

But in spite of the overwhelming heat, I felt freer than I had in months. It was like the weight of the world had been lifted from my shoulders. I no longer had to hide my feelings about Jackson from Maisie. Yes, I was in love with him. No, I didn't have to act on those feelings. Maybe I was just confused. Hopefully I could move on, with or without Jilo's meddling. I owed it to my sister to try, and I certainly owed it to Peter. Truth was, I owed it to myself. Maisie and Peter had been the two most loving constants in my life.

After picking up lunch at the grocery store, I dug deep into my bike's pedals, eager to get to Chatham Square as fast as I could. I didn't register any more of my surroundings than my basic survival instincts required, and as I neared the square, I hopped off my bike and started walking, already scanning the area for Peter.

"Mercy!" A sleazy voice pulled me out of my thoughts. I was approaching the northeast corner of the square when a new red Mercedes convertible pulled up beside me. "Mercy." This time the voice came more softly, teetering on the tightrope between greeting and proposition. The car came to a full stop. It was Tucker Perry. Great. "How are you, darlin'? My condolences about Ginny. Terrible business this all is."

"Thank you, Mr. Perry." I kept walking, but the car slid predatorily alongside me.

"I sure wish there were something I could do to make you feel better. Take your mind off everything." His smile was crooked, causing his right eye to squint a tad. I felt the sudden need for a shower. The thought of my lovely Ellen submitting to Perry's touch made me shudder.

"The thought is much appreciated." I forced a smile. "But I should be on my way now." Relief flooded over me as I saw Peter crossing the square toward us with a protective look on his face. He was bare chested, with his T-shirt clutched in his right hand.

"My offer to take you to the next Tillandsia still stands," Tucker said, taking note of Peter's approach. "Bringing you in would be completing the circle in a way. Your mama always enjoyed it so." Peter crossed the road and came up beside me. "We could use some fresh blood. You'd both be more than welcome. You and your young man there too."

"Thank you Mr. Perry, but I don't think so," I said, biting my tongue so I wouldn't say more. I was itching to tell him off.

"Everything good here?" Peter said, his eyes glued on Tucker.

"It all looks good to me." Tucker looked us both up and down and made that same crooked grin. "Well, I'd better be getting on. You let me know if you reconsider, Mercy." He sped off without another word.

"What the hell was that all about?" Peter asked, watching as the Mercedes disappeared from sight.

"Tillandsia," I responded. "Tucker seems to think we'd want to waste our nights drinking with him."

"Well, he could not be more wrong about that," Peter said, then turned to face me. He leaned in and surprised me with a kiss. "What are you doing around here?"

To hell with nonchalance, I decided. Here in front of me was a simple, wholesome man who loved me. No strings tying him to anyone else. No ulterior motives. "I missed you, so I came to see you. Is that all right?"

"That is way more than all right," he responded, his face lighting up with a smile. "Come sit with me." He took charge of my bike with his right hand and slid his left hand to the small of my back, guiding me gently into the square. He carefully set my bike down under the shade of one of the live oak trees and sat down next to it. "Pull up some turf," he said, patting the ground next to him. I carefully dropped the backpack of food in between us. "Any news about Ginny's funeral yet? I'll try to get off, but the boss said I had to give him a few days' notice."

"No, we aren't sure when her body will be released."

"I still don't understand how it could have happened," he said. "And why your family can't just do their hocus-pocus to find who did it." His untroubled acceptance of my family's powers made me smile. We had grown up together, but even with full knowledge of who my family was, and what they could do, he had never once pulled away from us like most normal people did.

"I am right there with you," I said. "A few weeks ago, I would have thought it was impossible for anything to harm Ginny. They've been trying to track down the murderer, but so far no luck, either for my family or for the police."

The rest of the crew had found their way to the park, and the men were spilling in around us. "Hey, Pete," one of them called. "That your dessert?"

"Damn, and all I got was a pudding cup," another of the guys hooted.

"Can I have a taste, Petey?" a short wiry guy called out.

"Ignore them. Those bastards would give anything to be sitting here with you. And I can't blame them," he said, but I could tell from the way he looked at the other men that they were pushing their luck. He noticed the backpack. "You doing a tour today?" he asked.

I opened my backpack and handed him his sandwich. "I brought you lunch," I said, suddenly self-conscious. Exposed and vulnerable in a way that a few catcalls could never make me.

"Lunch, huh," he smiled happily. "This really was premeditated, then?"

"Yeah, I guess it was." An innocent joy washed over him, and on his face I saw real love, not some horrible Hoodoo counterfeit. He deserved the real kind too, and I was determined to try to find it in myself to give it to him. And if I couldn't, I'd just have to find the strength to set him free. I cursed myself for ever going to Jilo. I pushed the thought of her away, only to find my thoughts returning to an equally undesirable person—Tucker. "Tucker told me that my mother was the one who got him involved in Tillandsia," I said. "Maybe that's where she met my father."

"Okay," Peter said. "What are you thinking?"

"That I might be able to learn something if I take him up on his offer to introduce me to the club. Maybe it would help me figure out who my dad is."

He was quiet for a moment, his face a kaleidoscope of conflicting emotions. "Listen," he said. "I don't think that would be a very good idea."

"Why not?"

"It's just that I don't know what went on in the club when your mama was in it. I'm sure it wasn't anything like the stuff they get up to today, but . . ." He paused.

"But what?"

"Well I've heard talk around the bar. They get up to some pretty wild things in Tillandsia these days. It's turned into a kind of swingers club." He looked guilty, as if he'd been forced to tell me there was no such thing as Santa. "You know I love Ellen, and I don't mean to judge her, but Mercy, Tillandsia is no place for you."

"But if what you say about Tillandsia is true, and it was like that when my mama was involved, any of the men in the club could be my father, even Tucker Perry."

"Not a chance," Peter said through his sandwich. "If Tucker thought you and Maisie could be his girls, he wouldn't be sniffing around the two of you so much."

"You sure about that?" I asked him. "'Cause I am not so sure myself."

Peter's face turned gray, and he lowered his sandwich. "I think I lost my appetite." He wrapped the sandwich back in its cellophane. "Naw, even Tucker Perry isn't that much of a perv," he said after a moment, trying to convince me, and probably even himself. "Listen. I could talk to Tucker. I *should* talk to Tucker. I've been wanting to, but I didn't want to overstep my boundaries."

"What boundaries?" I asked.

"My boundaries with you," he said. "I didn't know for sure if you would want me to stand up to Tucker as your . . ."

"As my what?" I prompted him.

"As your man," he said, and a nervous look came into his eyes, crowned by a twitch in his forehead. "I'm not sure if that's how you see me, but I do know you well enough never to just presume."

I took it all in—the warm light from his mismatched eyes, the sun setting his hair on fire, and his strength and kindness. Still I hesitated an instant too long.

"I always thought the two of us were bound to end up together sooner or later," he said. "Until Jackson came to town, that is." I didn't know what to say. It was one thing for Maisie to read me, but if my feelings were so obvious to Peter, the most normal man I had ever met, I stunk at hiding my emotions. "I don't mind that

I'm not your first choice, Mercy," he said, saving me from the silence. "Not as long you eventually get around to choosing me."

I felt a stirring in my heart, but I knew it wasn't the result of any Hoodoo—it was a recognition of Peter's goodness. I crossed the few feet over to him on my knees, then pressed my lips against his, wrapping my arms around him. He kissed me back and pulled me to his chest, like he was trying to pull me into him. Peter was a wonderful man. He'd be a good husband and a good father when the time came. Instead of a magical passion, I felt a sudden peace growing in me, a knowledge that somehow we were going to make our relationship work, whatever it took.

I stopped kissing Peter and looked him dead in the eye. "I think you need to go have a man-to-man talk with Tucker."

"Oh, and I am going to do just that," he said and began kissing me again.

"I would tell them to get a room," I heard one of Peter's coworkers say to the others, "but truth is, I'd kind of like to watch."

NINE

The day was hot, and only going to get hotter, so I was grateful for the air-conditioning in the limo, particularly since I was wearing black. We were on the way to Greenwich Cemetery, where Ginny would be laid to rest. Ginny had insisted that she wanted to be buried on her own, away from the rest of the family. Since we wouldn't give her a moment's peace in life, she'd say, she was going to be damned sure that death would allow her a little privacy. Unlike so many who died in Savannah, Ginny's spirit had not lingered. Her essence had passed on to another plane, and I said a silent prayer that she would find happiness wherever she was.

Oliver, Iris, and Ellen were riding with the body, and Connor, Maisie, Jackson, and I were following in a second vehicle. I looked at my reflection in the limo's window, and watched the world go by through my own image. Outside there were tourists in Hawaiian print shirts lining up to board a trolley. Inside there were black outfits and pearls and somber ties. Outside, in Forsyth Park, a few children ran ahead of their mothers and then stopped dead in their tracks at the sound of a voice I couldn't hear. Inside, I was doing my best not to listen as Connor droned on to Jackson about this, that, and everything—none of it important. I wanted to be able to listen to my own thoughts, but Connor's drivel lined my skull like ugly wallpaper.

Surrounded by my nearest blood, I felt entirely alone. I wished Peter could be here with me, but the site foreman had given him a very clear choice: show up for work as usual or never show up again. I offered to have Oliver pay the man a visit, but Peter seemed somewhat offended by the idea. "People like me, Mercy, like us, we don't rely on those kinds of tricks. We come by things honestly." I respected him for that, and even though I wished he were here to hold my hand, the way I knew—without even looking—that Jackson was holding my sister's, I was glad he felt the way he did.

I turned away from the window and my gaze fell on Maisie. It didn't take a mind reader to know that her mind was focused on one thing, the drawing of the lots. It was scheduled for tonight. I closed my eyes and said another silent prayer, this time for Maisie. I hoped that the power would settle itself on another. She thought she was prepared for the responsibility, but I wanted her to have her own life. A life that wasn't anchored to the line. And in my heart, I felt a sudden conviction that my prayer would be answered, that Maisie would be spared the burden of assuming Ginny's mantle, at least for now.

I felt the weight of Jackson's gaze fall on me. My heart began to pound when our eyes met, and the temperature around me soared. I always thought it was a joke when people said that you hear violin music when you're looking at your true love, but I swear I heard the rush of strings. I tried to look away, but his eyes held mine like a vise. Could that look in them be longing? I wondered if Maisie was right, and he really was torn between us. There had been that moment at the hospital after all . . . For a second I was lost, drowning in desire for him. The flame that I'd tried to smother was rekindled, and it burned all around me.

Then I noticed that Jackson was indeed holding Maisie's right hand in his left. A dark red shame filled me as I acknowledged that my thoughts were a betrayal of both my sister and Peter. I would not pursue my interest in Jackson, nor would I do anything to encourage him.

Guilt forced me to look away, and I returned my focus to my surroundings. The quirky, historic Savannah that I loved faded quickly into a no-man's-land of generic strip malls and discount stores. The road to the cemetery seemed too suburban to belong to Savannah proper, and I only felt a returning sense of home as we drew near the gates of the far more famous Bonaventure Cemetery, where my own mother and grandparents were interred. You can't reach Greenwich without passing by Bonaventure, and I promised myself that once the heat broke, I'd bike out and bring flowers for their graves, and maybe even a few for Ginny's.

The sun had reached its apogee, so the minister took mercy on us, speeding through a prayer that we all knew would mean little if anything to Ginny and then sprinkling the first handful of earth over the coffin. I broke away from the gathering and returned to the car, praying that the driver still had the air-conditioning running.

I was within yards of the waiting limo when an elderly man approached me. His face was familiar, but I couldn't quite place it.

"Miss Taylor, I would appreciate you coming with me."

Three things stopped me dead in my tracks: his calm demeanor, his gentle voice, and the terror in his eyes. My heart started beating like mad. I'd been around witches my entire life, and I instantly knew that he was being compelled, and through him, so was I. His request was no request, and I had no choice but to comply. That sure didn't stop me from trying. I lifted a foot and told it to move backward. It carried me forward instead, bringing me one step closer to the car. I turned my head, hoping that someone from the family had followed me and would figure out what was going on, but no luck. They were probably still gathered around Ginny's grave. The only other people in sight were a group of ghost hunters. They were shooting pictures of one of the more elaborate gravestones, desperately hoping to catch a glimpse of the supernatural yet completely oblivious to what was going on right under their noses.

I tried to call out to them, but instead heard myself saying, "Thank you, I'd love a ride" loud enough for all the ghost hunters to hear. I took a few lunging steps forward, walking awkwardly enough to cause someone in their group to comment on my sobriety. Within moments, they lost all interest in me and went back to taking pictures of illuminated dust.

The driver helped me into the passenger's seat of the car, then leaned in over me. "This ain't permanent," he said. He passed his hand over my eyes, and my vision instantly went black. "That is only until I get you where we going. Now you gonna sit still for me and don't make any fuss."

I felt my body go rigid. My adrenaline-induced sweat chilled in the car's air-conditioning and started to trickle down my spine. He buckled me in and closed the door for me.

"I sure am sorry about all this, Miss Taylor," he said as he took his place behind the wheel. "I'm sure you'll understand when I say I ain't got no more choice about this than you do. Jilo making me take you, just like she making you come." He shifted the car into drive and turned right.

"What does Jilo want from me? Where are you taking me?" I asked, fear mixing with anger.

"She won't let me talk to you about that, miss," he said.

"Then tell me how I know you," I demanded. "You look familiar."

"Why, you don't know me at all," he responded. "But I believe you have met my grandson. He's a policeman." Pride played in his voice, overcoming the forced circumstances that brought us together.

"Detective Cook is your grandson?" I heard myself ask. Now that I knew, the resemblance was unmistakable. They shared the same warm skin and tea-colored eyes. Jilo must have felt pretty confident in herself to use Cook's grandfather as a pawn in her game.

"That's right, miss."

"Can you call him? Tell him where you are taking me?"

"Oh, miss, you know Mother Jilo is cleverer than that," he responded. "I'd love nothing better than to help you, but she got me on a very short leash. And I can't fight against her power any more than you can."

I followed as best I could the turns we made, sure that once or twice we must have looped back. Oddly, we never stopped. Not for a stop sign. Not for a light. I lost any hope of knowing where we were headed.

We continued driving for what seemed like hours. Then I felt the asphalt give way to loose stones beneath us, and after a while we finally slowed and stopped. He opened my door, and the car was flooded with heat and the sound of cicadas.

"Allow me," he said, reaching in to take my hand. He helped me out of the car, and I began to listen intently for any sounds that might betray our whereabouts. I heard only the insects and the crunch of gravel beneath my feet. "We gotta walk the rest of the way from here, but it ain't far."

Suddenly I knew I was going to die in this place. He had taken me out to a grave, where he would kill me and leave me, and my body would decay. I wouldn't even see it coming. Maybe in time,

Connor would track down my remains with his flaccid pendulum. But it would be way too late. I'd be as dead as Ginny was.

"You're going to kill me, aren't you?" I heard my disembodied voice ask.

"Good lord, sweet girl! No, I ain't going to harm a hair on your pretty red head." We continued on down the path, the gravel changing to sandy soil that began to filter into my shoes.

"Unless she makes you," I responded after a few more steps.

"She can't make me do that. I'm a bus driver. She can make me drive, 'cause that comes natural to me. I sure ain't no killer, though. She can't make me hurt you."

"But that doesn't mean she doesn't have someone that killing comes natural to waiting for me," I said.

That he said nothing to the contrary told me he agreed that it was a possibility. We continued on in silence for a few moments longer. "But you a Taylor, my girl. Ain't they nothin' you can do to protect yourself?"

"Sorry. Shooting blanks," I said, laughing in spite of myself.

"Well, you know I be praying for you. If my prayers count for anything, you will see the sun rise tomorrow," he said and then stopped. "We here. They gonna be a few steps up now." He guided me up onto a porch. I felt a bug strike my face and nearly jumped out of my skin. "It's okay, girl. You be brave. Now, she say this is as far as I can take you." I heard a screen door screech open, and he guided me over the threshold. Another set of stronger and rougher hands took charge of me, and I was swept through the entrance and into another room. The door slammed shut behind me.

"You can see again now," a sorghum-sweet voice allowed. My vision returned instantly, and I felt my limbs return to my own control. The room, walls, and floor were all the same color, the aquamarine shade known around these parts as "haint blue," prized for its efficacy in repelling insects and unfriendly spirits. In the center of the room sat a single chair, and on that chair sat Mother Jilo, resplendent in shades of blue and purple that could arouse envy in a morning glory. On her lap sat a three-legged cat that purred as she scratched its head. The recipe for true haint blue called for the ashes of a cat's left back leg. I had a feeling that I knew what had happened to the feline's missing appendage.

"Why did you bring me here?" I asked. Jilo ignored my question.

"Come closer," she commanded.

"I told you I don't want your spells," I protested, even as my feet obeyed. They carried me within arm's length of her throne. "I should have never come to you in the first place, and I don't want anything more to do with you." Even though my body was under Jilo's control, my hands still had enough will of their own to clench into fists. I leaned as far back from her as her powers would allow.

She surveyed me up and down slowly then said, "So you wondering why Jilo brought you here. And I am sure you are wondering where 'here' even is, but I tell you these are the wrong things to be wondering. What you should be asking yourself is why your people never even taught you how to defend yo'self against being taken. Why you think that is, girl? Go on, you answer Jilo."

"I guess they thought folk would have more sense than to mess with me." The sound of my voice shocked me. I sounded angry . . . no, I sounded downright pissed. Jilo laughed, a deep and hearty sound that told me she really was amused.

"That's okay, girl. You should be mad. But you shouldn't be mad at Mother. You should be mad at that high and mighty family of yours. They the ones who left you defenseless. Not Jilo." Shadows formed at the edge of the room and began to advance on me, bumping up against my legs and sniffing at me like wild dogs. My instincts told me not to move.

"Back!" Jilo screamed, and the shadows scurried away and cowered in the corner. The individual gray shadows merged together, forming a single black mass.

"What are those things?" I asked and then corrected myself. "That thing?"

"That none of your concern," she responded. "Old Ginny in the ground now. That mean Jilo wins." She laughed her laugh that sounded like something between amusement and a death rattle.

"Did you kill her?" I demanded.

Jilo stopped laughing and leaned in close to me. "Jilo told you the spell she workin' for you took blood." Her eyes widened, and she began to cackle. My knees turned to jelly at the old woman's words. If Maisie hadn't assured me that blood was never really used in love spells, I might have collapsed completely. She winded herself with her laughter, and it took her a few moments to catch her breath. "Maybe Jilo killed the old woman, and maybe she didn't. What you willing to sacrifice to find out?" she asked, the cat on her lap stretching and licking its phantom limb. "I've seen you going around town, telling your lies for money. You charge for lies. Jilo gonna charge you for the truth."

I was relieved that she wanted something from me. The fact that I had something to offer bettered my chances of not ending up being planted at her crossroads. "I don't have any money. At least not now. I will after my birthday. If you let me live. Me and Detective Cook's grandfather. You let us live, and I'll let you have everything coming to me."

"Girl, Jilo don't need or want your dirty Taylor money," she said, disgusted. "And Henry is well beyond any help you can offer him."

"Then why do you want to hurt me?" I asked.

"Jilo got no need to hurt you. Jilo got better use for you. And that is for you to let her show you the ways. Let her teach you like Ginny oughta done."

"And what if I don't want that?"

"Then you ain't as smart as Jilo gave you credit for." She paused. "And you won't be under her protection no more." The shadow in the corner of the room moved a foot closer, but Jilo held up her hand to stop its progress. "I know your family," she said. "I know they secrets, things they shouldn't be keeping secret from you. Every time you come to Jilo, she send you away with one truth. We see how much truth you can take."

"But why are you doing this? Why would you care if I can do magic or learn my family's secrets?"

"'Cause, my girl, I want to hurt them. And I want to hurt them in a way that no killin' can. I want them to see themselves reflected in the hate shining through yo' pretty green eyes. Once you know them the way Jilo know them, you will understand why." Hatred carved wrinkles in her forehead and around the edges of her mouth. Her lips curled back into a hiss.

"I don't want to hurt them. I don't care what they've done," I said.

"You say that 'cause you don't have any idea what they done. Not just what they done to Jilo, but what they done to *you*. You come to me, you come to me willingly next time, and Jilo tell you what happened to your precious Ginny. Not that Jilo understand why you care what happened to her. The old one sure didn't care about you. You decide. You come to Jilo if you want to know.

"Now to show you Jilo acting in good faith, she give you one secret for free. You go ask that fairy uncle of yours why my grand-baby walked into the river and she never come back out." With that, Jilo snapped her fingers and the room went black. I groped along the wall, feeling for the door, and my fingers brushed over a light switch. When I flicked it on, I nearly fell back in shock. The chair was gone, and the room was no longer cyan. I was in the room of shared secrets, the linen closet on the upper floor of the house where I'd been raised. Jilo had made her point. If she could reach into our home, into the heart of my childhood, she had all the power she needed, borrowed or not.

TEN

As I rushed to my bedroom, I heard voices coming up from the ground floor. I must have been gone for hours, but apparently the post-funeral potluck was still in full swing. I locked the door behind me; it wouldn't stand a chance at keeping Jilo out, but it might at least encourage my cousins to respect my privacy. My glowing digital alarm clock caught my eye, and I gasped out loud. Only an hour had passed since I'd first laid eyes on Adam's grandfather at the cemetery. I wondered if magic had bent time or if my perception had been twisted by fear.

I shed the clothes I had worn to the funeral, promising myself I would burn them, and sat on the edge of my bed, more tired than I had ever felt in my life. I wondered if Jilo had "borrowed" some of my own life force to put on her little magic show for me. The urge to lie down for a few minutes hit me, and I was too tired to hit back. I scooted up onto the bed and closed my eyes.

Seconds later I opened them. To my surprise, the clock next to me revealed that two hours had passed. My skin was tingling slightly, and I felt disoriented and a little nauseated. The objects in my field of vision seemed to exist in more than one spot at a time, as if several versions of the same thing were slightly overlapping each other. Jilo had definitely stretched time a bit; my exhaustion and disorientation were signs that it was snapping itself back into shape around me. From what my family had always said, this kind of manipulation was above Jilo's pay grade, but she had managed to get the juice from somewhere. Maybe she'd done it so that my absence from the house would go unnoticed, but more likely she'd just wanted to show me what she could do. Sometimes I really hated magic, especially since I was always on the receiving end.

I could still hear a large group of people conversing on the ground floor. Most of the nonrelated mourners would undoubtedly have made their excuses by now and headed home, but the cousins weren't going anywhere until Ginny's replacement, the new anchor, was selected tonight. I felt desperate for an escape, and seeing as Jilo could reach directly into my house, I figured I'd be as safe on the streets of Savannah as I was in my own room. The thought of visiting Peter flitted through my mind, but he wouldn't be done with work for a few hours, and I didn't want to get him in trouble with his boss.

I wanted more than anything to turn this into as normal a day as possible. It was a bit after two, plenty of time for me to get out for a while and still be back for the drawing of the lots that would determine who took over for Ginny. I'd use my window escape route to avoid the family gathering.

I rolled off the bed and went to my mirror. My hair had turned into a tangled mess as I slept, so I did my best to work through the worst bits, tugging it back into a ponytail. I'd have to make more of an effort for tonight's ceremony, but for now, I pulled on an old T-shirt and a pair of comfortable cutoffs.

The heat roiled into the room the moment I opened the window. I took a deep breath and plunged into it headfirst, feeling like I was climbing into an oven. I grabbed hold of the trellis with my right hand and swung my right leg out. Once I had my feet safely in position, I leaned back and used my left hand to slide the window mostly closed, leaving just enough of an opening for my fingers so that I could go back in the same way I had come out. The bougainvillea scraped against my exposed skin, but all of the practice from my teenage years served me well. I made it to the ground without a single scratch. I heard a few people talking out front, so I scanned the yard to make sure none of the guests were lingering between me and the garage. No one was in sight, so I crept over to it to retrieve my bike.

The heat was so intense that visible waves rose up not only from the paved area, but from the sandy soil beyond the reach of our lawn sprinklers. I was about to grab my bike and head out when I sensed something strange in my field of vision. I returned my attention to the gray and gritty dirt and realized that my first impression had been off. The ground wasn't reflecting heat—it was actually pulsating. Before common sense could trump curiosity, my feet led me over for a closer look.

The soil pulsed like there was a heartbeat just beneath the surface and as I watched, the particles started to attach themselves to each other. At first, there were only five little ridges, like five anthills forcing themselves upward. But within moments, the ridges grew and a distinctly human shape began to form in their place. A scream started to form in my lungs, but the sound didn't pass my lips as anything more than a muted, "Meeep." My mouth opened and closed, like a fish gasping in the air. A hand began to reach up from the earth in front of me. No, it wasn't reaching up from beneath the surface, it was forming itself from the powdery dirt. A wrist and then a forearm grew before my eyes, stretching up toward the sun. I couldn't move. A shoulder formed and then in one forceful jerk, a roughly hewn head and neck tore themselves from the ground. As gray as the soil from which it came, the creature's skin was smooth, and it glistened in the sun. Then its eyes opened, soulless and streaked like large amber cat's-eye marbles.

I finally found my voice. Screaming at the top of my lungs, I fell back onto the ground, frantically crawling away from the creature that was coming to life before me. Its upper body and torso were fully formed now, and it continued to watch with glassy eyes as I scrambled backward. I felt arms wrap around me from behind, pulling me up from the ground. I screamed and started striking wildly with my hands.

"It's me, Mercy," Jackson spoke into my ear. "I've got you. I've got you." He swung me up into his steely arms like I was a small child. "What the hell is that thing?" he asked, backing away.

"I don't know. I don't know." Sobbing, I buried my head between Jackson's neck and shoulder. I could feel his pulse against my skin, and his scent was calming. I looked back up when someone bumped into us.

A steady stream of cousins had started to pour off the front porch and out of the house, coming to a stop directly in front of us. The creature was complete, and it took a couple of hesitant steps, as if it were trying to orient its body to its surroundings. A sinkhole had formed in the earth that had given it birth. Even though the cousins had formed an impromptu wall between us and the creature, I still had a prime view. The thing had to be almost seven feet tall.

"Well I will be damned!" I heard Connor's voice and then saw him force his way to the front of the group, pushing cousins aside as he went. "I've heard of these things, but I never thought I'd live to see one." He walked right up to the creature and touched it.

"What is it?" I felt Jackson's chest rumble as he asked Connor the question, holding me tightly all the while.

"A golem," I heard Maisie's voice reply. My eyes sought her

out, and I was surprised by how cold her expression was. "It's an animated body made from inanimate matter." She made her way over to us. "You can put my sister down now; she's safe." Jackson hesitated for just a moment. From the expression on her face, Maisie had taken note of his hesitation and read a whole lot of something she didn't like into it. Jackson lowered me gently until my feet felt the ground. My knees were still wobbly, but considering the way Maisie's eyes were narrowed, I knew better than to lean against Jackson for support.

"It scared the crap out of me," I said by way of explanation, or maybe even apology. "It just started forming from the ground with no warning."

The cousins had joined Connor in admiring the thing, and they were no longer paying us any mind. "Okay, so it's a golem," Jackson addressed Maisie with a noticeable edge to his voice. I could tell that he had been frightened too. "What's it doing here?"

"The families," she responded, her shoulders slumped a little when she took in Jackson's tone. I knew she was referring to the nine other witch families who wouldn't be present for the ceremony. "The families created the golem to house the energies from their representatives. You are seeing one body," she explained, "but there are nine intelligences inside of it. They're the families' witnesses to the drawing of the lots."

"You knew this thing was coming?" I asked.

"We only found out like an hour ago," she responded impatiently. "I came up to your room to warn you, but your door was locked, and you wouldn't answer. I figured you were hiding out with your earphones on." She looked up at Jackson. "And I couldn't find you anywhere."

"What? I was outside on the porch having a beer with your cousin from Athens. We were talking football."

Maisie eyed him up and down. "Well, I would appreciate your

support. Today of all days." She shot me a quick, sharp look. "And I mean both of you. I couldn't get to either of you, and then I come out here to see you looking like the cover of some cheap romance novel." She turned and started back toward the house in a huff.

Jackson followed on her heels. "Now, baby, don't be that way," I heard him calling after her. Meanwhile the group surrounding the golem shifted as the creature began walking toward the house.

With the wall to my back, I inched farther and farther away. Its movements were halting and cumbersome at first, but after a few more steps, it began to proceed at a nearly human gait. I realized that its features had refined themselves quite a bit over the past few moments. It no longer looked like a roughly hewn statue. Except for its unnatural color, it might have been mistaken for an actual human being from a distance. A large and naked human being. I prayed that the creature wouldn't be anatomically correct, but as the cousins moved to give him a wider berth, I realized that nothing was going to go my way today. Its skin was turning a Mediterranean olive, and for some reason the realistic new skin tone made the whole naked thing more of an issue.

Although I couldn't tear my eyes away from the creature, I gladly lifted them and focused on its face instead. It was beautiful, and I recognized it instantly—it was the spitting image of Bernini's *David*. Dark eyebrows had taken shape on the thing's well-formed skull, and its scalp was filling in with curly black hair. After some indeterminate point in the transformation, I found myself thinking of the creature as a "he" rather than an "it." All the same, I didn't like the idea of being too close to him. After a few more moments had passed, he fixed his gaze on me and took a few confident steps right up to me. The cousins who had been entranced by his metamorphosis crowded in on us.

"You are Emily's child," he said, and it sounded as if many

voices were speaking at once. Baritone and tenor, soprano and bass mixed into an unnatural wave of sound.

"One of them," I responded, pushing my back closer to the wall. "But you are probably looking for my sister."

He drew nearer, and I noticed that the amber in his eyes had begun to recede, whites forming around them. The cat's eye swirl had coalesced into a large but fairly normal looking pupil. Those eyes took me in from head to toe. "Do you consider your outfit appropriate mourning attire?" the multilayered voice asked.

At that moment all my fear dissipated, and I wanted nothing more in the world than to kick him in his newly formed testicles. "Do you consider your outfit appropriate mourning attire?" I parroted, poking him in the chest with my finger. He was warm to the touch. Very warm. I pulled my hand back quickly.

"No, you are correct," he replied, and the air around him began to shimmer. A well-tailored, single-breasted dark suit wrapped around him. Under it, a crisp white shirt and an expertly knotted tie. He had gone from Georgia dust to male model in mere minutes. "Please change into something better suited to the occasion. Something that shows respect for Ginny's memory and for the role you will be playing in selecting her replacement. We will wait for you inside."

"How about you go straight to hell?" I put my hands on my hips and dug my heels in.

Although the golem stood stock still, the voices burst from the golem, this time not in chorus, but like an angry debate. For a moment I thought the golem might be coming undone. Then the voices paused. "You are angry because we frightened you," he said—*they* said—in a unified and reasonable baritone. "It was not our intention. It was unfortunate that you witnessed our arrival without warning."

"And this is the point where you apologize for your bad attitude, young lady," commanded Connor, who had drawn up near us.

I realized what the families had said through their mouthpiece was as close to an apology as I'd ever get. I wasn't sorry, but I knew my life would be easier if I gave them what they wanted. "You're right. I apologize," I said, mentally adding *for being scared out of my wits twice today and thinking there was a rule of one person per body.* Without another word to acknowledge my apology, the golem turned from me and headed toward the front door.

"Do as he says—change into something appropriate," Connor barked as he pushed past me. "And then meet us in the kitchen."

ELEVEN

I ignored the request for a wardrobe change. I was not about to be bossed around by a mud pie with an attitude. When I entered the kitchen, the creature and my family were sitting around the table with a bunch of tiles spread out between them. They were the size of dominoes and all but one were white. The odd one out had been stained red. Maisie was gingerly running her finger over the red lot, fascinated but cautious, as if she expected it to deliver a shock. None of the cousins had joined us, and Jackson was nowhere to be seen. He would undoubtedly be glued to Maisie's side if he hadn't been purposely excluded. I wondered who had done the excluding, the rest of the family or Maisie herself.

The creature scanned me with emotionless eyes. "She is an insolent creature," he said as I sat in the last empty chair. His voice modulated between a few different tones at first, but then seemed to settle on one.

"She sure as hell is," Connor said.

"And that is why we love her," Oliver said, pulling me close and planting a kiss on my cheek. "Quite a day we're having here, huh?" he asked me.

"And you don't know the half of it," I responded, wondering when or even if I should ask him Jilo's question. I turned toward the visitor. "What are we supposed to call you anyway?"

"The body does not have a name," he responded. "The body is only a shell." He looked at me as if he were considering a grave problem. "The child is ignorant of our ways," the creature said, speaking about me as if I weren't in the room. "Why have you not taught her?" My heart beat faster as I heard him echo Jilo's words.

"She's got no power," Connor stated as if that explained everything.

"It is what Ginny wanted," Iris added, a heaviness in her voice. "I always questioned the wisdom in it, but Ginny had her mind set. And I never questioned my aunt's commitment to maintaining the line."

I looked at Maisie, whose expression was inscrutable. With a sinking heart, I realized that she had been as much a part of Ginny's conspiracy as the rest. "Ginny taught me," she began. "She told me that I'd gotten all the power, and because of that, all the burden." She looked up at me. "She told me it would be unfair to burden you with knowledge that you would never be able to use."

"By leaving her in the dark, you have left her open to danger," the golem said. I wondered if he were making a blanket statement or if he knew something about my dealings with Jilo.

"It's true," Oliver said. "But Ginny demanded that Mercy wouldn't be taught our secrets because she wasn't born of the power. She worried that what Mercy knew, Mercy could be forced to betray."

"Or choose to betray," Connor said.

"I'd never willingly betray the family," I started to say, but the golem interrupted me.

"So you chose to leave her defenseless?" he asked.

"No, not defenseless," Ellen said, looking around the room at everyone, even me, for corroboration. "Ginny set up protection charms for her."

"But Ginny is gone, and with her, her charms," the creature replied. "Which of you has renewed them?" An embarrassed silence fell over the table. Ellen grasped my hand. A tear plopped down Iris's cheek.

Oliver gave me a guilty look. "I am so sorry, Gingersnap."

"I'm not sure what good these charms are anyway," I responded. "They sure didn't help Ginny."

"Ginny had no such charms for herself," Iris said. "She thought she could take on any comers without them."

"We will renew and strengthen the charms," the golem said.

Maisie turned to address the golem. "I've spent my entire life training with Ginny to take over for her when the time came. I am ready to take over as anchor, and I will always protect my sister."

"You may have chosen the power," the creature responded, "but we will not know until tonight if the power has chosen you." Maisie's face betrayed her surprise—it was clear that she hadn't seriously considered the possibility that anyone else would be chosen. He turned to Ellen. "You will see to it that Ginny's folly is rectified. You will teach her."

"Of course," Oliver responded for Ellen. "We all will. And there's no time to start like the present," he said, shifting to face me. "You already understand the fundamentals of the lottery. All of us with shared blood will take turns drawing a tile," he said, motioning to the tiles on the table with a wave of his hand. "Connor, of course, won't be involved, but the two of you will be." He gave Connor a loaded glance. I knew without asking that Connor had supported Ginny's decision to keep me ignorant, and I could tell that Oliver enjoyed putting the older man in his place. It was rare for any of us to have that opportunity. Connor noisily pushed his chair back from the table and got up to pour himself some coffee.

"But what would lead the power to select a specific person anyway?" I asked. "I mean, why would it pick one of us over one of the Duvals?"

I expected the golem to offer his opinion, but he remained silent.

"I honestly cannot say that anyone knows why a particular person would be picked over another," Iris responded after a pause. She had evidently expected the nine families to put in their two cents as well. "I suspect that the power may have chosen Ginny because it knew she would be willing to sacrifice her entire life to focus on her role as anchor. She was truly single-minded in performing her duty, and I doubt that any other anchor has ever served as loyally. But whatever reasons the power may have behind selecting an anchor, it has chosen a Savannah Taylor for generations, so it's a pretty safe bet that it will choose one of us at this table."

"The important thing for all of us to remember"—Ellen said "us," but her gaze was plainly fixed on Maisie—"is that we don't have to consider Ginny as any kind of role model for how the anchor should live his or her life. Being the anchor was Ginny's entire life. She chose to cut herself off, and her own choices embittered her. Some of the other witch families have anchors who remain very engaged in the world around them. They have careers and children, and anything a body could want from living."

"Of course," Iris said as she turned to face her brother, "if Oliver were selected, he would have to move home. Finally."

"Well, let's burn that bridge when and if we get to it," Oliver replied tersely.

"You are not exactly telling Maisie the truth," Connor said falling heavily back into his chair. "These anchors with careers and children and bright and shiny lives, they are able to have these careers and children because they A, pick a career that allows them enough freedom to be where they need to be when they need to be there and B, marry someone like them. Another witch who can help share the burden of maintaining the line." He looked over at Maisie. "That Jackson boy of yours, he'd get his fuses blown before the rice even got thrown. You'd have to marry into one of the other witch bloodlines."

"It is true," the golem said. "Should Maisie be chosen, the boy would not prove a suitable mate."

Maisie looked at me with panicked eyes. The thought had never occurred to her that becoming the anchor might interfere with the future she wanted with Jackson.

"But what if you don't want it?" I asked for Maisie's sake. "What if you don't want to be chosen?" Maisie was bracing herself to be selected, but I felt certain that she didn't really want it. She wanted the freedom to live her life as she saw fit. She wanted Jackson. Oliver looked at me, and then at Maisie, his eyes zeroing in on the ring hiding beneath Maisie's shirt. Damn it, he was reading me again! I silently pleaded for him to keep quiet.

"Then you are just plumb out of luck," Connor said.

"You don't reason with a lightning bolt or negotiate with a hurricane," Iris said. "The power is a force of nature; witches didn't create it, we merely found a way to ally ourselves with it. I know on the surface it seems like the power is something witches control, but more often than not I think it controls us." She shook her head. "Sometimes it seems to me like there is a sentience, a mind behind it. Sometimes it seems like it's just a current. Either way, it will not be denied."

"Well," Oliver said. "Let's see how things play out before any of us get our panties twisted."

Out of the blue, a new line of reasoning hit me. "What if it were possible for the job to be shared by more than one person?" I asked, still eager for an out.

"It isn't a 'job,'" Iris corrected me. "It's a duty. A calling."

"Besides, sweetie," Ellen added, "there is only so long that a group of people can share a focus strongly enough to hold the line in place."

"But Connor just said that the anchors who married other witches could share," I objected.

"Yes, but for a day at a time or, at most, a week. Small breaks, not on a permanent basis. And it only works then when the two are totally in sync. Almost like twins . . ." She stopped dead.

We all knew what she was thinking, but not even Connor was callous enough to finish her thought. "And if I had any power?" I asked, forcing her to continue.

"Well, then who knows, perhaps you two could have shared the burden successfully. But that obviously wasn't meant to be."

"Mercy, it ain't your fault." I was shocked to hear the words coming from Connor. "You couldn't have chosen to have the power in you any more than Maisie could choose not to. Regardless of who is chosen, your part will end with the drawing of the lots," Connor said, but not in his usual scornful tone. For once he seemed like he was trying to be kind to me. "And that is all you really need to know."

There was silence at the table. "Well, am I lying to the girl?" Connor barked.

"No, you aren't," Iris responded calmly.

"Listen, girl." Connor eyed me. "I know I am not the best uncle a girl like you could want. I know I am a mean old bastard.

And yes, I try to exclude you from things like this. But maybe, just maybe, I exclude you because you are the only one who can be excluded. Who doesn't have to be involved. Look at your sister. You don't think I would love to be able to chase the both of you outside with a fly swatter? Let you both get out in the world and live outside of this bullshit? I may not be kind and I may not be patient, but that doesn't mean I don't want the best for you. Be grateful you don't have to be any more involved in this mess than you are."

"It is her birthright," the golem said coolly. "You have no say in this." Connor and the creature stared at each other. My uncle's face turned purple with rage, and I knew he was about to let loose. A loud knock on the side door made me jump and lanced the tension from the moment. Oliver jumped up and opened the door before the rest of us could blink.

TWELVE

"Adam," Oliver said and stepped aside to reveal Detective Cook.

"I'm sorry to bother y'all today," Cook said. "But I have some news."

"Come on in," Oliver replied. For a brief second Oliver's eyes locked with the detective's and a nearly electrical charge shot between them, heavy with regret, false pride, and hunger. Oliver looked at Cook the same way I knew I looked at Jackson, guilt and desire wrestling it out in his gaze.

"Hello," Cook half said, half asked as he took note of the golem. There remained nothing overtly supernatural about his appearance, so Cook seemed to accept him as a natural, if unknown quantity. "Uh, I have something I'd like to discuss with the immediate family, if that is all right."

"It's all right, Detective Cook," Iris said, labeling the policeman for the golem's benefit. "This is a dear friend of the family, and you can say anything you need to in front of him."

"Okay," Cook responded. "Pleased to meet you . . ."

"Clay," I interjected. "Emmet Clay."

"Mr. Clay," Adam said. I looked over at the golem, surprised to see the corner of his mouth turned up into a sly smile. Emmet appeared to appreciate my humor, and I was glad to have a label for him.

"Detective," he responded.

"So have you come to arrest us, officer?" Connor drawled, pushing his chair onto its back legs and resting his hands on his impressive stomach. He was itching for a fight, and right now he didn't care whom it was with.

"No. Not at all." Cook looked at me, his warm eyes filled with regret. "I'm sorry if I was rough on you the other day. Like I said, in these cases there is usually a family member involved."

"And in this case?" Maisie asked with a defiance I hadn't heard in her voice since we were teens.

"No. Not in this case, Miss Taylor. As a matter of fact, I came to let you all know we have made an arrest."

"You have the killer?" Ellen asked, her voice hopeful, relieved.

"We believe we do. A bit of good luck, actually. There was a break-in a few blocks away from Ginny's. An officer caught a young man trying to sell some of the stolen items. When he searched the suspect's car, he found a tire iron wrapped up in a towel. There was blood and bits of bone fragment both on the iron and in the fabric."

"Ginny's?" Maisie asked, deflating into her chair, all her defiance draining away.

"Yes. We got results back from the lab a short time ago. I've been holding this under my hat for a few days while we were waiting on them. The suspect left no fingerprints at the crime scene, but we found the tire iron in his possession. When he saw it, he started screaming like he'd seen a ghost. Passed out right in front of the arresting officer and had to be transported to the emergency room to be stabilized."

"He on something? Meth?" Connor asked, leaning back toward the table. "Them damned meth heads are taking over the whole goddamned world around here."

"No, sir. He tested negative for any drugs, but he seemed pretty near scared out of his mind. We had him on psychiatric restraint until we could get the results."

"I thought those were usually only good for seventy-two hours," I said.

"Well, you know how persuasive your Uncle Oliver can be. He convinced the judge to stretch the rules a little."

"You knew about this, Oliver?" Connor spat out.

"Yes. I contacted Adam to chew him a new asshole for upsetting Mercy. As it happened, they had just pulled this guy in. I went and visited Judge Matthews to see if we could arrange for the bastard to stay behind bars until we knew for sure."

"And you didn't share this because?" Connor continued.

"Because you and Iris have already done enough to hurt the detective's case. I figured the less you knew, the less damage you could do."

The two men stared at each other with all the warmth and kindness of junkyard dogs greeting strangers at the gate. Connor broke his gaze and turned to Cook. "So who the hell is the prick, anyway?"

Cook flipped open his black notebook. "His name is Martell Burke. Does the name ring a bell with anyone?"

"Never heard it," Iris responded. "Have you?" she asked her husband. Connor responded by shifting his chair back and shrugging his shoulders.

Ellen frowned slightly as she tried to match the name with a face. "No," she responded after a few moments of quiet consideration. "I don't think so."

"No," I seconded Ellen. "Me either."

Maisie said nothing, but Cook didn't press her. "I didn't expect as much," Cook continued. "He was raised up north, came to Savannah a few months ago. Has a pretty long record, reaching back to juvenile, but mostly small time offenses. Nothing violent," Cook added.

"So maybe he broke into Ginny's not knowing who he was taking on?" Maisie asked.

"That is where it gets interesting. Burke may be new to the area, but he has people here. People with deep roots." Cook paused. "I am sure you are all acquainted with Jilo Wills."

"Mother Jilo," Ellen exhaled.

The blood drained from my face as I remembered Jilo's promise to work the spell I had requested of her. My feelings toward Peter had not changed since my visit to the crossroads, but even with Maisie's assurance that Ginny's death had had nothing to do with me, I felt sick. I forced myself to concentrate on what the others were saying, hoping my thoughts wouldn't betray me. I felt as though I should say something about being with Jilo the night before the murder, but I couldn't, at least not for now. I looked at Maisie, but her eyes warned me to stay silent.

"That's right. Martell is Mother Jilo's great-grandson. So it's looking much less like this was simply a home invasion turned violent."

"Well, I can't imagine why Jilo would want to harm Ginny," Iris said. "Ginny never interfered with Jilo. She never even took her too seriously."

"And that could be reason enough for some folk," Connor offered.

"Wounded pride," the officer considered. "You could be right there, Mr. Flynn."

"Have you questioned him? What is he saying about what happened?" Ellen demanded.

"He admits to being at Ginny's, but swears he never stepped foot inside. We can't get anything else out of him."

"Well, let Oliver have a little time with him. That'll get him talking. And if that don't work, let me have him for a while," Connor said, leaning back in his chair again.

"I already proposed that," Oliver said. "The part about my questioning him, not the part where you try to hold onto the illusion of being a young cock. Detective Cook here would have none of it." All eyes turned toward Cook.

"Listen, I don't pretend to understand how y'all do this 'woo-woo' stuff that you are into, but I know it's real. When I was a little boy my grandmother told me that if I couldn't avoid you Taylors, I'd better make it my business to befriend y'all. I can't let Oliver near this guy. If I did, I could never be sure that Oliver hadn't influenced him not only to talk, but also on what to say."

"You saying you don't trust me, Adam?" Oliver asked.

"I'm saying I can't trust you, and Mister, you know why."

Oliver and Cook locked eyes, and a long moment of silence stretched out as we waited to see who would call chicken first. Cook let it drop. "Burke says he'll tell us everything after he talks to Mother, but we can't find her. No one's seen her at her usual haunt in Colonial lately, and she's done a good job of staying off the grid other than her appearances at the cemetery."

"You won't find her unless she wants to be found," Iris said.

"That may well be," Cook responded, "but I was hoping that perhaps Mr. Flynn would be able to give us a lead on where she might be located. Your reputation," he addressed Connor, "for tracking things down is legendary, and with your vested interest in the matter, I thought perhaps you would be willing to do a little off the record investigating of your own."

Connor puffed up with the praise, but his response was cautious. "Jilo is a slippery one, Detective. I'll be happy to give it a go, but I suspect that if she don't want to be found, I ain't going to find her."

"I'd appreciate any help you can offer in the matter—" Cook's sentence was cut short by the ringing of his cell. He pulled the phone out of its holder, his gaze drifting back to Oliver. He seemed to have a hard time *not* looking at Oliver; it was as if his eyes were hungry for the sight.

"Cook," the detective answered his phone. "Yes. That's correct. I am here with the family now." As he listened, his reaction indicated bad news—his nostrils flared and his eyes widened. "He what? How the hell could he do that? All right. You sure as hell had better. You tell March I want to talk to him the second I get there." He turned off his phone and looked at us. "Martell Burke disappeared—literally disappeared—from his cell, and I want you all to tell me just how the hell that could have happened."

"Detective Cook," Aunt Iris said with raised eyebrows, smiling with only the right side of her mouth. "We want Ginny's killer brought to justice. I certainly hope you're not suggesting that we would free the man you suspect of killing her?"

"No ma'am, I don't think you'd free him, but I sure as hell better not find myself stumbling over his body in a day or two. I need to get back to the station, but y'all can help me by getting me the names and contact information of any relatives who've been here for the funeral in case I need to get in touch with them."

He gave Oliver a cold and pointed look. "And don't you even think of leaving town, Mr. Taylor. If my suspect turns up looking any less than healthy, you, sir, will be the first person I pay a visit. I would suggest you send up a little prayer for Martell's prompt and safe return to custody." Cook stared at Oliver for a moment more before slamming out the door.

"We should all keep an eye on each other until they catch this guy," Connor stated flatly as the sound of Cook's steps faded away.

"But how could this Burke fellow up and disappear?" Ellen asked. "Unless Mother's behind it?"

Connor laughed. "Mother ain't got the juice to pull this kind of stunt off."

"It appears you are mistaken," Emmet responded, "as it is unlikely anyone else would have had the motivation to free the man."

Iris shocked us all by slamming her hands down on the table. "Oliver. Tell me you had nothing to do with this disappearance! You swear to me!"

Oliver's eyes widened as he shrugged and tried to look innocent. For once he succeeded. "I didn't Iris. I swear. I didn't do a thing to Burke." We all fell quiet and waited. "Nor," Oliver continued in a somewhat hurt tone, "did I convince anyone else, including Burke himself, to do anything. I really and truly have no idea where he is, or how he managed his Houdini, unless Mother somehow pulled it off."

"Damned shame." Connor chuckled. "I would have respected you more if you had. But it is what it is, and we have bigger fish to fry. Let Cook try to round Burke up. We need to deal with the lot drawing. Once we get that handled, we can turn our attention to Burke."

"He's right," Iris said. "We must deal with the matter at hand, and then if the detective still hasn't apprehended this man, we can deal with the situation ourselves."

"Wow, you light up the torches and I'll grab the pitchforks." Oliver smirked, but Iris's expression told him she was having none of her little brother's nonsense at the moment.

"We'll give the law their chance, but if they can't handle it, we will," she replied, stressing the word "we" to let Oliver know that he was indeed part of that pronoun. "Ginny's blood is crying out for justice, and I for one will not ignore its call."

THIRTEEN

I had a lot of processing to do, so I took the first possible opportunity to excuse myself and go back upstairs. The nine families seemed scandalized that Ginny had kept me ignorant. I wondered what they'd think if they knew they were singing from the same song sheet as Mother Jilo.

Now that enough time had passed for the golem to understand that I was changing for my own reasons and not anyone else's, I put on a light cotton dress and some comfortable shoes. Nice, not disrespectful by any standards, but also not making any more of a display in Ginny's honor than was necessary. One of the cousins knocked tentatively at my door and told me that I had a visitor, a young redheaded man who seemed quite anxious to see me. I gave myself a quick look in the mirror and headed downstairs.

Freshly showered and dressed in jeans and a white T-shirt, Peter was a fresh breath of air in the sepulchre that our home had become. He beamed when he laid eyes on me, and I noticed that the pulse in his neck became visible as he took me in.

"I'm sorry I couldn't be here today. I came as soon as I could."
I hurried over to him and kissed him on the cheek. As happy as I

was to see him, this wasn't the time or place for more. His disappointed face showed that he'd been hoping for a more impassioned greeting, but he settled for it, placing a gentle kiss on the top of my head.

"Well if it isn't little Peter Tierney," Uncle Oliver said, walking up from the direction of the library. "All grown up, and nicely too, might I add." He gave Peter a big theatrical wink.

"Will you stop flirting with my boyfriend?" I blurted out. It felt odd to call him that . . . but appropriate. Somehow he was so much more to me than a simple boyfriend; boyfriends could come and go, but Peter was a true friend, a fixture, someone I'd always want in my life in some capacity. It wasn't passion, but a conscious decision that had led me to choose him as my own. But simply saying the word had made me see him in a more romantic light, as sure as if I had uttered a magical incantation.

"Oh, now, Mercy." Oliver feigned hurt. "I'm simply appraising, perhaps complimenting, but never flirting."

"Don't worry, Mr. Taylor." Peter laughed. "If I ever go gay, it will be for you."

"I'm going to hold you to that," Oliver responded. "But I'd rather you make that little girl there happy."

"Gonna do my best to do just that, sir."

"Sir." Oliver chuckled and walked away.

"He can really be too much," I said, shaking my head in disbelief.

"Ah, he isn't that bad," Peter responded. "And he sure does love you." He wrapped his arms around me and nuzzled his face in my hair. I took a deep breath and let myself relax in his embrace.

"Yeah, I know he does," I said. "In his own way at least."

Peter spun me around in his arms. "I like the sound of that, you know. You calling me your boyfriend."

"I kind of like the sound of it myself," I responded and rose up on my toes to kiss his lips. I let my kiss linger, and then pressed my head into his chest. His T-shirt felt soft against my skin.

"Peter." I heard Maisie's voice call out as she descended the stairs. I turned just enough to see her coming down, Jackson following on her heels. Maisie had changed from her funeral clothes into a black cocktail dress. So she had chosen to go formal for the evening. Next to her, I would look totally underdressed, but next to her, I would always come in second place anyway. Even in an old gray T-shirt and cutoff shorts she was astoundingly beautiful. Dressed like this, it didn't seem possible that any straight man could resist her. Flawless skin, a small straight nose, and heart-shaped lips that looked great even with no lipstick. Her honey blond hair hung loose, falling for a moment over her sapphire eyes. She brushed it back with her hand.

"Hello, Maisie," Peter responded. I didn't want to see his reaction to her—I was sure he'd be as dazzled as any other man—but I couldn't help myself. I turned to look at him. And in his eyes I saw nothing other than an honest friendliness. Then he looked back at me, and I saw fire. Something rushed from my head all the way to the soles of my feet, and if he hadn't been holding me, I could very well have keeled over.

"Jackson. Good to see you," Peter said, his eyes still locked on me. I turned to face the staircase when I heard Jackson's name. His beautiful features were twisted into a combination of jealousy and barely suppressed rage that I would only have expected if he'd walked in on Peter and Maisie going at it.

Maisie read something in my expression and turned in time to catch what I had seen on Jackson's face. She swiveled around quickly, pretending not to have noticed, but I knew her too well. I had seen her angry often, and this kind of anger, the cold kind, was the most frightening. "If you are hungry, Peter, there are a ton of leftovers in the kitchen," she said, descending the rest of the stairs. "You should hurry on back and have some before Iris chases you out of here, though. Family business is going on tonight, and Iris is very limited in her definition of family."

"I was kind of hoping we could get you out of here for a bit," Peter said to me. "Mom and Dad asked if we'd stop by the tavern for a while tonight to see them."

"Nothing doing, son," Jackson boomed. "Haven't you heard? Killer on the loose and all that?"

"No, I haven't heard anything. What the hell's going on?" he asked, addressing me as if we were the only two people in the room.

"The police caught the man they think killed Ginny," Jackson answered for me. "Some guy named Burke. But he escaped."

"They aren't sure he's through with us yet," Maisie said. Her mouth pulled into a slight frown and her eyes focused on an empty point a few inches in front of her. Perhaps she was trying to scry, trying to foresee any future danger.

"You have got to be kidding me," Peter exclaimed, pulling my attention back to him. "How did he escape?"

"Detective Cook said that he just plain disappeared," I answered.

"He disappeared?" Peter asked. A slight shake of his head and arched eyebrows illuminated his incredulity.

"Poof," Jackson responded. "Right out of his cell. Mother Jilo done worked her Hoodoo."

"Mother Jilo?" Peter looked to me for an explanation.

"Burke is her great-grandson," I responded.

That seemed to be explanation enough for him, although I sure would have liked more information for my own account. I wouldn't feel right about anything until I knew whether Mother Jilo was responsible for Ginny's death. "But if they couldn't keep him in jail," he asked, "how do they plan to keep him out of this house?"

"My thinking, exactly," Jackson responded. "That's why I am going to be staying here until they catch the bastard again. Keep an eye on things."

"You will have to run that by Connor," I said. "He and Aunt Iris may have their own opinion—"

Maisie interrupted me. "Connor and Iris have agreed to allow it."

"But with the 'family business' . . . ?"

"They aren't very happy about it, but we've told them, Mercy. We've told everyone now." Maisie held up her left hand, proudly displaying the ring she had been wearing around her neck.

"Congratulations, you two!" Peter exclaimed. I knew he was genuinely happy for Maisie, but I suspected he was even happier that Jackson had been officially claimed. I knew it gave him more hope about our own relationship. He let go of me and stepped forward, offering Jackson his hand.

Jackson leaned away from Peter, and looked at him through narrowed eyes. There was no warmth on his face as he gave Peter's hand a single pump. "Thanks," he said, letting Peter's hand fall.

Maisie's face froze as she took note of Jackson's lack of enthusiasm. "Yes, thank you so much," she said. "We are very happy not to be keeping it a secret any longer. We waited for a while out of respect for Ginny, but it seemed like the family could use a little good news."

"Good news? Hell, I say it's great news!" Peter said. He reached out and pulled Maisie into a hug, nearly lifting her off the ground. "When's the wedding?" He was beaming.

"We haven't discussed that yet," Maisie responded. She seemed a bit put off by the degree of his gusto.

"Let her go," Jackson said, but Peter didn't seem to notice the other man's threatening tone. Still smiling, he released Maisie from his embrace and took me into his arms, rocking me a little from side to side. Jackson's expression of annoyance hardened into a look of hate. I'd never thought that Jackson was capable of looking ugly, but the set of his jaw combined with the loathing in his eyes changed him.

"Hello, Peter." I heard Ellen's voice call out from behind us. She was coming from the direction of the library.

"And good-bye, Peter." Connor was right on Ellen's heels, and his protruding stomach was practically pushing her along. Iris circled in front of him, shaking her head. "Really, Connor, there's no need to be rude," she said and then she addressed Peter. "I want you to know you are always welcome here, my dear, but I am afraid you have chosen a bad time to come calling. We'd love to have you back for dinner tomorrow, but we have things that the family must attend to tonight. I'm sure you understand."

"Yes, ma'am. I do understand, and I do not mean to intrude, but Jackson was telling me about this Burke guy. If you wouldn't mind, I'd like to stay so that I can help keep an eye on . . . things," he looked warmly at me, making it clear that I was his only concern. "I promise I won't interfere with whatever it is y'all need to handle tonight. I'll stay out of the way. I just want to be nearby in case I'm needed." He paused and put his arm around my shoulders. "I think Mercy would like me to stay." He looked to me for confirmation, and I realized that I did want him near. I was confused all right, but one thing I knew was that Peter always had—and always would—make me feel safe.

Jackson advanced on us, not to the point of being within striking distance, but not far from it. "Mrs. Flynn has asked you to leave," he said, accentuating every word.

Peter flushed red, and in one fluid movement he removed his arm from my shoulder and moved me behind him. Safely out of the way, I watched as Peter cooled himself down, unclenching his fists and taking a deep calming breath. I realized he was doing everything he could to put me first, even stifling his hot Irish head. "And I have asked her to reconsider. If there is any chance that Ginny's death was anything other than a random killing, I'd like to be here to help keep Mercy safe."

"You don't got to worry about Mercy, son," Connor chimed in. "We'll take care of her. We've got ways to protect our own."

"We didn't protect Ginny," Ellen responded. "And none of us gave Mercy a second thought when we needed to renew the charms. Let Peter stay. Mercy will feel safer with him around."

"Ellen," Iris responded. "You know that it is simply not possible tonight. Tomorrow, yes. The day after, certainly. But not tonight. Now, I promise you, young man, your Mercy will be as safe as can be tonight. I personally guarantee it," she said, smiling at him reassuringly.

"It's only that . . ." Peter began to protest, but Jackson took another step toward him, crowding him back.

"Mrs. Flynn said she'd like you to leave."

"Jackson, this really isn't necessary," Iris said trying to calm him.

He ignored her and pushed Peter. "Get," he said. "I can take care of Mercy. She doesn't need you."

"Don't touch me, man," Peter warned, tensing. "And don't pretend you know what Mercy needs."

Jackson shoved him again, but this time Peter was braced and couldn't be budged. "I said you need to get," Jackson snarled, his face taking on an ugly sheen again.

"That's the last time. Don't touch me again," Peter growled back.

"Boys." Ellen laughed nervously. "Enough of this nonsense." Without warning, Jackson pulled back and swung at Peter. Instinctively, Peter weaved out the way of the punch, and Jackson's fist swung past him and lightly grazed my temple. I barely felt a thing, but Peter registered what had happened and tore at Jackson like a wild man. Before I could blink, he had pounced on Jackson and was pummeling him.

"Stop it! Stop it!" Maisie began screaming at the two, tearing at the back of Peter's shirt.

Suddenly Oliver reappeared. "Freeze," he commanded with authority, and the two fighters instantly stopped. I tried to go and coax Peter off Jackson, but to my surprise, I found that I couldn't move either—I couldn't even blink. All I could do was focus on the tableau of Peter sitting on Jackson's chest, his hand frozen mid-punch. Maisie backed away from the men as the cousins reappeared en masse, most of them happy to have a bit of entertainment.

"What the hell is going on here?" Oliver demanded.

"A couple of young bucks butting horns, I'd say," Connor said.

When Oliver looked to me for explanation, he realized that I was caught up in his freeze frame. "You're good," he said, and I was finally free to move again. I was surprised to see Emmet towering over the rest of the crowd, a smile of amusement on his face.

"Mercy," Iris addressed me. "You understand why I say your young man cannot be here tonight? It's for his own good. Things may go on tonight that he is not ready to understand. He wants to protect you, but you need to protect him. Things may go smooth as silk with the lot drawing, or they might not. If they don't . . . well, who knows what could happen."

"Yes, ma'am, I do understand," I replied.

"Good." Iris smiled. "And he's welcome here at any other time."

"Jackson might have other thoughts on that subject." Connor smirked.

"Speaking of Jackson," Iris continued. "He has shown that he is not mature enough to be a part of tonight's business." She held up a hand in a preemption of Maisie's anticipated protest. "Don't you say a word. He started the fight, and by any rights I should toss him out on his ear. That ring on your finger is the only reason I am not. He doesn't have to leave the house, but he cannot participate. I'm sorry, but until he learns to communicate with his words and not his fists, it's too dangerous to have him involved." Maisie didn't respond. She just looked at Jackson and then back at me with narrowed, angry eyes.

"Okay. It's decided then," Oliver said. "Peter goes home, and Jackson sits tonight out." He snapped his fingers, and the duo on the floor fell apart. "Enough," Oliver addressed them. They moved in slow motion, never taking their eyes off Oliver, still under his thrall. "Peter. Like they say at last call, you don't have to go home but you can't stay here. You will return tomorrow for dinner with roses for your girl and a bottle of good scotch—exceptionally good scotch—for the rest us. Good night." Without a word, Peter rose and exited. Jackson's eyes followed him as he left, anger still smoldering just beneath the surface.

"And now it's your turn," Oliver began.

"Wait!" Maisie called out. "Please, Uncle Oliver, let him be. I'll talk to him." Oliver looked at Iris.

"All right, missy," Iris responded. "But make sure he stays out of the way tonight, and that he shows up at dinner tomorrow with a brand new attitude." Oliver sighed and snapped his fingers a second time. Jackson shook his head, hungover from the toxic combination of Oliver's spell and Peter's fists. Maisie rushed to his side and knelt down beside him. I was surprised that he wasn't more bruised than he was. My temple was slightly throbbing, and

I reached up to touch it. It had started to swell a little. Jackson followed my movement with his eyes, and his face clouded over with regret.

"Mercy, I'm so sorry, I didn't mean to hurt you. I'd never want to hurt you." Maisie froze as surely as if Oliver had hexed her and looked up at me. I said nothing.

"No, you just meant to beat the holy shit out of her boyfriend," Connor said.

"It doesn't matter what your intentions were," Ellen said. "You've hurt Mercy physically, but she'll mend. I'll see to that. What you are doing to Maisie . . . that, I can't cure."

Jackson turned his attention to his fiancée. He started to speak, but Maisie jumped up and ran upstairs. Jackson watched helplessly as she fled, his shoulders falling and his head drooping. A nearly inaudible curse parted his lips.

"It looks to me that you have some damage to repair," Iris said. "But I am afraid tonight isn't the night to do that. Maisie has enough on her mind." Iris eyed him coldly. She looked from him to me and then back at him. "What was this about?" she asked him. "Is it jealousy? You can't have them both."

"You got the pick of the two anyway," Connor added. "Why would you go messing things up now?" Coming from anyone else, the words might have hurt me. Coming from Connor, not so much. They were what I'd learned to expect. I guess I'd already seen the end of the kinder, gentler version of him.

Iris gave her husband a venomous look; she didn't need to say a word to him, he knew to keep his peace. She turned back to Jackson. "You've given Maisie your ring. That means your mind has been made up, understand?"

Jackson lowered his eyes.

"Do you understand?" she pressed.

"Yes, ma'am," he responded.

"And if you haven't in fact decided, you need to make up your mind once and for all, right quick," Oliver added.

Jackson looked at me, his face betraying that he hadn't really made up his mind, not at all. I thought of my sister crying upstairs and realized that the part of me that might have been happy about his indecision was long since gone.

"Show's over," Oliver said to the assorted group who had gathered to witness the drama. "Meet you all right back here in an hour for the drawing."

FOURTEEN

Instead of a few strays, this time the entire clan was gathered as close as possible to the foot of the stairs. On each side of the foyer, the doors to the library and the formal living room had been thrown open, so that those who couldn't manage to crowd in and see could at least strain an ear to hear. The stairs and the landing were also littered with cousins. As the eldest family member present, Michael MacGregor had been chosen to serve as the master of ceremonies. He stood near the grandfather clock, whose pendulum had been stopped so as not to distract from the proceedings. The golem, nearly as tall as the clock, stood silently beside him.

Michael had always been a man of action, so none of us was shocked to hear him start by saying, "Y'all know why we're here. No need to drag this thing out." His backwoods accent might make an outsider think of him as slow, but his mind was razor sharp. He may have been rough around the edges, but roughness belied an intellect worthy of the Ivy League. "No disrespect to Ginny, but I'm ready to get back to Tennessee."

"We'll go in alphabetical order. Not one of the traditions," he added, "but since I suspect we all know how this is going to play out, it will add to the drama." His comment was met with chuckles and nods from some and overtly angry glances from others. The anchor had been a Savannah Taylor for generations, and most of the group seemed to feel pretty sure that the tradition would not be broken. There were others, especially some of the younger cousins, who were positively itching to get their hands on the line's power.

"Now it's time for the representatives to come forward. Who is representing the Duval family?" he asked loudly.

"I am," Lionel, a slight, middle-aged father of three raised his hand and came forward. The Duval branch had been dealt a heavy blow to their egos when Katrina ravaged New Orleans. They were hungry to reestablish themselves, hoping that the line would select one of them, restoring honor to the family. I liked the Duvals. It would be nice to have that branch return to Savannah.

"My son Micah has been selected to represent us MacGregors," Michael stated proudly as a younger version of himself pressed forward. The MacGregors couldn't care less who got picked. They were simply fulfilling a duty by being here. Checking the box. "I believe I overheard that Teague Ryan is representing your group?"

"That's correct," a decidedly non-southern accent responded, as Teague stepped forward to shake MacGregor's free hand. Teague scanned the room, doing his best to meet the eyes of every member of my immediate family, as if he were issuing an open challenge. The intensity of his desire for control scared me. Even though I prayed that the line would indeed pass my family over as Teague had suggested it would, I prayed that it wouldn't pick him. He wasn't a man who would use the power well.

"I'm here for the Taylors. The 'hick' Taylors, that is, not the fancy city Taylors," said Abby, an ample yet kind-looking woman about Ellen's age. It was true, the extended Taylors were pretty rustic in their manners and dress. But we really didn't look down on them, at least not much. As she brushed past Connor, his eyes latched onto her. He seemed genuinely amused by her comment, and more than a bit drawn to her curvy figure. He made no attempt to hide his appreciation from Iris, nor from Iris's family. My aunt had long ago grown accustomed to her husband's wandering eye, and Abby wasn't interested enough in Connor to notice him, so his leering didn't cause anyone undue concern.

"And the Savannah Taylors?" MacGregor asked.

"I will do the honors," Oliver said, looking at his sisters, who offered their consent through silence.

"All right. Let's get to it. Thirteen lots in the bag. Five people to draw and for you young ones out there, I can guarantee you the red lot will be picked by one of them. 'Cause it ain't the person that's choosing the lot, it's the lot that's choosing the person. Lionel," he said, offering the bag to the Duval branch.

Lionel closed his eyes and reached into the old pillowcase that was being used to hold the lots. His shoulders fell as he drew one out. He handed it to MacGregor, who proclaimed, "White. The lot is white. The Duval family has been exempted." He dropped the lot back into the cloth and shook it before extending it toward his own son. Micah reached into the bag and pulled out an identical white lot, holding it up for all to see. The hint of a smile crossed Michael's face, and his shoulders relaxed. "White. The lot is white. The MacGregor family has been exempted," the elder MacGregor called out loudly enough for everyone to hear.

I scanned the room for Maisie and spotted her in the corner next to the library doors. She was whiter than any of the lots in Ginny's old pillowcase. I smiled at her, and tried to send out waves of reassurance, but she didn't seem to notice. I could hear the lots click against each other as MacGregor shook the case vigorously before offering it to the Ryan's envoy. Teague reached inside and drew out a lot.

"White. The lot is white. The Ryan family has been exempted."

"Wait," Teague nearly shouted. "I need to go again."

"Sorry, son," Michael said. "One draw per family head." He held the case out to Teague, who dropped the lot back in, angry disappointment coming off him in waves.

As soon as the lot had been returned to the case, Abby pushed forward and shot her hand into the bag. "Anyone care to make a little wager before I pull this out?" she asked, laughing. When no one responded, she added, "Well then y'all are smarter than y'all look." She whisked out the lot. MacGregor started to speak, but Abby cut him off. "Yeah, yeah, we all get the drill. It's white, and the white trash Taylors are exempt." She tossed it carelessly back into the bag and it clicked loudly against its companions. "Preliminaries are over; let's get on with the main event."

MacGregor shook the bag once more and offered it to Oliver. His manicured hand moved carefully in and retrieved the lot. "It's red," he said quietly. MacGregor took the lot from him and held it high. "Red. The lot is red. Not much of a surprise, but we had to follow through with the 'preliminaries,' to borrow Abby's term." He returned the lot to the case and handed it to Oliver. As he returned to the center of the crowd, he patted Oliver on the back. "It's all yours, cousin."

Holding up the pillowcase, Oliver addressed the crowd. "It's strange, you know, you feel the little bugger force itself into your hand." He looked around the room. "No offense to Michael, but we're going to have a slight break with both tradition and the theatre of suspense. I know we usually go from eldest to youngest, but we all know what we're thinking here, and I don't want to prolong the misery for Maisie any longer than need be. Come on, sweetie," he said addressing Maisie. "Let's end this thing."

"I can't," Maisie responded flatly. "I can't do it."

"Sure you can, honey," Ellen reassured her.

"Mercy. Go help your sister." Iris called to me. The cousins cleared a pathway for me as I moved across the room toward Maisie. "You two came into the world together, you two can draw together."

"You're not in this alone. I promise you, sis. We'll face things together no matter what." Something played on Maisie's face, a look that said something like "Easy for you to say."

"I don't need you to hold my hand," Maisie said, her voice scarcely loudly enough for me to hear. She pulled back her shoulders and raised her chin. She looked nearly regal as she walked over to Oliver. I followed on her heels, just like I'd been doing since I could walk.

I knew she was angry with me, but after this was over, we'd talk it out. Jackson loved her. Maybe he was a little confused, a little afraid of the commitment he'd made to her. But what he felt for me wasn't real. It was just a way for him to maintain a bit of his bachelorhood, keep one little toe out of the water. That's all it was, I told myself, not letting myself consider whether it was true or merely a crutch I was using to help us all over this rough patch. They would marry, and I would marry Peter. The four of us would grow old together and sit out on the porch of this very house laughing about what had happened today.

"But I do need you," I told her. "I need you to hold my hand." She held my gaze, and the irritation on her face melted away.

"Together?" she asked, her voice quavering.

"Together," I responded and took her hand. Oliver held the case out to us. Still holding onto each other, we reached into the bag with our free hands. I squeezed her hand tightly as we pulled our respective lots from the bag. My heart soared as I saw the lot she had drawn. White. She was free.

I squealed and hugged her, starting to dance around. Oliver's sharp, "Mercy!" cut into me, and I swiveled to look at him, a bit confused by his severity. That was when I saw it. The lot I was holding was *red*. I looked at Maisie and was astounded to see the look of shock in her eyes harden into an expression of absolute hatred. Her forehead was pinched, and her teeth were exposed in an open mouth grimace. She ripped her hand from my grasp.

"You put a magnet on the end of a nail, and the nail becomes a magnet too," Connor announced into the stunned silence. "You girls shouldn't have gone together, and you shouldn't have been holding hands."

"I'm not so sure," Abby responded. "The power picks the one it wants. Maybe we should stop and think about this. It could be a sign."

"Maybe it's a sign we need to start all over," Teague called out, pushing his way back to the front of the room.

"Why are you so angry?" I whispered to Maisie. "I thought you didn't want this."

She pulled away from me, stepping back a few steps. Then she whipped her hair around and faced me like she was about to pounce, her hands bent into claws. I felt like I was looking at a total stranger. Not someone I had known even before birth. "Because it's mine!" she hissed back at me. "I've spent my whole life preparing for this!"

I shook my head, totally confused. The only reason she wanted to be the anchor was because she thought I might get to be. None of this computed with the sister I thought I knew. "You've always had everything. But that isn't enough for you. Now you want my man. You want my place." The words came out in quiet but barbed hisses.

"No, Maisie," I said. "You're wrong. I just want you to be happy." I tried to approach her, but she stepped back again.

"Don't touch me!" she warned, her voice like a slap. I stopped dead in my tracks.

"We've never questioned the draw before," MacGregor ventured tentatively. "I know on the surface this looks a little odd, but . . ."

"Listen," Oliver interrupted impatiently. "There's an easy way to settle this. We'll have them both go again, separately this time."

"I second that." Connor started to step forward, sucking in his stomach and puffing out his chest in one quick move.

"But you ain't part of this decision." Abby spun on him. Connor's admiration for the woman evaporated from his face.

"Then I second it," Iris stated, moving out from behind her husband's shadow. "Come on, girls, let's have a redo."

I reached over and dropped the red tile back into the bag. I was totally stunned. By the tile. By my sister. I just wanted this day to end.

"No," I responded. "This is silly. We all know that I'm not the right one to replace Ginny. My presence here is only a formality." I gave Maisie a sidelong look, trying to find some warmth in her face. "I'm sorry I upset you. I didn't think you wanted this. Maybe the power thought the same thing. But it's over. It's yours." I turned and started for the door, but Oliver stopped me.

"You all are up to something," Teague said, shaking a thick finger at my uncle. "You all know the power is through with you Savannah Taylors, and you are doing your best to hide it."

"Step down, Teague," his father called out. Resentment flooded Teague's face, but he obeyed.

Oliver shook his head and then looked at me. "No, Mercy. It has to be official. We can't have anyone question the choice. It would weaken the line."

"Okay, Uncle Oliver," Maisie began in a tone I had never heard come from her before. Her sweet voice had been replaced by ice. Venom seemed to drip from every syllable. "You want to

THE LINE

make sure there isn't a question about who should be the anchor? Fine, let me settle it for you."

The house filled with an inescapable beating sound, like when you're holding your breath underwater and you need to rise for air. The pulsing in my head became as loud as thunder in an August storm, and the pressure was unbearable. I felt as if my head were being crushed.

Even the golem had been affected. He lay on the floor, bucking up and down as if he were having a seizure. Everyone except for Maisie put their hands to their ears, but even with covered ears the pulsing continued, growing louder and louder. I realized it wasn't from an external source—it was coming from within each of us. Ellen screamed and fell to the floor, and I saw blood trickle from her ear. I wanted to run to her side, but I couldn't move, frozen in place by a gravity that centered on Maisie.

"Maisie!" I shouted, barely able to hear my own voice. "You're hurting us! Stop!" She looked at me with eyes I did not know, filled with a coldness I could never have imagined. She knew she was hurting us, and she was taking pleasure in our pain—no, not just that, she was gaining strength from it.

The smell of ozone filled the air, and static electricity sizzled all around us. Wisps of blue electric fire jumped from person to person. There was a moment of total silence as Maisie rose up into the air. She levitated toward the ceiling, the short silence broken as stones began to fall from nowhere, pounding on the roof and crashing through the windows like cement raindrops.

Overhead, the pipes burst, sending spurts of water everywhere, and the very foundation of our century-and-a-half-old home, the seat of my family, began to rumble and shake. The room twisted on its foundation and its tortured beams were ripped screaming from their plaster skin.

128

Maisie clasped her palms together and a roar of fire shot from her to Oliver. The pillowcase in his hand burst into flames, and he dropped it, yelping as his fingers blistered. Maisie held the final tile, the white one she had drawn, up into the air, and it crumbled into a fine dust.

And then it was over. The stones stopped. The house was still and whole. There was no water falling from overhead, and Maisie stood quietly before us. I saw Oliver peer at his hand, which was completely fine, no burns. It was as if nothing had ever happened. I realized that in our reality nothing had happened. Maisie had simply opened a window into what *could* happen, so that we could all peer in, and then she'd shut it off like flipping a switch. The only true victim of the episode was the case of lots, which remained a pile of ashes near Oliver's feet.

"Does anyone have any questions?" Maisie asked, her eyes glowing in triumph, her body still hovering a few inches from the ground. She was electric. A numinous fire. She was not my sister. She was a fearful angel. I turned and forced my way to the front door. I turned the knob, but the door wouldn't budge. It seemed to be jammed in its frame or frozen by a difference in pressure on the other side. I shook it hard a few times, but it stayed wedged in place. Then a wild strength welled up in me, and I flung the door open wide. As the warm night air reached in to touch my face, I ran.

FIFTEEN

I ran for blocks, paying no attention to traffic or crosswalks, and when exhaustion overcame adrenaline, I walked. My subconscious mind was in charge, leading me south, and my conscious mind only clued in to my destination as I drew near Sackville, and the house that Peter had been renting since moving out of his parents' place a couple of years ago. When I found myself standing before it, I realized that something had changed inside of me. I felt like a different woman. I went up the steps of the small, wooden-frame house and knocked on the door.

Peter opened the door wearing nothing but a pair of boxers. At first he just blinked at me, but then his mouth fell open. "What the hell?" he asked, reaching out to pull me in from the night. "Are you all right?"

I stumbled through the door and into his arms. I understood his surprise when I caught sight of my reflection in a wall mirror. My hair was standing on end, still electrified by Maisie's power. My skin was as pale as death and giving off a faint blue glow. "Don't tell Maisie I'm here," I said, my voice sounding somehow wrong to my own ears. "Don't tell any of them."

"I won't tell anyone anything," he said. Putting a hand on each of my forearms, he held me back to look at me. His nose flared as if he could smell Maisie's magic on me.

"Come on," he said, guiding me gently to the couch. "Tell me what happened. Talk to me."

"I don't want to talk," I said, and then I kissed him. I kissed him again. He pulled me tighter to him, and I breathed in his clean scent. I pressed my face against his chest, and kissed him there too. My tongue darted out and tapped his nipple. "I need you," I marveled at the sudden urgency of my words. "I love you," I said, and the words were true. At that moment what I felt for Peter was vivid and intense, and my feelings for Jackson seemed like something left over from a nearly forgotten dream. I wrapped my arms around his neck and went up on my toes. I coaxed his tongue into my mouth, and felt his growing stiffness press into me.

"Whoa, Mercy," he said, forcing himself to gain control. "I love you too. God knows I do," he said, his mismatched eyes fixing on mine. "I want this. I want it more than you could know. But something's wrong. I can tell. If we do this now, you'll regret it tomorrow."

Looking into his eyes, I had one of those rare moments of clarity. "You're right. There is something wrong. There are more things wrong than you can even begin to imagine," I said. "But this. Us. There will never be anything more right in my life." I kissed him hard and took him in my hand. He shuddered, and his eyes asked me the question his lips wouldn't form. I nodded, and he swept me up into his arms, carrying me into his bedroom, to his bed. He laid me down gently and carefully lowered himself on top of me.

He propped his torso up on his arms and looked down at me hungrily. "This means something to me, Mercy. This means we belong to each other. I don't want to do this if you have even the slightest doubt," he said.

I looked up into his beautiful face. "No doubts," I said.

He leaned in and kissed me deeply. "There's never been anyone but you," he whispered into my ear. "I've never," he confessed quietly. "I've waited . . ." he said. "I hoped you . . ." I reached up and pulled his mouth from my ear to my lips.

Later, as Peter slept, I rested next to him, wrapped in his embrace. I closed my eyes and experienced a moment of the purest peace I had ever known. But as I started to drift off, I was pulled back from my dreams by the sound of Jilo's dark cackle dancing in the air all around me. Then I knew that it was Jilo's magic that had drawn me here.

Despite Peter's nearness, I lay there silent and alone as my heart turned into stone and fell into the pit of my stomach.

SIXTEEN

"You gonna be okay?" Peter asked as we pulled up in front of my house. "I can take you back to my place if you aren't ready to face them. You can hang out, relax. I'll come back here with you after work." His face was glowing with happiness in spite of the concern he felt for me.

I considered his proposal. "No. I think it would be better for me to get this over with. No sense in avoiding the inevitable." I needed to fix whatever was wrong between Maisie and me. Then I needed to consider the ramifications of the spell Jilo had settled on me.

"I love you," he said, kissing my lips, my forehead, my eyelids. "I don't want to leave you, but I have to get to work."

"I love you too," I said. It was true, even if the passionate side of that love had been magically induced. Perhaps my feelings for Peter ran deeper than I had ever known. Maybe we would have eventually come to this without the spell? He kissed me again, and I felt my body respond. With a supreme effort of will, I reached over for the door handle and hopped out of his truck. "I'll see you tonight?"

"Ain't nothing or nobody gonna stop me." He smiled. I shut the door, and he started to drive off. He stopped again a few feet down the road and put his truck in park. He jumped out of the cab and ran back to me, yanking me into his arms and spinning me in the air as he kissed me long and hard. "I love you, Mercy Taylor. I do," he said before returning to his truck and driving away. I watched until he was out of sight, and then I braced myself.

The door was locked, but before I could ring the bell, I heard the lock click and the door eased open. No one was visible on the other side. I poked my head in and scanned the hall, but it seemed to be empty too. I figured that the door must have been charmed to open for me. The house was quiet for the first time since Ginny's death. The cousins had evidently fled to higher ground.

"Maisie's gone," Wren said from behind me. I gasped and swung around.

"Wren, you're going to be the death of me one of these days!" I said.

"She asked me to tell you she's sorry."

"Where did she go?" I asked. My exhaustion and a sudden concern for Maisie made my voice project more loudly than I'd intended.

"She's gone to apprentice with another anchor," Iris responded, appearing from the shadows behind Wren. "A very strong one who can teach her to control her emotions, so that we will never face another episode like last night's." Although she tolerated Wren, Iris had no sense of attachment to him. She dismissed him with a tap on the shoulder, causing him to dissipate like fog.

Iris pulled her robe tightly around herself and motioned me into the library. She sat on the edge of the love seat and patted the space next to her. I took the hint and sat. "I'm so relieved to see you. When you ran out . . ." She paused. "Maisie short-circuited us completely. Connor had to recover before he could find you, and when we tracked you down at Peter's, I figured we should leave you there. It seemed like the safest place for you. If anything had happened to you . . ."

A tear formed in the corner of her eye, and she visibly shuddered. After a long moment, she took my hand in hers. "She is sorry, you know. And it's only her true contrition that saved her from a binding."

"A binding? I didn't think that was still done," I said. A binding would block a witch from using her powers and from affecting the line.

"Just because it hasn't been done in a long time doesn't mean it can't or won't be done," Iris said.

"But if she's the anchor and a binding were done on her?" The morning sun pierced the room, and Iris rose to shut the curtains against its rays before returning to sit next to me.

"The energy would take her over. It would use her as a receptacle, but it would wipe away the part of her that we all recognize as your sister. In effect, she'd be lobotomized."

"You couldn't do that!"

"No, my dear, we couldn't, but that isn't to say some of the other witch families wouldn't," Iris said, toying nervously with her wedding ring. "The tremor Maisie set off last night was felt around the world. We call it a line, but it's more of a web. You pluck it here, and witches all around will feel the vibrations." She looked me in the eye. "Maisie is very young, but very powerful. She must learn how to manage herself, so it was decided to send her off for training."

"I didn't think she wanted to be the anchor. I don't understand why she got so angry last night. Especially over such an obvious mistake."

Iris sighed. "Well, it wasn't such an obvious mistake to everyone. There were those who questioned whether the power was telling us that the arrangement we have had for so long needs some changing. By making such a completely . . . unexpected choice, perhaps it was telling us that it's time for an alteration."

"What do you think?"

Iris took a few moments to consider. "Honey, after last night, I don't know what to think. For now, though, I say we count ourselves lucky. You're safe and home. And although she's far away for now, we'll have Maisie back safe and sound in a couple of weeks. She's going to need you when she comes home."

"I'm not sure she even wants me around. I think it would be best for me to go away for a while," I said, wondering if I could convince Peter to leave with me. Just the two of us, traveling as far from Savannah as we could. He'd always dreamed of seeing Alaska.

"And how long is a while?"

"I don't know. Just a while."

"No," Iris said, her voice firm. "Your sister needs you here. We all need you here."

"But the way she looked at me last night," I said. "Aunt Iris, last night she hated me."

"Last night was last night. When she left, you were the only person on her mind. She didn't even say a word about that young man of hers."

Guilt overwhelmed me again. I had to confess to someone. "Aunt Iris, it's partly because of Jackson that I should leave. I've been confused about my feelings for him, and I think he might be a little confused as well."

The disappointment in Iris's eyes was piercing. "Oh, I see," she said. "I had hoped that whatever was going on with Jackson was one sided, but you have . . . taken up with him?"

"No. Nothing like that. It's only that . . ."

"It's only that there is a possibility. And you need to follow your conscience and make the best possible decision for everyone involved. Now you have a better understanding of what it's like to anchor the line. You have to close some doors, honey, no matter how nice a yard they open out onto."

"I'm trying to close the door. I have closed that door. That's why I want to leave," I protested.

"No, honey. That's not deciding, that's running. Just like you did last night when you got scared. Choosing and then living with the consequences, that's what deciding really is." She reached up and ran her fingers through my hair. "You're the one who looks more like your mama, you know." Of course I knew that from the photos of my mother, but it always felt good to hear it. "And I'm afraid you may have more of Emily in you than I thought."

"What do you mean by that?" I asked, suddenly defensive.

"My sister had a taste for other women's men too. She made the wrong decision more than once, and her choices never brought anyone happiness. Especially her. I'm sorry, my dear. I never wanted to speak poorly of your mama to you, but I don't want to see you make the same mistakes she did." My arms drew involuntarily around me, forming a shield between my heart and her words. I hated hearing this about my mama. It fit in too well with what Tucker Perry had told me about her participation in Tillandsia.

"Listen, girl," she continued. "If you follow your true heart and the good sense you were born with, you'll see that Jackson isn't the right man for you. Maybe young Peter is, and maybe he isn't. But I know you. You would never find happiness if you broke Maisie's heart in the process. She means too much to you."

She was right. Despite the craziness of last night, I loved Maisie too much to take anything from her. And now I was committed to Peter. Even if Jilo's magic was at the root of my actions, I was the one who had gone seeking it. I couldn't hurt Peter. I considered telling Iris about what had happened with him, at least in broad strokes, but I wasn't ready to confess my connection with Jilo.

"I loved my little sister dearly," Iris said. "She sure wasn't perfect, but I loved her. And she gave me you and your sister. I've never asked you for anything like this before, and I hope I never have to again, but I am asking you now. You stay with us, Mercy. Stay until we can get things settled here. You may not have power like the rest of us, but you do have the power to help hold us together."

I couldn't look at her. I wanted to say yes, but I didn't want to make a promise I was afraid I might not be able to keep.

"Promise me you will at least think about it, and that you'll talk to me before you leave. No disappearing in the middle of the night. You can give me that, right?"

"Yes," I replied, the sleepless night having caught up to me. I was too tired to argue.

"Good, then," Iris said. "I'm going back to my room then before your Uncle Connor wakes up. He'll never stop pestering me with questions if he realizes you were at Peter's all night, and I'll have to tell him lies to shut him up. You get upstairs too and change clothes. Go on now." She swatted at me playfully.

When I leaned down to kiss her on the forehead, she smiled at me with so much love in her eyes. I wasn't sure what Jilo was selling, but I couldn't, wouldn't, believe that this woman who had raised me—or, for that matter, anyone in my family—had anything in their hearts for me other than the best of intentions. Iris glided out of the room, and I followed her up the stairs. When I reached my bedroom, I went inside and closed the door softly behind me. Dawn had begun to break, so I closed the blinds before slipping beneath the sheets. Within moments I was dead to the world.

SEVENTEEN

When I awoke, I knew that someone was in the room with me. I felt the weight of unfriendly eyes on me, and I scrambled up in bed with a gasp.

"No need for all of that," Connor said. "It's just me." He had pulled the chair from my makeup table over to the foot of my bed and was sitting there watching me sleep. The chain of his pendulum was laced through the fingers of his right hand.

"What do you want?" I asked.

"Now don't get all riled up," he said, letting the pendulum fall to its full length. "I wanted to have a talk with you in private."

"So you chose to sit there watching me sleep like some kind of boo hag?" I asked. The boo hag was the low country's own version of the boogeyman—well, maybe more of a cross between the boogeyman and a vampire. It was a creature that sucked the life out of you as it watched you sleep. Connor had cracked open the shutter behind him just enough for a sliver of light to pour in. Since it was coming from behind him, I could only see him in silhouette, his features were obscured by shadow. Flooding the room with sunlight might have helped dispel the sense of menace, but something told me not to risk walking by him to throw open the shutters. I reached over and snapped on my bedside lamp.

The light revealed an odd look in his eyes that I would never have expected to see there. Regret combined with tenderness, a caring that shook my sense of who this man was to me. "You sure are your mama made over," he said. "A little discipline would have done her good too," he said. The hardness I was accustomed to returned to his eyes.

I pulled a pillow in front of me and hugged it. "What do you want to talk about?" I asked, a sense of vulnerability adding an edge to my question.

He smiled. "I want to talk about the day Ginny was killed. Something's been bothering me about that day," he said, leaning forward a little. The chair squeaked beneath its heavy burden. "I was going to let it go, but then last night you pulled the anchor lot."

He allowed a pregnant pause, but I said nothing.

"It's just that my pendulum kept giving me some odd answers that day when I asked it to show me the location of the weapon used to kill Ginny."

"You said it wasn't there," I said.

"Well, that was a wee bit of a lie," he said and began to swing the pendulum in a slow circle. "Every time I asked for the location, it pointed at you." He stood up and came closer to my bed.

"I had nothing to do with Ginny's murder," I said. "And I'd really like you to leave my room now." I was afraid to hear what he might have to say.

"Are you so sure about that?" he asked. "Or maybe what you really want to do is to take this moment, when it's only the two of us, to tell me everything you know."

"I don't know anything I haven't already told you," I replied. "Now, please leave."

He ignored my request. "Ginny was angry with you. You were mad at Ginny."

"I didn't hurt her," I responded.

He sat next to me on the bed, and I pulled my arms more tightly around my body. "Oh, I believe you there," he said. "That's where things start to get interesting. The pendulum was so insistent about you that I asked it then and there if you had killed her." He stared deeply into my eyes, and damn it, I blinked. "It told me emphatically no." He stood abruptly, and the mattress squeaked as he moved.

He began to pace a bit back and forth. "So the message I got was that you were the weapon used, but not the hand that wielded the weapon. Any idea what that means?"

"None. Go ask your toy."

"I have, and I'll continue to ask for clarification, but I was hoping that you'd open up, maybe tell me what you were up to that was pissing Ginny off so much."

I glared at him. "Who knows? It was always something with Ginny."

"That's true," he allowed. "She was a touchy old bird." He stopped pacing and turned to face me. "Like I said, I would have let it all go, chalked it up to confused energies, except for the fact that you were chosen to take Ginny's place."

"You yourself said that was a mistake," I countered.

"I know what I said, but I was just trying to look out for you. And I was trying to right a wrong that was being done to Maisie. I don't know what you're up to, but somehow you have gotten in way over your head," he said, shaking a finger at me. "You should have never tried to take what was intended for you sister. You keep it up, and you are going to get yourself squashed like a bug."

"That's enough. We are done," I said and threw the pillow I had been holding across the room. I swung my feet onto the floor and stood, stretching as tall as I could make my body go. "I haven't done anything." I reached out and poked him hard in the chest. "And I haven't tried to take anything." I poked him again. "Anything. Period." I got right up in his face. "Now get out!"

He took a step back. There was a smile on his face, but no warmth in his eyes to back it up. He didn't say another word; his expression said it all. He knew I was guilty of something, even if he hadn't quite figured out what it was yet. I tried not to think of Jilo, but try not to think of an elephant, and all you see is trunk. Oliver could have read me with no problem, but thank God, Connor was weak. After a long moment, he turned and left the room. I shut the door behind him, locked it, and then I rushed over to the window to open the shutters and let the sunlight flood in.

EIGHTEEN

Several moments later there was a light knock on my door. "Everything okay in there?" Ellen asked. "I heard you yelling."

"I was having a bad dream. I'm okay," I said a little shakily and then added, "Everything's fine." I opened the door so that she could see for herself that I was in one piece.

"All right, then." She hesitated a moment. "Listen, I'd like to talk to you about last night if you feel up to it. Maybe we could get out of here for a while? We could get dressed up all girly, and I'll treat you to high tea at the Gryphon."

"I'd love that, but I need a shower first," I said.

Ellen was exactly the person I wanted to talk to about last night—not the drawing, but what had happened with Peter. In a normal world, I would have rushed upstairs this morning to tell Maisie about it. I wondered if not having her around was going to become the new normal.

"I'll be in my room," she said. "Come and get me when you're ready."

I showered and dressed in a vintage 1950s cocktail dress that Ellen herself had gotten for me. I let my hair hang loose and put on the string of pearls that Iris had given me for my eighteenth birthday. After adding on a pair of ballet flats I had excavated from my closet, I felt much more girly than I had since I turned twelve and stopped wearing princess costumes for Halloween.

When I reached Ellen's door, I could hear Wren's voice from inside. I was about to knock and ask Ellen if she was ready, but the opportunity to eavesdrop on the two was too tempting. I strained to hear through the thick oak door.

"Maisie scared you." Wren's falsetto was as clear as a bell through the wood.

"Yes, she did," Ellen replied, her voice more muffled.

"She scared me too," Wren confessed, and I suspected that Ellen had pulled him close to comfort him in the ensuing silence.

"I won't let anyone hurt you, baby," she said soothingly.

"I love you," Wren piped. I wondered if it was possible for Wren to feel real emotions.

"I love you too, little man." I bit my lip; she used to refer to Paul as her "little man." It didn't seem healthy for her to call Wren that.

"Is Maisie bad?"

"Why no, sweetheart," Ellen said, sounding surprised by the question. "She's young and confused. A lot of responsibility has fallen on her shoulders. But she's not bad—far from it."

"I think she is bad. She stole from Mercy," my ears pricked up at this comment, and I leaned closer to the door. "The power didn't want her, it wanted Mercy."

I suppressed the urge to laugh out loud at the ridiculous notion that the power might have chosen me after ignoring me so completely for nearly twenty-one years. I doubted that it had suddenly changed its mind and elected me homecoming queen.

Ellen stayed silent for a few seconds. "Maisie isn't bad," she pronounced summarily. "She's my baby niece. But I think you could be right. I don't understand what went on last night, but my gut tells me that the right sister drew the red lot. I can't explain it, but I'm certain that this isn't as settled as Iris would like to think. Nothing was ever cut-and-dried with Emily, so I wouldn't expect for anything to be cut-and-dried with her girls."

"Why is your hand shaking like that?" Wren changed the subject while I was still trying to grapple with what my aunt had said.

"It's nerves baby, just nerves," Ellen replied.

"You'd feel better if you had a drink," Wren said. My mouth gaped open.

"No. I need to keep the promises I've made to the family, to Mercy."

"I won't say anything. A little bit will help. It's Maisie's fault." That little bastard. Was he just giving voice to Ellen's own rationalizations, or was he afraid of losing his battery in the event that Ellen pulled herself together? I needed to talk to Iris and Oliver about him, and soon.

I tapped on the door, desperate to stop her before she gave in to Wren's advice.

"Yes?" Ellen called out.

"It's me," I responded.

"It's unlocked," she said, and I tried the knob. When the door swung open, she was sitting alone at her dresser. "I'm almost ready," she said. I suspected that Wren was still in the room but hiding himself from my view. I came in and stood behind her, looking at our combined reflections in the glass. She smiled at me and returned to her lip gloss. "What is it, sweetie?" she asked in mid-application.

I put my hands on her shoulders, and leaned in to kiss her cheek. "It's only that I believe in you. I really do."

She smeared the gloss above her lip and reached for a tissue. Wiping away her error without comment, she reapplied the gloss, using the action to mask her shock. Turning to face me when she was done, she immediately changed the topic. "I sense something different about you today," she said.

I felt a blush of warmth flush my cheeks—it wasn't embarrassment, it was happiness. I smiled and sat on the edge of her bed. "Last night," I began. "Peter and I—"

It was all I could manage to get out before Ellen rushed over to the bed and took me in her arms.

"I am so happy for you!" she said and then she paused, giving me a weighing look. "We are happy about this, right?"

I smiled and nodded my head yes. "Well, no wonder you're glowing today. Tell me all about it—well, obviously not all about it," she sputtered. "Oh, hell, just tell me you're in love."

She seemed so happy for me that I couldn't bear to bring Jilo into the picture. "Yes," I responded. "I am."

"That should really help settle things with Jackson then," Ellen said to herself. She shrugged when she realized that she'd said it out loud. "Sorry."

"No, it's okay. You're right. This does help clarify our relationship," I said. "I'm not like her that way, you know?" Ellen didn't make the connection. "My mother that is. I don't intentionally go after other women's men."

"Why sweetheart, I know you don't!" she said. "Who has been telling you tales about Emily?"

"Iris said that she was worried that I had inherited the gene for man stealing," I said, trying to make light of my concerns.

"Well pardon me, but Iris doesn't have any idea what her fool mouth is saying. You are like your mother in many ways, but all of them good." She put her arms around me and squeezed me tight.

"Tucker Perry said that my mother introduced him to Tillandsia," I said. Ellen released me, her expression alarmed. "Is Tucker my father?"

"Dear God, no!" Ellen said.

"Then you know who my father is?"

"I'm sorry, darling. I don't. I really don't."

"Were there too many men to guess which?"

"I'm sorry. It's true that Emily was a part of Tillandsia. And it's true that she had many men in her life." She bit her lip, then looked with narrowed eyes. "When were you talking to Tucker anyway?"

"He's kind of been following me around lately," I responded, searching Ellen's eyes to see if Tucker's stalking ways made her angry or jealous.

"I'm sorry he's bothered you," Ellen said. She looked away in shame. "I've told him that you and Maisie are strictly off limits unless he wants to end up like Wesley Espy and wear his genitalia for a boutonniere." Wesley was a judge's son who'd had an unfortunate taste for gangsters' girlfriends. The fathers of Savannah's daughters have been offering up his story as a cautionary tale to prom dates for going on eighty years. "I'll see him tonight and set the record straight once and for all."

"I think Peter plans to pay him a visit as well," I said.

"That's good, but the bastard needs to hear it from me too."

"How can you bear to let him touch you?" The words came out of my mouth before my brain could censor them.

Ellen didn't appear shocked or offended. "Since I've stopped drinking, I've been asking myself that very same question. And now that I know he's been soliciting you, I can guarantee that he'll never touch me again." She was quiet for a moment, and the animation fell from her face. "After Erik and Paul died, I stopped caring about what was right or wrong. I didn't give a damn what happened to me. Tucker was so attentive, and he was fun. He distracted me from the pain a little."

"I am so sorry to have brought this up," I said.

"No, don't be. It's good to get it out. I've been thinking about them a lot after what happened to Ginny." Ellen looked me in the eyes. "Mercy, I know this is a terrible thing to say, but I hope that if they find this Martell Burke guy, they give him a medal. And Jilo too, if she sent him to do the deed." I was shocked by her words, but the floodgates had opened, and Ellen wasn't through. "Erik died at the scene of the accident, but my boy was still alive. Barely alive, but there was enough of a spark left in him for me to save him. I could have done it, I know it. But she stopped me."

"How?" I asked. "Why?"

"You were young, but you probably remember. The week before Erik and Paul died, a young man was hit by a car outside my old flower shop."

"Yes, I do remember—" I replied, but she wasn't listening.

"The car went right over him. He was mangled. I didn't think. I just reacted," she said. "I went to him and held him in this world." She looked up at me with wonder in her eyes. "He was so close to death that I saw it, Mercy, I saw that tunnel they talk about and the light. I could hear voices coming from that light, but then he opened his eyes and asked me to please save him." She shook her head, and closed her eyes, the memory taking her someplace else. "Somehow I did it. I pulled enough juice to heal his worst injuries. By the time the ambulance arrived, all he had left was a couple of broken legs and a cracked rib. Ginny was furious. She said I had damaged the balance of nature by saving that boy."

"But how could she have stopped you from saving your own son?" I asked.

"She was an anchor, but sometimes she confused being an anchor with being God. She used her control to dampen my powers that day. It was kind of like she put a kink in my hose. Truth is, my ability has been waning ever since."

"No, I mean how could she have just let Paul die?"

"Honestly, I think she was afraid of him," Ellen said. "You know the ten main families, the ones who are linked together and maintain the line. But there are three other families that we don't talk about much."

"The three who helped create the line but then regretted it."

"Oh it's more than regret. They've tried to break the line more than once. Bring the whole system down."

"But why would they do that? Why would they want to turn the world back over to demons?"

Ellen leaned over and picked up a framed picture of her son and husband from the nightstand. She placed it in my hands. "Because when our reality was controlled by the demons, the thirteen families held a special place in the hierarchy of things. The demons were the kings, but the thirteen families were the lords. Revolution led to democratization. When we shifted our reality out from under the demons' control, we wiped out a social hierarchy that had existed since the first humans. And although the three families were happy to be free from their bosses, they didn't like losing control of those below them." She paused. "Erik was from one of those families."

"Uncle Erik?" I asked, having a hard time wrapping my head around it. I nearly dropped the photograph.

She took the picture from my hands and returned it to her nightstand. "Yes, but he was nothing like his family. He had broken allegiance with them and joined the ten families long before the two of us met."

"And Ginny was scared of Paul because his father was from one of the three adversarial families?"

"No, Ginny was scared of Paul because of a prophecy that was made when the three families separated from the rest of us. After Paul was born, Ginny learned that it had been predicted that the mingling of our immediate bloodlines would lead to the birth of a witch capable of reuniting the thirteen families. Neither of us had heard of it until Ginny started flipping out."

"You think Ginny sacrificed Paul because she didn't want the families to reunite?" I reached out and gently tugged at her hand.

She rejoined me on the bed. "Who knows what she wanted. I'm not even sure she cared about the families. I don't think she wanted any light to outshine her own, and she knew she'd end up a dim comparison to my son."

"Do you think Ginny might have done something to cause the accident?" I asked, surprised that I'd even let myself have such a thought.

"No," Ellen said. "If I did, I would have killed her myself years ago." Ellen spoke with such cool clarity that I didn't doubt her. "Ginny tried to pass herself off as a saint, as some great martyr, but she was a miserable, controlling bitch. And I am glad she's dead, so three cheers for Mother Jilo or whoever did her in."

"So you do think Jilo might have done it?" I asked. I knew for a fact that Jilo hated Ginny enough—she hated all the Taylors enough. Ellen just nodded her head in response. "But why would Jilo hate Ginny enough to kill her?"

Ellen crossed her arms as if she had felt a chill. "Oh, darlin', people like Jilo always walk around with a laundry list of perceived offenses. I am sure that in all the years she and Ginny bumped heads, Jilo found reason enough."

"I heard Oliver was close to her family at one time. That he was friends with her granddaughter, the one who drowned herself," I said, fishing for answers. I hoped that Ellen could tell me what had happened so that I wouldn't have to ask Oliver himself.

"You're talking about Grace," Ellen said after a few moments. "Where did you dig up that ancient history?"

"People talk," I responded vaguely.

"Well, yes, he and Grace used to hang with the same group of friends, but that was way back when he was a teenager," she said, visibly calculating the years that had passed since. "That was back when he and Adam Cook were buddies. Rumor was that the girl had an abortion and then regretted it. It was a very sad situation, but it had nothing to do with us. I'm sure I don't need to explain to you that your uncle had nothing to do with her getting pregnant," she said, smirking at me.

"No, ma'am, I am very sure Uncle Oliver had nothing to do with that," I said and returned her smile. I wanted to believe that Oliver wouldn't harm a fly, that he'd done nothing to this Grace. With all that had gone on over the last several hours, I was willing to take comfort where I could find it.

"I've been giving it a lot of thought, though," Ellen said. "And if Jilo *was* responsible for Ginny's death, revenge might not have had a thing to do with it."

"What do you mean?"

"Only that Jilo works a lot of dark magic, blood magic. Ginny was a powerful witch. Jilo could get a lot of mojo out of Ginny's blood. Maybe we've been looking at it all wrong. Maybe it wasn't a murder. Maybe it was a sacrifice."

"But what kind of spell would require a human sacrifice?"

"Oh, sweetheart, conjurers like Jilo know how to store up energy from a bloodletting. She could expend it all attempting something big like a resurrection, or she might parse it out over years, using it little by little for money spells, revenge spells, love spells—"

"But I thought you don't use blood in love spells." I thought I would be ill. I had been so willing to accept Maisie's assurances that Ginny's death could not possibly have been related to the spell I'd asked Jilo to do.

"Well, of course I wouldn't. You'd have to be pretty crazy or desperate to mess around with love spells anyway. But even the real witches who do them would never use blood. For someone who only borrows power, though, like Jilo, sometimes blood is the only way. Oh, I am sorry. I've upset you." Ellen forced a smile. "Enough of this. Look at the two of us! The past is the past. We shouldn't be wasting all this feminine beauty and grace on a walk down bad memory lane. Let's go get that tea."

"No, I'm sorry. I'm suddenly not feeling well. Maybe another time?"

Ellen regarded me with concern. She placed her palm on my forehead. I knew I couldn't fake a physical illness with her. "Of course," she said. "I'm sorry. I should have kept my theories to myself."

"No. I'm glad you shared your thoughts with me. I just need a little time to process them."

She traced my jawline with her finger. "We'll try this again soon."

NINETEEN

I headed back to my room, the tomboy in me desperate to ditch the dress and pearls. I wanted to put on some shorts. Find my bike. Ride as hard as I could until the sick feeling I was carrying fell away. Maisie had lied to me, and I had lapped it up. I realized now that I had to find Jilo. Go to her and demand the truth. I'd never be able to live with myself wondering if I had Ginny's blood on my hands. I'd start with Colonial Park Cemetery. If she wasn't there, I'd return to her crossroads. I no longer felt safe going there alone, but I couldn't let another night fall without my knowing the truth.

As I passed the door to the linen closet, I heard it creak open behind me. I turned back to look. Through the narrow opening of the door, I could see the aura of haint blue telling me that another world awaited me on the other side. Jilo's world. Somehow she knew I'd be ready for her. Ripe for the plucking. The thought that she had such intimate knowledge about me terrified me. I hesitated in the rippling strip of aquamarine light. Jilo had made it clear that her sole interest in me was to use me to bring pain to my family. She might still be doing her best to make me like her, or maybe she'd moved past that idea and on to plan B. If Jilo was behind Ginny's death, I might be walking right into my own execution.

But I *had* to know what had happened to Ginny. The door swung all the way open, the blue scintillating like a swimming pool in full sun, and without letting myself think another thought, I stepped across the threshold. The door closed behind me of its own accord, and for a moment I was blinded by the bright sun as it reflected off the river. I recognized the spot, of course—it was the bend where the river met Bonaventure Cemetery.

"Savannah," Jilo began without looking at me. "Whole damned place a graveyard. Funny thing is we got a whole mess of bodies with no markers, and then we got markers that ain't got no bodies." She laughed at her own joke, finally turning to me.

I was desperate to ask her whether or not she had killed Ginny to set the spell in motion, but before I could get the words out, she asked me a question of her own.

"You ask your sweet uncle about my Grace yet?" She bent over, picked up a stone, and began rolling it smoothly through her fingers.

"No," I responded. "The timing hasn't seemed right." And then the words "Did he do it? Did Martell kill Ginny?" burst out of me.

"No." She paused and held the stone still in her palm. "My Martell did not kill your Ginny, and that all Jilo has to say on the matter for now."

"Connor said that you wouldn't have enough power to free Martell on your own," I pressed her.

"Oh do he now?" she laughed, her whole body shaking.

"Yes. He thinks you couldn't siphon off enough power to physically transport him from one place to another."

"But you know otherwise, don't you?" she asked, her eyes narrowing as her mood quickly morphed from mirth to anger. "Oh don't you worry, sweet little princess," she hissed. "Jilo know you think she killed Ginny for yo' little love spell, but those lily hands are clean. Jilo ain't no fool. If they a price to pay for stealing a little bit of power, what do you think gonna happen to someone who take out an anchor? Jilo, she might be up for a skirmish with a witch or two from time to time, but they ain't no way she taking on every last damned last one of them. Killing Ginny, whoever done that signed they own death sentence."

I wanted to believe her, but I'd also wanted to believe Maisie. My family seemed so certain that transporting Martell was beyond anything she should be able to do. If I found out how she'd worked this particular feat, it might help me figure out the true depth of her power. Whether she really could work miracles under her own steam, or whether she was lying to me too. "But you moved him like you moved me. How do you find the power to do that unless you took it from Ginny?" I asked.

She looked me up and down, "If Jilo tell you, can she trust you not to go blabbing to your people?"

I knew she expected a lie, so I tried to take her off guard. "Of course not. I'll tell Aunt Iris as soon as I get within earshot of her," I responded.

My words were met with laughter. "You all right, girl." She winked at me. "And it a good thing you tell me the truth, 'cause Jilo was gonna lie to you anyway. Someday, when you know what your people been up to, then Jilo gonna be able to trust you. And then she tell you. But for now, she gonna let you in on a little secret. Just 'cause something look the same don't mean it is the same."

"What do you mean?" I asked.

She began to move the stone between her fingers again, rippling it over and under each digit smoothly before returning it to its starting point. "I mean that what Jilo done with her gran'baby ain't the same thing she do with you. All I had to do with Martell was bend the light around him so that no one see him. When they open the doors, he walk out on his own."

"You made him invisible?"

"That's right, and it don't take no power at all to do that. Well, at least not much. There now. Jilo done hand you enough on good faith. You want the rest of what Jilo know about the day Ginny killed, you gotta give a little back. You ready for your first lesson?"

"Yes, ma'am, I am ready." I felt nervous and distrustful, but my pulse raced at the thought of finally touching magic. Suddenly I found myself questioning my true motivation for having risked this visit with Jilo. There was no doubt that I felt guilt over Ginny's death, but the thought of having my own magic was seductive.

The slightest smile curved on her lips. She held the stone up to me. "You see this here rock?"

"Yes, I see it."

"Good, now you look real good at it. Don't you take your eyes off it, you hear?"

"Yes, ma'am," I replied.

"You lookin'?"

"Yes, ma'am," I responded again.

"Good," she replied and then threw the stone right at me. I yelped as it bounced off my shoulder and onto the ground.

"Why are you throwing stones at me?"

"Just 'cause it felt so good to do so." She was bent over with laughter.

"Well I am not going to stand here and let you hit me with rocks," I spat out, turning to leave.

"Wait girl, don't go off all mad, I didn't hit you with no rock." She continued laughing. "I just threw it. You did all the hitting yourself."

"What the hell is that supposed to mean?" I asked. My shoulder was visibly starting to bruise. Jilo stopped laughing and walked cautiously toward me, like she was approaching a spooked animal; at that moment it wasn't far from the truth. She reached out slowly and brushed my shoulder with one wrinkled hand. The pain disappeared, and the bruising faded before my eyes.

"There now," she said patting me. "What that mean is that Jilo threw that rock, and she threw it at you. But you stop and think, though. You slow it down in your head. What happened?"

"You hit me with a stone," I replied tersely.

"No, think it through. You see Jilo with the stone. You see her throw the stone at you, but what did you think when she threw it?"

I stopped and let the event run through my mind. "I thought the stone was going to hit me, and then it did."

"That's right. Jilo put the energy in by throwing the stone, but they ain't no reason it had to hit you. It coulda fallen to the ground. Hell, it coulda flew cross the river. The power was Jilo's until she threw. When that stone left her hand, the power went with it. It was you who took that energy and hit yourself with it."

"Wait. You're blaming me for being hurt? I didn't do anything wrong. You're the one who threw the stone."

"You want to talk about right and wrong, you go to Sunday school. This ain't about right and wrong. Someone try to hurt you, sure they doin' wrong. But when they attack you, they are sending energy your way. Strong energy. And that energy belongs to you. You have every right to use it for your own purposes."

"But that's blaming the victim," I rebutted. "You're saying that they take the energy that's sent toward them and then hurt themselves with it."

"You ain't listening, girl. It ain't about fault. This victim you talk about, he accept the intention of the person trying to hurt him. He accept it out of fear. He accept it 'cause he don't know he don't have to accept it. You got to start small. You start with a stone, not a bullet," she said and chuckled. "It take a lot more energy to stop a bullet, your own common sense should tell you that much. Now I admit, this only work if you aware of the dangers around you. Someone sneak up on you, that one thing. But when you see the danger coming head on, then you got the time to turn the energy to your advantage."

"But if you don't know someone's trying to hurt you, what then?"

"Girl, the trick is paying attention. Always being aware and keeping guard on your blind spots. Jilo, she gonna show you how to do that, but it take practice. It don't just come to you overnight. There. That your first lesson." She turned from me and watched the river around the bend. "Sorry, you gonna have to find your own way home. Jilo got not more juice for you today."

"But you promised me that you'd tell me everything you knew about Ginny if I came to you."

"That may be, but I never said when I would tell you. I done told you Martell ain't done nothing, so you go on home now. Jilo need her some time alone."

"You promised me," I said, feet planted firm.

"Do not make me angry, girl!" Jilo hissed. "Get movin'!"

My feet turned of their own impetus, as if they had more sense than my head did, and I had taken a few quick steps toward the cemetery path before I even registered what was happening.

"Mercy!" Jilo's voice called out to me, and I turned in time to see her hurl a large flat river rock at my head. I felt a burst of anger, and the stone stopped in its course, hanging in midair. For a moment I sensed the rock as part of the air that was holding it, and then my rational mind said that air and rock were very different things. The stone fell to the ground in front of me. I had worked magic. Real magic. I was no longer on the outside looking in. The power may have been borrowed power, but it felt good.

"You passed, all right," Jilo said with what I could almost have taken for respect. "I believe you came for the lesson and for the truth. You can leave without the truth. It's your last chance."

"No," I responded, wondering if I was making the right choice. "Tell me what happened to Ginny."

"All right then," Jilo said. She produced a small string bag in her hand and dangled it in front of me. "You know what this is?" she asked.

"I guess it's one of the juju bags you make," I said. Jilo was famous for her spell mixtures. "You got herbs and stones and things like that in there, right?"

"Dirt," she responded. "I got dirt in this bag." With a wave of her hand the bag disappeared back to wherever she had drawn it from. "Dirt from the old woman's yard."

"But why would you have dirt from Ginny's yard?"

"Like draws like. When Jilo do a spell for money, she take a little dirt from the bank and mix it in her juju. She do a spell for love or sex, she take it from where you young folk park your cars. She do a spell for death"—she paused, looking around us—"she take from a cemetery. But always, no matter what kind of spell she doin', she add a sprinkle from the old woman's yard, 'cause that where the power lie. That's why Jilo's juju work better than any of the others who try to do Jilo's work. Course you gotta remember when you take from someone, like I took from Ginny, you gotta leave something in return, or what you taking loses its power."

"But what does this have to do with Ginny's murder?"

"Jilo do her own diggin'. Everywhere that is but the old woman's place. She done told Jilo not to come around her place no more, and Jilo respected that. She never said nothin' though about Jilo sending someone else to dig."

"Martell," I interjected.

"That's right. I sent my Martell," she said, shaking her head. "I sent him at sunrise, so he could dig when the sun first hit the earth. He heard the old lady yelling. He crept up to the window, and when he look in, well, he saw Ginny getting hit with a tire iron. Thing is, they weren't nobody holding that iron. At least nobody he could see."

"So someone was bending the light, like how you helped Martell disappear?" I asked, trying to wrap my head around it.

"Maybe. Maybe not. You gonna have to figure that out for yourself."

"But what I don't get is that Ginny must have known how to protect herself from whatever was attacking her. Based on what you've told me, she must have accepted the intention of her attacker."

Jilo smiled like a proud teacher. "That's right, my girl. You seeing the big picture now. Who would that old woman have accepted her death from? That's the question you need to be askin'." And with that I was standing by the river alone, as alone as if Jilo had never been there at all. The air was as hot and moist as a dog's breath as I started making my way through the cemetery. A storm was brewing, and I just hoped to make it home before it broke.

TWENTY

The sky turned the orange of ripe cantaloupe, and the wind began to swirl around me, pelting me with hail. A bolt of lightning zipped overhead, followed by the peal of distant thunder. Then the clouds opened up, rain falling in buckets as the quickening lightning chased it from the sky. I must have been living right, because I managed to catch an empty taxi that had just let off a bunch of fool tourists at the gates of Bonaventure. I knew the driver, and she refused to turn the meter on. "I got a hotel pickup on Bay anyway; I'll drop you off on my way," she said. "Sorry about all of your family's troubles of late." I thanked her and forced her to take a five for an after work drink before letting her drive off.

By then the worst of the wind had blown through, and the sky had gone from sherbet to gunmetal. Even though the wind had relented, rain was still falling all around me as I tore up the steps to the front door.

"Mercy." Jackson's voice surprised me. I hadn't even noticed his presence until I heard my name. He was soaked and shivering in the rain that was still whipping through the porch's columns. His car was nowhere in sight, so he must have walked here in the storm. "I've been waiting for you. We need to talk."

"Sure," I replied. "About Maisie?"

"No. About us." Lightning flashed around us like a strobe light with a migraine, and I wanted to be inside.

"There is no 'us.'" I wanted to put a barrier between myself and the elements. I wanted to put a barrier between myself and Jackson too, but I wasn't sure why. Had Jilo's magic worked so completely? Thunder trampled on the lightning's heel, with hardly a second between them. I couldn't just leave him out here. I reached out and tried the door.

"It's locked," he said. "I rang a few times. No one's home."

I found my key and opened the door. "Let's get you a towel," I said and stepped into the dim foyer. I tried to switch on the lights, but nothing happened. "Looks like we've lost power."

Jackson followed me inside and closed the door behind us, leaving us nearly in the dark. My eyes were slow to adjust, dazzled as they had been by the lightning. I felt him draw close to me, placing a tentative touch on my shoulder. He pulled me to him— gently at first, but with increasing urgency. I tried to extract myself, but his other hand reached for me too, and before I knew it, I was in his arms. His skin was hot beneath the chill of his wet shirt, and I could feel his heart thudding against mine. My body began to respond to his, fire building between us, but as my body's will weakened, my conscience took over. I could not— would not—betray Maisie. I reached up to push him away, my hands pressing against the steel of his chest, his shoulders, but his mouth found mine. His tongue forced its way past my lips, and for a moment all of the old feelings were there, as sharp and as intoxicating as they had always been. My scruples deserted me. He should be mine.

But even as that thought burned its way into my consciousness, my body began to strain to free itself from his grasp. Jilo's magic wrestled with my emotions, repressing my ardor for

Jackson, making its color drain away until I felt nothing. Peter's face rose up in my mind, and the warm glow I felt for him once again transformed itself into the passion I had sold my soul to Jilo to kindle.

"Stop," I said, and then again more forcefully, "*Stop.*"

He loosened his hold, and I pushed away from him. Even in the dark, my eyes had no difficulty registering the disappointment on his face. "I know you feel it too," he said. "I know . . ."

A flash of lightning flared through the window, lighting up the room around us. There was a bloody stain on the wall behind him. A handprint. Adrenaline flooded my body. I tried to speak but couldn't find my voice. I pounded on his chest with one hand, pointing over with his shoulder with the other. At first he wrinkled his forehead in confusion, but then he turned. Another less furious flash illuminated the print once again.

"Stay here," he said, scanning the entrance way for a viable weapon. There was nothing.

"No way," I replied, reaching out to take his hand. This time he was the one to pull away. "Stay behind me if you're going to come," he said.

I followed him into the library, my view blocked by his broad shoulders. He banged into an end table. "Damn," he said under his breath. "Can't see a thing."

"In the desk," I said. "Connor usually keeps a flashlight in the top right drawer."

Jackson carefully made his way to the desk and rummaged for the flashlight as noiselessly as possible. After a moment, he pulled it out and flicked it on, its beam hitting my eyes and temporarily blinding me. He turned and ran the beam over the room. "Nothing," he said and led me back across the foyer and into the living room. Jackson swept the room with the light, and I stepped out from behind him and took in the scene. A struggle, a fierce one, had taken place here. The poker from the fireplace lay in the center of the room, and the rug beneath it was stained black.

"Don't touch it," Jackson commanded before I even realized that I'd bent over to pick it up. I took a step back and surveyed the room. Furniture had been knocked aside, and there were shards of broken crystal everywhere—the remnants of Iris's favorite vase. Jackson shone the light on the floor, revealing a trail of blood drops that led from the room to the handprint on the foyer wall. He crossed over to the fireplace, grabbing the log tongs. "Take the light," he said, handing it to me. It was only when I took it that I realized my hands were shaking.

Jackson returned to the foyer, and I followed close behind. Drops of blood led us the first few steps down the hall, and then the drops turned into a smear. Someone had fallen and been dragged away from the spot. The smear served as a bloody marker, pointing us in the direction of the kitchen. We crept up to the swinging door that separated the kitchen from the hallway. Jackson turned to face me and raised the tongs in his hands like he was holding a baseball bat. He nodded at me and then kicked open the door, which hit the wall behind it with a *whack* as loud as the dying thunder. He dove through the opening, but the door swung back through the frame before I could join him, flapping until it came to rest.

"Oh, my God," his voice carried over to me. It felt like an eternity had passed since he'd crossed into the kitchen. "My God," he kept repeating, his tone keening and filled with panic. I didn't want to see what was on the other side, but I stepped forward and eased the door open with the gentlest of pressure, and my feet carried me across the threshold.

My brain had a hard time processing the scene before me. Oliver was lying on his back, tied to the tabletop. Each arm and leg had been tightly secured to one of the table's legs. His clothing had been shredded, and what was left of it hung from him in blood-soaked tatters. Iris crouched in the shadows in the corner of the room, a straight razor dangling from her fingertips.

"Iris," I said, my voice rough and shaky at the same time. "What have you done?" She bounded from the shadows and crossed the room in a furious leap. Her eyes glowed red, her lips curled back to reveal her canines, and she swiped at me with the razor. I jumped back. I knew then that Iris wasn't acting of her own will. Her body twisted around on itself in a way no human body was meant to bend as she leaped onto Oliver, perching herself on his chest. The moan that escaped him told me that he was still alive.

Jackson pressed up next to me. I had almost forgotten that he was there. "What do we do?"

"You leave!" Iris raged. "He need to pay. He gonna pay. Pain for pain. Life for life."

To say that we were dealing with an angry spirit—whether it was a ghost or demon or what—was an obvious understatement. So it was angry. It felt wronged. Maybe encouraging it to air its grievances would keep it from inflicting any more damage on Oliver. But I realized that I'd be taking away its role as a victim if I asked it why it was doing this to Oliver. Instead I asked, "What did he do to you?" My tone intimated that his crime must have surely matched the punishment she was meting out.

She looked at me, and although her eyes were still wild, the red glow toned down. I knew I had come up with the right incantation. "He murdered my baby is what he did," she said with a flat intonation, as if she were trying the words on for the first time. She must have read the shock and disbelief on my face. "He made *me*"—she emphasized the pronoun—"murder my baby. And when I came to and knew what I done . . ."

"You walked into the river and didn't come out," I finished for her, the pieces coming together in my mind. Had Grace and her child come between Oliver and something he wanted? I had seen him trample over the will of others time and again and had often wondered how far he'd go to get what he wanted. I asked myself if I believed Oliver's moral compass was damaged enough to allow him to commit murder. Possibly, under the right—or wrong—circumstances, was the answer that turned up. "You're Grace, aren't you?"

At the mention of her name, she halted. "Yes," she said, but then a howl tore from her and she began swiping at Oliver with the blade, slicing him open with indiscriminate blows, some deeper than others.

"Help, help, help," I pleaded in my mind, not even knowing whom I was addressing. Maybe it was a prayer. Maybe my mind was just trying to muster up its own courage. I rushed forward, reaching for the blade. She swiped at me and would have cut me, but Jackson swung the tongs at her hand with such force that I heard the radius in Iris's forearm crack. The razor skidded across the floor, and Jackson dove at her. She struck him with her good arm, and he was knocked back across the room.

Before either of us could recover, she lifted her good arm and the razor flew back into her hand. "Fine then. I'll let you watch," she said, poising her hand over Oliver's throat.

"No!" I said and was surprised to hear it come out as a command. "You will not do that. You will drop the razor." I gave my words all the authority I could muster. Grace shot me a ferocious look over her shoulder. Iris's face was twisted beyond recognition by the force of Grace's fury. I turned the flashlight fully on her. Her skin was nearly purple, the veins bulging behind the skin. She labored and strained, growling and spitting, every ounce of the spirit's power focused on forcing Iris to make the final cut. But Iris's hand remained locked a mere inch or two above her brother's jugular.

"The young lady told you to drop the knife," the words were followed by a shimmer in the air that resolved into the golem. I dropped the flashlight in shock. "And you will vacate Mrs. Flynn's body immediately." Iris instantly fell limp on top of Oliver.

I heard the squeal of brakes and a slamming door, and within moments Ellen was by my side. She stopped dead at the sight of her siblings. Her eyes fixed on me for a moment, wide with confusion, but instead of waiting for answers, she rushed over to the table. "Get Iris off him," she commanded, and Jackson obeyed, lifting Iris's dead weight off Oliver. The blood that had bathed Iris now coated Jackson, and he shuddered at the sensation.

"He's dying. Call an ambulance. I don't think I can help him. He's almost gone," Ellen said, the words spilling out with no inflection. "He's lost so much blood, and I don't have it in me to heal him." She placed her hands on Oliver and closed her eyes. "I said call an ambulance!" This time the words were an order. I turned and ran to the old landline that Connor had insisted we keep, slipping in the blood that had formed a puddle around the table. Emmet's hand shot out and righted me before I toppled over.

"Stay," he said to me. "You have the power, Ellen. We just need to reconnect you to it." Emmet let go of me and laid his hand on Ellen's head. She bolted off the ground an inch or so, suffused with a golden light. "The blockage has been removed. Another one of Ginny's many follies."

Ellen's suspicions about Ginny had been right all along. Her face grew radiant as the power surged through her. "That bitch," was all she said before turning her attention to Oliver. Light emanated from her fingers, from her hands, and then from her whole being. The bulbs in the overhead light began to glow as if electricity had been restored to them, and the room went from gloomy to intensely bright. Within seconds Oliver's chest began to move up and down as his breathing returned to normal. The wounds closed and scarred over, and after a moment he opened his eyes. He looked around the room and started to say something, but then his eyes caught hold of mine. A look of shame washed over him, and he held his peace. The physical healing was miraculous, but I knew that the emotional healing was going to take much longer.

Iris had begun to stir, and she came to with a horrified look on her face. "What have I done? What have I done?" she wailed, staring down at her clothes, which were covered with her brother's blood. She collapsed sobbing against Jackson, who recoiled from her, pushing her away. His blue eyes were wide as he looked from Ellen to Emmet to Iris to me, his face gray and sickly. I couldn't tell if it was from the blood that covered him or the magic that was crackling in the air around us. He lowered his head and pushed past me. I heard his quick and heavy footsteps echo down the hall, the front door banged open, and he was gone.

Emmet walked over to Ellen and removed her hands from Oliver's chest. "He'll mend nicely now. You should turn your attention to your sister."

Ellen was still on a high from the energies that had been restored to her, and her expression resembled Saint Teresa in her ecstasy. There was such beauty in the moment that I nearly forgot about the horrors that surrounded us. Carried by a wave of healing light, Ellen glided toward Iris. She took her sister into her arms and rocked her gently. "No harm done, no harm done," she kept repeating in a singsong voice. In seconds Iris too was bathed in Ellen's light.

"No harm indeed," Emmet said to me under his breath as he retrieved the straight razor, using it to cut the ropes that bound Oliver to the table. "Let's get you into bed," he said. One moment

Oliver was there in front of me, and the next he was gone. "Don't worry about your uncle. We'll watch over him while he rests."

"But how did you know?" I asked him. "How did you know to come?"

"We heard your call, and we summoned your family to return home," Emmet replied. He sensed that I wanted more of an explanation, so he continued. "We promised we would renew and strengthen the charms Ginny was using to protect you. If ever you are in true danger, we will come to you, at least as long as this body still has form."

Something began to gnaw at the edge of my consciousness. "You said you summoned my family?"

"Yes," Emmet replied.

"Then where is Connor?" I asked. Iris gasped and ran from the room, apparently alarmed by the mention of her husband.

"You had better follow her," Emmet said to Ellen, and, reluctantly returning from the high she had been experiencing, she went after her sister.

For the first time, I was left alone with the golem. His dark eyes surveyed me, and he traced the back of my hand with his index finger. His touch was warm. "You enjoyed taking charge," Emmet said. "And you did it well. You stopped that spirit from ending your uncle's life."

"I was bluffing. You were the one who stopped her."

"No," he said. "We did not. You were the one who stayed her hand." Before I could object, he continued, "There is magic in the air from Oliver's blood and the spirit's rage. None of it came from you, but you made it yours. A part of it still lingers in you," he said. "It was your will that kept the spirit from killing Oliver. When you saw us, you relinquished control, but you were wielding the power when we arrived."

"What are you saying?" I asked.

"We are saying that for one not born of the power, you channel it as naturally as if you were. You do it instinctively," he said.

"Well good for me," I said, "but I've had enough for one day. I'm going to go make sure Connor is all right, and if he is, I'm going to bed. And frankly, I might stay there for a while."

"Then we wish you sweet dreams, young witch," Emmet said, bowing to me in a courtly manner.

"Yeah, right," I responded and padded down the hall. When I reached the second floor, the sight of the linen closet door made me wonder if my visit to Jilo was somehow linked to the timing of Grace's attack. But that possibility was going to have to wait until tomorrow to be considered. I needed sleep.

TWENTY-ONE

I was dreaming of Peter—his touch and the feel and scent of his skin—when I awoke to an unfamiliar sound. I tried to place it without opening my eyes. I wasn't sure if I could take anything remotely similar to what I had encountered yesterday, so I refused to budge from beneath my covers. The sound repeated again and again, a rhythmic whack like someone felling a tree. Realizing that it wasn't going to stop, I clambered out of bed and over to the window, opening it wide enough so that I could lean out. Oliver was down below, swinging an ax into what was left of our kitchen table, splintering it into so much kindling. He was shirtless and glistening from his exertions. I watched as he swung again, his muscles playing beneath his taut and flawless skin, the same skin that had been hanging from him in shreds only a few hours ago. Wearing running shorts and shoes, he looked like he was dressed for a marathon rather than a stint as a lumberjack, but then again, what do you wear to destroy a family heirloom that's stained with your own blood? I leaned back in and closed the window.

I called Peter, but it went straight to voice mail, which meant that the supervisor of the building site must be on hand. I texted him a quick "I love you," pushing aside the guilt I felt about Jackson, then brushed my teeth and pulled on an old T-shirt and a pair of cutoff sweatpants. I was pretty sure that Aunt Iris was going to need help cleaning this morning. I had stumbled to bed without giving the carnage in the kitchen further thought, and I figured that the residue would be grisly. When I got to the kitchen, the windows and the door were wide open. The air smelled of burned sage, but other than that it was bright and spotless. Not a single drop of blood. The room was completely empty of furniture, which indicated that the chairs must have gone on the chopping block along with the table. I went around to the back, where Oliver had stopped hacking up the table. He dropped bits of it into a large barrel, squirting them with lighter fluid before dropping in a match. The wood burst into flame like a sacrifice to some angry god.

"I was eighteen," he said, although he hadn't done anything to show that he'd acknowledged my presence. "You were a newborn, and we had recently lost your mama. I don't say that as an excuse. I just want you to understand how long I've been living with my guilt over one stupid, angry decision." I said nothing, but went and sat on the ground next to him.

"It was a different world back then," he continued. "Not the kind of world where a football player could invite his boyfriend to homecoming." He tossed a few more chunks of wood into the barrel. "This all has to be burned," he said, nodding at the pile of wood that was all that was left of the table where I had grown up eating my breakfast. The chairs were already broken up and lying at the bottom of the pile. "My blood has soaked into it, and unless it's burned, someone could use it to control me or steal my power. I'll have to get a hold of the clothes Jackson was wearing and burn them too." He surveyed the shards of broken furniture all around him. "Jilo would sell her soul for this pile," he said.

I wondered again if Jilo had kept Grace from breaking through until I was safely out of the way. Could she have created the storm

172

to slow me down? The lesson she gave me, being aware of danger and fending off attacks, would indeed have been appropriate if she had suspected I would get home before Grace was finished. Could Jilo have really intended to allow Grace to kill Oliver—or maybe even my entire family?

"Adam was never comfortable with being gay." Oliver shifted gears again without warning. "He still isn't, but it was much worse back then. He wanted to go into the military and then become a cop after his service was completed. Being gay didn't fit into his plans at all. But then he made the mistake of falling in love with me, and I loved him right back."

"Don't be angry," I had to say. "I don't want to hurt you by saying this, but maybe you loved him so much that you—"

"That I 'bent' him?" Oliver's laugh was bitter. "No, Gingersnap, Adam was plenty bent long before I laid eyes on him. Don't let his butchness fool you. It's the real knuckle draggers who can't wait to get on their knees." I couldn't think of a single thing to say to that. Oliver looked at me and tossed another bit of wood into the fire. "To make a long story short, I loved Adam. As a matter of fact he's the only man I have ever loved, although now I am damned if I know why." He stopped poking the fire and turned to meet my gaze. "Truth is, I will go to my grave loving him. Hell, I came pretty close to doing that last night." The right side of his mouth edged up in an attempted smile, but it fell flat. "And now," he continued, "I have to live the rest of my life seeing you look at me the same way he does."

It was exactly what Jilo had hoped for when she'd mentioned Grace to me. "Tell me what happened," I said, hoping against hope that I would find some extenuating circumstance that would allow me to pardon Oliver.

"You already know. Grace wasn't lying," he said.

"But you tell me. You tell me anyway."

He moved away from the barrel and sat down next to me. He leaned back on his elbows as sweat beaded up and slid down his bare chest. "Grace said Adam and I were sick. Men weren't supposed to be doing the things we did. Men shouldn't love each other. She wanted Adam, and she figured she could fix whatever was broken in him."

"Did she have Mother Jilo charm him?" I asked.

"There was no need. Adam and I had been together for over a year. He had grown a little bored with me by then anyway, I guess. He liked Grace's attention; he was flattered by it. But mostly he believed the same things she believed. That there was something wrong with us. And when she promised to cure him, he went for it like the fire in that barrel is going after the wood. Problem is, it didn't work." He looked up at the blue sky and watched a large cumulus cloud move closer. "He came back after a few months, going on about how much he loved me, how much he missed me. He swore to me, swore to me, that we would be together somehow. And then a few days later he up and disappeared.

"I went to his house, but his mother told me to go away. Grace was pregnant, and she and Adam were going to get married. Her son didn't have time for any more of our 'little games.' He was grown up, and he was going to be a man now. It was time for me to do the same. She slammed the door in my face, and then I saw the curtain in Adam's window move. I knew he was there. I should have been angry. I should have walked away, but I was . . ."

"Heartbroken," I said when he wasn't able to find the word.

"No, darker than that. I was heartbroken, but my conscience was broken too. I sat down on their steps, and the darkness grew inside of me. I couldn't move, and I felt like I was growing heavier and denser with each breath. After a few minutes, Adam's grandfather Henry came out and sat next to me." Oliver swiveled to look at me again. "Henry was the most decent man who ever walked this earth. He put his arm around me and told me that I needed to be tougher for my own good, but that I was going to get through it. And then he pulled me close and told me that his grandson was a fool not to love me like I deserved to be loved."

"I met Henry once; he's a good guy," I said.

"But Henry died right after you were born." Oliver started to shake his head, but then he sighed. "Savannah."

It hadn't occurred to me that Henry was a spirit. He had held onto me, driven a car for me. Jilo must have lent some mojo to his apparition to make it capable of the physical feats he had performed. I should have been shocked, but it was getting hard to surprise me anymore. "Savannah," I responded.

"Things would probably have worked out," Oliver continued. "Sure, Adam would have married Grace, but I doubt it would have lasted. Probably in a year or two, he would have decided to move on from Grace as easily as he had moved on from me, proud of the fact that at least once, he'd managed to get his dick hard enough for a girl to plant a baby in her." Anger simmered very close to the surface. "That kid would have been his cover for life."

"Is that why—" I started to ask.

"No." Oliver stopped me. "Winning wasn't good enough for Grace. She had to come here to rub my nose in it. We fought, and I told her that the only reason Adam was marrying her was because she was knocked up. She said that Adam wanted a normal life, not a perverted one. I snapped and told her that if she was so sure of that, she should abort the baby and see if Adam was still interested in a wedding. I compelled her to have that abortion."

"You were angry." I found myself rationalizing for him. "They were just words."

"So it wasn't premeditated. It was still murder. I knew what I was doing. I didn't care. Maybe the baby would have been more real to me if she had been showing. Maybe . . ." He paused. He'd obviously traveled this road many times. "She wasn't a woman who decided what was right for her own body, Mercy. I decided for her, and there is no way to redeem what I did."

"No," I said. "I reckon there isn't. But I don't believe you truly intended for her to do what she did. I don't believe you meant to compel her. I think you were grieving and angry. Maybe it was manslaughter, but I don't believe it was intentional. You are not a murderer." I stood and walked over to the fire barrel, where the wood was turning to ash. I tossed in a couple of extra pieces of the table.

"And I wonder if you're too willing to turn a blind eye to the faults of those you love," Oliver said.

"Come on and help me," I said. "This is burning out." He stood and dusted off his shorts. I bent down to grab another chunk of wood, and my hand touched a piece that was much smaller than the rest—a splinter about the size of my palm. It was stained deep garnet with my uncle's blood, like it had absorbed more than the rest. I picked it up and glanced at Oliver, who had turned and was reaching for one of the table's legs. Without consciously understanding why, I slid the piece into my pocket and then returned to feeding the fire.

"Did Grace kill Ginny?" I asked after he poked the table leg into the fire. Sparks flew up and the heat of the fire combined with the heat of the day forced us a few feet away from the barrel.

"No. When Iris put her hand on Ginny's body, she opened a door to the other side, and Grace stepped right in. She was just biding her time until she could break through."

"Maybe Jilo killed Ginny to trick Iris into opening the door?" I asked, wondering if I had been duped into helping that happen.

"No one knew about my part in Grace's suicide besides Jilo and Ginny," Oliver replied. "Jilo used her granddaughter's death as a negotiating tool. They made a pact, Ginny and Jilo. Jilo wouldn't try to seek revenge if I agreed to move away from Savannah. That's the reason I only come home a few weeks each year, and why I had to miss out on most of your childhood. The pact only allows me four weeks a year in Savannah. But getting rid of me was just icing on the cake."

"What do you mean?"

"Jilo got her hands on a big chunk of power. I don't know the mechanics of how it was done, but Ginny charged up a piece of quartz for her. About the size of my fist," he said, holding up his hand to demonstrate. "It glowed bright enough to light a football field. I swear. I couldn't even bear to look at it. Ginny told her to bury it where it couldn't be found, and to use it carefully. I bet that rock has been powering her tricks for over twenty years now." He grabbed another leg of the table and added it to the crackling pyre. "No, Jilo cares more for power than she ever did for Grace. She's fat and happy, and she'd never do anything to risk the comfortable little setup she has around here."

"So you don't think she had anything to do with Ginny's death?" I asked.

"No. I wondered at first, when her grandson Martell was spotted with the murder weapon, but the more I think about it, the more my gut tells me no." He shook his head at me. "Nothing more concrete than that, just my intuition."

I looked deeply into his blue eyes, trying to see the old Oliver, the one who Grace had unintentionally excised on our table. His confidence, maybe even callousness, had all but evaporated. I sensed that the Oliver I'd known was gone, and although part of me would miss him, I suspected that my uncle might become a better man now that he'd been freed of the secret he had been carrying all these years. "Will Jilo let you stay now that Ginny's gone?"

"Fuck Jilo," Oliver stated flatly. "And fuck any deals she made with Ginny. I'm not denying I'm guilty, but after last night, I think I've sure as hell served my sentence." He grabbed the ax and punctuated his statement with a quick whack at a large chunk of the table.

"You seem to have this under control," I said. "I guess I'll leave you to it."

"All right then," he said, but as I started to leave, he called out after me. "Gingersnap, that wood you have in your pocket . . ." he said, and I felt the blood rush hot to my cheeks, as hot as the fire popping in the barrel. "No," he said. "It's okay; I'd say I owe you at least that much after last night. Just take it up to your room for now, and I'll be up later to show you how to use it right. Don't try anything till I've shown you, okay?"

"Yes," I responded, my eyes dropping guiltily to the ground. I couldn't bring myself to look him in the eye. I turned on my heel and fled through the kitchen door. I heard Oliver chuckling as he tossed another bit of wood into the can. His laughter sounded truly happy.

TWENTY-TWO

By lunchtime, Iris and Connor had returned, having purchased a new kitchen table and chairs that would be delivered in the afternoon. The air was thick with awkwardness. Iris walked in with her head hanging low, her arms pulled tightly against her sides as if she were afraid of bumping into things. Connor was still angry, smarting from having been hogtied and gagged by his own wife, even though she'd been under Grace's control at the time. Ellen had found him naked in a closet, a sock duct taped in his mouth.

Connor opened a cabinet and grabbed a glass, then slammed the cabinet shut. The remaining glasses rattled against each other. He yanked open the refrigerator and poured himself a sweet tea. He tried to slam the refrigerator door too, but the insulation strip muffled his tirade. He made no attempt to hide the fact that he blamed Iris for the whole situation, glaring at her between each gulp of his tea. Iris clearly blamed herself too; she stayed quiet and braced herself against the counter by the sink, staring blankly out the window. I went over and wrapped my arm around her shoulders, but she pulled away.

"I knew the risk I was taking when I laid hands on Ginny. Especially after you . . ." Iris stopped short.

"After I what?"

179

She and Connor looked at each other. "Are you gonna answer her, or do you want me to?" her husband asked, slamming his glass onto the counter. Tea splashed everywhere, and Iris reached for a towel and began dabbing at it without even looking up at us.

I had almost stopped waiting for a response when she turned to me and said, "Your reaction when you found Ginny was rather intense. Your distress destabilized the energies I needed for my reading, and I knew it. I also knew that in all probability you wouldn't be strong enough to help ground me, to help keep anything from getting into this world." She paused. "Into me. Connor tried to stop me from doing it, but I wouldn't listen."

"I'm sorry," I said. "I didn't know. I just reacted."

"Don't blame yourself, sweet girl. None of this is your fault. I'm responsible for everything that happened here yesterday." I tried to pull her into my arms, but she wouldn't allow it. "I don't deserve your comfort," she said, shrugging off my embrace.

"You sure as hell don't," Connor replied. He grabbed the newspaper off the counter and stomped out of the room, hitting the kitchen door hard enough that it swung back and forth three or four times before settling itself closed.

"Well God save us all from getting what we deserve," I said, loudly enough for him to hear me. I hugged my aunt anyway. Her body felt different to me today, as if a certain frailness had crept into her bones.

"Amen," Emmet said, stepping in through the door to the backyard, which was still open.

"Bless you, baby," Iris said to me and then fled from the room, her face lined with tears.

"She'll be fine," Emmet said. "She made a mistake, a huge mistake, but nothing we were not able to rectify. Your family is careless, impulsive when using their powers. They are weak and emotional."

"Yeah, well thank you for your input," I said. Whatever my family was, we had been through enough, and the last thing we needed was the criticism of someone who had once been a pile of dust.

"We don't mean to anger you," Emmet said. "The fault does not lie with your family. The fault lies with us. An anchor should cultivate the witches around them. Help the weaker powers to grow and learn to function responsibly. Instead of offering guidance and light, Ginny created an atmosphere of darkness. She kept your family weak and you ignorant. In so doing, she failed you all, and we failed you by not seeing that earlier. We are here to rectify these wrongs."

"What about Grace?" I asked.

"The spirit will not be able to return," he said. "She can either move on to the next realm or she can remain in the shadows of Savannah as an angry spirit. The choice is hers. But she will not be able to break through and make another attack on Oliver or anyone else in your family." Emmet closed his eyes and broke into a discordant inner discourse—I'd never get used to that as long as I lived. After a few unnerving moments he looked at me. "We have spoken to Oliver," he said and held his large hand out to me. "Show us the remnant of wood that you claimed." I obeyed him without even giving it a single thought, reaching into the pocket of my cutoff sweatpants and handing him the scrap of wood. He hadn't compelled me to do it, I simply did.

"Glamour and persuasion," he said as he turned the piece in his hand. The splinter's sharp edges rounded as he touched them, leaving the piece perfectly smooth. "Those are Oliver's strong suits, and for a brief while they will be yours too."

Oliver appeared in the open doorway, as if he had been called by name. He took the piece from Emmet's hand, and held it silently for a few moments before placing it in my palm. It was warm, and it gave off a tingling sensation. As I watched, three symbols etched themselves onto its face.

"*Gebo* shows that I have given this to you freely," Oliver explained, "for stealing power comes with a consequence that I could not bear to see you pay. *Uruz*, here," he said, pointing at the second symbol, "has the double meaning that it is my power that I am giving, and that it is within my rights to do so. The last one is *Dagaz*, and it limits the time the power is available to you to one day. And with that, a share of my powers are yours. Your buddy Emmet here will explain the rest," he said. "Don't do most of the things I've done with them," he added and went back outside.

The tingling moved from my hand through my arm and then dispersed in a blink throughout the rest of my body. My knees went weak, and I started to tumble forward, but Emmet caught me in his arms before I could even blink. I righted myself and stepped away from him. I had never felt so powerful or so lost. I had dreamed all my life about having a day, just a single day, to know what it felt like to be Maisie. To have the world at my fingertips. And here I was stumbling around in the kitchen without a clue what to do with the power now that I had it.

"It's overwhelming," I said, more to myself than to Emmet.

"This is good for you, Mercy," he said. "This power you feel overwhelmed by. It is only a tiny fraction of what's surging inside Oliver, Iris, or Ellen. Even Connor for that matter. And when you compare it to Maisie's power, it's nothing. Nothing." He let the word sink in. "Tell us, Mercy, how does it feel? Does the power frighten you?"

"No," I said. I stopped and considered how it really felt to have the energy flowing through me. "I feel alive, I feel like a picture coming into focus. It feels good."

"You are a mystery, Mercy Taylor, to all of us," he said. "The power slides into you with none of the ill effects that we would have expected to witness in an average human. You fit the power like a glove. It fills you beautifully, as if you had been made to hold it, but still—"

"But still I never did," I finished for him.

"You do today," he said. "And now you must show yourself worthy of this gift. Whatever magic you work today, you must work on your own. We wish neither to impede any action your conscience allows you, nor to give you ideas that might distract you from your intuitive course. You are a natural vessel, and the magic is merely awaiting your command."

TWENTY-THREE

Standing in my room, I could still sense the bit of wood vibrating in my hand. When I looked down at it, it was visibly quivering and giving off faint blue sparks. Everything about me felt changed. No, not changed—heightened, intensified. I tested the power I felt surging through me, using it to bore a small hole in the tip of the shim so that I could wear it as a pendant. I watched as the wood pulled itself apart, cell by cell, leaving a perfectly shaped circle through which I strung some hemp. I knotted the hemp a few times to make sure it would hold, and then pulled the loop around my neck. The string was long enough that the tip of the wood rested near my heart. As the wood slid between my breasts, the vibrations spread all over my body.

Liquid fire coursed through my veins. I slid my hand over the pendant and looked at myself in the mirror, amazed at the self-assured face that was reflected back at me. I felt like a fish that had been tossed into water for the first time after somehow managing to survive its entire life on dry land. I had been waiting for this feeling my entire life. For once, I felt like I could truly breathe.

I was saddened by the knowledge that this power was only borrowed. Tomorrow I would be back to floundering on the shore, even though the river would continue to flow right next to me. One second I regretted ever taking the power into me, and the next I wondered what I'd be willing to sacrifice to hold onto it. The memory of Jilo's words plagued my conscience. I pulled the necklace up over my head and tossed it down onto the table. I tried to walk away and leave it there, but my hand reached out of its own volition, my fingers hovering over the wood, wanting so badly to touch it, to hold it. I wondered how it would change me if I let it fill me for even a day, if I let myself see the world through the eyes it gave me.

"You need this," I heard Ellen's voice. She had been watching me from the doorway. I wasn't sure how long she'd been there, but I was sure it was long enough. "You need to feel the magic, if only this once. I know you've always wanted this experience, and the other families might not allow it again. This is a special dispensation. This is your opportunity to walk in a witch's shoes, Mercy. It may make it easier for you to understand your family and forgive us for our gargantuan shortcomings."

I could have been angry with her for spying on me, but I wasn't. I was glad that someone was here to share this with me, to be my confessor. "I'm afraid," I said. "I don't want to feel this good, this powerful, knowing that I'll never experience it again. It's worse than a drug."

"No, it isn't a drug at all. It's the power that naturally flows through a witch . . . and you sense that it should be flowing through you."

A few moments had been enough to convince me that my hunger for magic was too great for me to withstand. "But this is too strong," I still said. "I can't let it fill me today only to leave me tomorrow. I won't be strong enough to let it go. I won't be strong enough to go back to being me after I've been . . ."

"Maisie. After you've been Maisie," she said, and I acknowledged the truth of this statement with a nod of my head. Tears had begun to well up in my eyes, and I couldn't find my voice.

She reached out and took the necklace, opened the loop wide, and hung it over my head. She lifted my hair up over the cord and then let it fall gently down my back. The wood touched my heart, and once again I was part of the magic and it was part of me.

"I'm not sure I'll be able to let this go," I said again, but my will to protest faded before I even finished the words. I looked away from Ellen and back at my own reflection. As my eyes adjusted, I noticed that an odd shimmer was dancing around me. Concentrated around my heart, it flitted between red and green, with bits of black speckled throughout. It was as if I were enveloped by a field of living color.

"Try something, anything," Ellen said. "See how it responds to you."

I was heartsick for Maisie. I missed her desperately, and I had to let her know that I forgave her for what had happened during the drawing of lots. I needed to see her for myself; I needed to know that she was okay. I held out my hand and touched the mirror. It rippled for a moment and then the reflection changed. I could see Maisie talking with a dark-haired woman I didn't recognize. I caught the woman's notice instantly, and with a wave of her hand she broke the connection.

"Amazing," Ellen whispered. "You shouldn't have been able to create a portal to Maisie. How did you do it?"

"I just thought of her and how much I wanted to see her," I said.

"And with a simple thought and only a jigger of Oliver's power, you were able to reach into another world, another dimension."

"Dimension?"

"It was felt that it would be best to move Maisie out of contact with the line while she works things through."

"Who was the woman?"

"Woman? She is less of a woman and more of a force of nature," Ellen said, the corners of her mouth pulling downward. "She's the anchor with whom Maisie is training. It would be best for you not to draw her attention again, sweetie." She smiled at me, but the smile seemed forced. "So what are you going to do today?" she asked, quickly changing the subject. "Surely you aren't going to waste it by standing in front of the mirror."

Her question caused me to focus on the red and dappled green aura I had noticed earlier. I hesitated, but then said, "I think I've made a mistake," pointing at the concentration of vibrant colors that hovered near my heart.

"Yes," she said, stepping closer. "I can scarcely make it out, but I can tell that there is a magic there that's at odds with your own." Ellen reached out and brushed away the pendant to place her fingers over my heart, her touch gentle. "This is artificial magic. This is not witch magic."

I knew we were both sensing Jilo's spell. I also knew that I needed to use this day to rectify the wrong I had committed by going to her. I needed to find a way to end the spell she had placed on me even if it meant breaking Peter's heart. I had to believe it was better for him than living a lie. "It's Mother Jilo's magic," I confessed.

"Yes," Ellen said. "Jilo's signature is all over it, powerful yet amateur. Foolishly constructed and open to a whole bunch of negative side effects. Who asked her to place this on you?"

I didn't respond, but Ellen seemed to guess the truth. "I see," she said. Questions flitted across her face, but she chose not to pose any of them.

"Can I break this spell?" I asked.

"Yes, the spell can be broken," she said after some consideration. "But it is a blood spell. In order to break it, you need to have the blood of the one who cast it."

"How much of her blood?" I asked, a cold shudder shaking through me. I remembered the sackcloth bag that Jilo had been carrying when I went to see her at the crossroads; the poor hen inside had been destined for something much darker than Sunday dinner.

Ellen removed her hand and the pendant slid back into place. I felt myself grow stronger and more confident when it touched my chest.

"Not much," she said. "Only as much as she used in her original casting."

"So all I need to do is hunt down Jilo and ask her for a donation," I said. I was strangely certain I could find her, but I wondered if even Oliver's power for compelling would help me extract blood from the old stone.

"It would be best if she revoked the spell on her own, making it like she never cast it," Ellen responded. "But if she's unwilling, you could break it yourself with a bit of her blood mixed with a bit of the blood of the person who requested the spell."

"But how?" I asked.

"Trust your instincts," she said. "You don't need my help for this one. If you can reach across worlds to find your sister, you can handle Jilo."

I was still staring at my newly enhanced reflection when she left the room, but she was right. I was not going to waste another moment of my day. I placed my hand over the pendant and felt the fire circulate in my veins once more. When I slipped it beneath my shirt, I experienced a feeling barely short of vertigo. The world rushed up around me, and I was completely enveloped in the power. Finally the energy settled inside me, and I could think clearly again. Time to deal with Jilo.

I walked down the hall to the linen closet, halfway expecting it to creak open and radiate shimmering haint blue light, just like it had yesterday. The door remained shut. I stood before it for a few moments and then took the knob in hand. When I opened it, a completely normal room lay in front of me—no aquamarine, no amputee cat, and certainly no Jilo. I stepped in and closed the door behind me. I went to the center of the room, trying to sense Jilo's magic, but the room felt blank. The only magic I sensed within its walls was what I had brought in with me. *This* was why my family had never sensed that Jilo had created a portal in our home. It was hidden from those who were filled with magic.

I left the room and followed my instincts downstairs and out of the house. Jilo was hiding from the police, who were a mere inconvenience to her, and from my family, who could pose a more serious threat. As guilty as Iris may have been for carelessly letting Grace slip into our world, I was guilty too. I had given Jilo a purchase from which to take aim at my family. I needed to convince her to break the spell that she had cast and then break off relations with her entirely. It was wrong for me to put my desire for knowledge and power before my family's well-being.

I briefly considered taking my bike, but I needed to feel Savannah beneath my feet. After a few steps, I kicked off my shoes. I needed the stones and the sandy soil, the sun-baked concrete, and the tabby sidewalks to guide me. The surfaces tugged at my feet, their energy merging with my own, their molecules communicating directly with mine in a way that couldn't be explained by the rational world. The sun was nearly overhead, and I knew the ground beneath me must be infernally hot, but I felt no pain. I felt only the pull of Savannah as she guided my feet toward my destination.

Through the lens of the power, I felt as if I were seeing the city for the first time in many ways. Periods of the past interlaced with future possibilities in a way that was confusing at first. Houses rose and fell, the street was paved and then it wasn't. Towers I had never imagined seeing in Savannah sprouted and then faded. Everything was jumbled up before me, but with each step my focus was narrowing in on the now.

I let my feet carry me forward without questioning their steps. I realized that I was moving away from my home in an ever-expanding spiral. I felt as if I were once again a little girl, playing blind man's bluff. Savannah called "warmer" or "cooler" to me as I continued along. I approached Whitfield Square, and its gazebo was like an arrow pointing me farther south. My pace quickened as I continued down Habersham past the small liquor store. Instinctually I drew closer and closer to the broadcasting tower on Huntington. And then I knew. I turned onto Huntington, moving as if the air itself were carrying me back toward Drayton, toward Forsyth Park.

I felt her nearby—her vibrations and the scent of her magic, ripe with earth and ash. It pulled me closer and closer to old Candler Hospital. Georgia's oldest hospital, it had opened decades before the Civil War began. The misery of the past roiled from the building like heat off a blacktop. Victims of the yellow fever epidemic had passed through its doors on their way to their final reward—or were sometimes hurried toward it by the doctors who coveted their bodies for dissection. The indigent and the mad had also been hastened inside, few of them ever to leave. During the Civil War, piles of amputated limbs had practically reached the second floor. Even today, thirty-something years after it had been closed as a hospital, Candler seemed glutted, choked on the wretchedness it had absorbed for centuries. Toxins both real and spectral emanated from the building, and the rusted and peeling ironwork seemed to threaten tetanus if you so much as glanced at it.

As I circled to the front of the hospital, I sensed a barrier that separated the building from the world around it. The faculty with which I sensed this barrier was almost sight, almost touch, but independent from both. As I focused on the barrier, I caught a fleeting glimpse of it, a wall of cold blue flame that encapsulated the building.

A spirit on the other side of the barrier flung itself against it again and again, reaching out to me in supplication. He crouched there, naked and unwashed, and my sympathy for his plight drowned out my own fear and disgust. One instant he was there, on his knees, his bloodied hands beating against the wall that held him. The next he and the barrier had vanished from my sight, and the building was bathed in normal late morning light. He must be the soul of one of the madmen who had lost their lives there, I realized. I continued to circle the building until I reached the Drayton Street side. I had seen the defunct hospital so many times while walking in Forsyth Park, but I had never really taken it in before. Well, maybe I had, but only with ordinary human eyes.

The large Candler Oak stood sentinel before it, its Spanish moss–covered limbs nearly three hundred years old. It was an old friend of mine, having served me in many games of hide-and-go-seek over the years. I felt compelled to touch it, to run my hand against its bark and experience it as a witch. I tentatively traced its side with my index finger, and the tree shimmered its welcome, seeming to recognize my touch and invite it. I splayed my whole hand against it, letting my palm scrape against the immense trunk. Suddenly dozens of vivid impressions crossed my mind. I closed my eyes. The ancient oak was trying to communicate with me by sharing the feeling of its deep roots in the cool soil, the sensation of hot sun on its leaves, and the deep sense of place it knew, which could never be understood by those who moved across the face of the earth.

I opened my eyes, and burning in the wood before me were two symbols, similar to those that Oliver had carved into the wood I was now wearing as a pendant. A spell had been placed here and, with the magic running through me, I could see it. The first symbol looked like the letter Y with a line drawn through its vertical center. *A defense, a source of protection, a warning.* The second looked something like a fish standing on its tail. *Property, a parcel of land.* I didn't know their names, but the magic within me explained their purpose. These runes strengthened the spell that held the mad and desperate energies of the old hospital in check, keeping them locked in place so that they couldn't spread out into the rest of the city.

I considered the wisdom of freeing those who were trapped on site. It wasn't the smartest or safest thing to do, but I couldn't bear the thought of leaving them there forever. Maybe this was the one unselfish thing I could accomplish today. I cast my mind out around the spell, checking for any weak spots, and as I did, a shrill and piercing sound rose in my ears. It was deafening from the start, and it kept getting louder and louder until the pain caused my knees to buckle. The warning was clear—I wasn't to meddle.

I was still on my knees looking up at the hospital when I felt strong hands grasp my shoulders. My sense of hearing returned in a rush of words.

"Mercy, are you okay?" I spun around to see Jackson. His eyes widened and then narrowed as he took in the new glow that Oliver's magic had given me. An angry crease formed on his forehead. "What's wrong with your eyes? What have they done to you? What have you done to yourself?" he asked, his voice full of misery. "I can feel the magic on you."

I looked into his eyes, feeling their blue warmth, and wanted to possess him, the strength of Oliver's need to seduce momentarily overpowering the effects of Jilo's spell. The look of distaste on his face was a cold slap that triggered my conscience and stopped me from acting. I knew that something had changed in him. I had seen him look at Maisie with adoration thousands of times, but he was repulsed by the power in me, even though it was inconsequential when compared to hers.

"Nothing," I said. "It's nothing permanent." I reached into my shirt and pulled out the wooden amulet. It was hard to summon the will to remove the necklace, but I managed to pull it off and let it fall to the ground beside me. The world around me faded, losing the vibrant colors and sharp edges that had been revealed by Oliver's magic. It was once again my simple, everyday world.

"Burn that thing," Jackson said, reaching down to grab the necklace.

"No!" I blocked him with a show of force I never would have thought myself capable of without the power. Then, more calmly, "Not yet. I'll destroy it tomorrow."

He backed a few steps away from me, surveying me for any remaining traces of the power. "This isn't meant for you, Mercy. This 'magic'"—he said the word with disgust—"is unnatural. It's wrong. I'm done with it."

"You can never be done with it," I said. "It's what Maisie is, what she's made from."

"That's why I've been looking for you," he said. "I'm through with the magic. And I'm through with Maisie. I've decided to break off our engagement." I started to protest, but he held up his hand to silence me. "I mean it. My eyes have been opened. I saw what Maisie turned into the night of the lot drawing. I've been asking myself if I could truly love her after what happened. The sight of her, floating above the ground, the way she enjoyed hurting us. The look in her eyes. It sickened me. *She* sickened me."

"You shouldn't have been there. You shouldn't have seen any of it."

"But I was. I did. And I don't know how to deal with it. The reason I showed up at your house yesterday is that I wanted to talk everything over with your family. I hoped it would help me figure out if I wanted to carry on with Maisie."

"You can't decide that by talking to anyone other than Maisie," I said, but Jackson just shook his head.

"No," he said. "I had my answer as soon as I laid eyes on you, and when we went into the house—I can't live with this weirdness in my life. As long as I'm with Maisie, it will be a part of my life, and I just can't abide by that. It took me a while, but I've finally gotten it through my thick head what your family is all about. And this magic is not natural. I'll never forget the things I saw yesterday. I'm sorry, but what I felt for Maisie is dead. I could never love her again." His face softened, and his eyes bore into me. "But you aren't like them. Not usually, at least. Mercy, I've got to say it. I wish to God that I'd met you first."

"You don't mean that," I protested out of loyalty for Maisie. Or was it only Jilo's spell that was keeping me from throwing my arms around him? In my secret and guilty dreams, I had heard him say these words to me thousands of times. But in my dreams there were never any consequences.

"I do mean it," he said. "You're real. You're human. Quite frankly, I don't know what Maisie is anymore, but I know I can't love her. I can't build a life with her. I sure as hell cannot make her the mother of my children." He hesitated a moment and then said, "I'm leaving Savannah, and I'd like you to come with me."

"I couldn't—"

"No, don't answer me now. Take some time and think it over. I know that you've made promises to Peter. I know you feel responsible for him and Maisie, but I think that deep down you know I'm right. We belong together, and the farther we get from this place, the clearer that truth is going to be to you. We could go anywhere, as long as it's far from here. Seattle, Los Angeles, you name it." His voice had been growing in intensity, but he stopped and ran his hand through his blond locks, taking a moment to compose himself.

I couldn't process his words. Jilo's magic made it impossible for me to consider leaving Peter, and my love for Maisie made the thought of breaking her heart even more impossible. But in my mind's eye, if only for a fleeting moment, I could see us together on that other coast, holding hands by the beach. I pushed the image away.

"But even if you don't choose to leave with me," Jackson said, "you still need to get away. You cannot let their magic poison you. Leave that thing here." He nodded toward my necklace on the ground. He stepped closer to me and took me into his arms. He didn't try to kiss me; he just nuzzled my hair, breathing in deeply. Then he whispered into my ear, "Sleep on it tonight. I'm leaving tomorrow. If you want to go with me, and I hope and pray you do, meet me at dawn in front of Saint John's. I won't see another day in Savannah." He turned away from me and hopped into his GTO, leaving behind a peel of rubber the length of a full good-bye.

I reached over and retrieved my necklace, putting it around my neck without even consciously thinking about it. As my eyes followed the trail of colors that Jackson had left in his wake, I felt a tug from Connor, the power of his pendulum seeking me out. Well, whatever he wanted could wait. I swatted his energy away like I would an annoying fly.

TWENTY-FOUR

I took a few steps toward the hospital, and the net of energy that surrounded it clung to me like a spider's web. I could feel Jilo nearby, but the closer I got to the building, the farther away she felt. I found myself zigzagging back and forth in the parking lot. After a few minutes of wandering around, a glimmer caught my eye—a wave of aquamarine reflecting off the hospital's exterior wall. I rushed over to it, hoping to find its source before it faded.

The glow intensified as I came closer, and I sensed that it was intended as a beacon to guide me to Jilo. I looked down and realized that the light was emanating from the entrance to a set of steps that led beneath the parking lot. The heavy sheet of metal that usually sealed the opening had been moved aside. I realized that Jilo must be hiding out in one of the yellow fever tunnels that had been dug under Savannah to hide the extent of the epidemic from the populace. As a child I had spent days exploring the hospital's grounds and the cool tunnel that went under Drayton Street and into Forsyth Park. Somehow I had never noticed this entrance before. I took one last hungry look at the light of day and descended into Jilo's magical gloaming.

The tunnel was impossibly long and lit in a way that made it seem less like a tunnel and more like a bridge through an eternal darkness. But that darkness was not empty; it was woven from the animated shadows that I'd first witnessed in Jilo's haint blue chamber. I could sense an endless number of them. They appeared to be seamlessly united, but each had a hunger all its own. Instinct told me that their realm fell outside the boundary of protection created by the spell that had been engraved on the Candler Oak. It was somehow both deeper and farther away. The darkness watched me with its black and countless eyes as I carried on, putting one foot before the other, wondering if Jilo's magic was the only thing protecting me from a quick death.

There was no sense of having crossed a boundary or stepped through a doorway, but I suddenly found myself in Jilo's haint blue room. With one step, I was in the tunnel, with the next, I was standing before her. My rational, non-magical mind protested that this room couldn't be anywhere near Forsyth Park. After all, Cook's grandfather had driven me up dirt roads to get to this room when Jilo had influenced him to abduct me. My witch knowledge explained that the room was not only a room; it was a hub that could open up onto any number of places.

"Took you long enough," Jilo's voice carried from the center of the room—a space that was at once as large as a football field and as small as our walk-in linen closet. "I guess you too busy for Jilo. How is yo' love life anyway?" She chuckled. She sat there on her aquamarine throne, dressed in a color I might have called crimson if it had been a tad less vibrant. "Come closer, little girl," she commanded. I stepped forward, but not because I had been compelled. Despite her show of power, I could sense that that the force within me was greater. I would never have this advantage again, so until sunrise tomorrow, Mother Jilo would have to answer to me for a change. "Pretty necklace you wearing, girl. Any chance you could get Jilo one like it?" She laughed.

"I don't think so," I responded.

She reached out and took the amulet into her hand to examine it, but a surge of electricity shot through her, leaving her gasping. "Damn, girl, Jilo wasn't gonna try and take it; she just wanted to see. Jilo ain't no fool. She ain't never stole no witch's power, and she sure ain't going to start by stealing from a Taylor. The penalty for stealing power is lot steeper than Jilo willing to pay for a half-day token." I stayed silent because I didn't want her to realize I was not completely in control of the power. After a moment, Jilo composed herself and leaned back on her throne. "So, they done made you queen for a day. Whose idea was that?"

"It's a long story," I said. "But the power is Oliver's."

Jilo smiled knowingly. "So he still with us then?"

"You *did* know about Grace," I said. "Why didn't you warn me?"

"Warn you? Warn you against my own blood? Jilo tried to protect you. She gave you what you needed to protect yourself. But Jilo ain't doin' a damn thing for the rest of yo' family. That uncle of yours, my Grace's blood is on his hands. Anything she done to him, he deserve. I wish to God she had killed that prissy little bastard," she said and spat on the ground without a lick of self-consciousness. "And Grace just the beginning of what yo' family done to Jilo's. Our families got history, my girl. Real history. Jilo shouldn't even waste her time on you. But you different from the rest of 'em, that why Jilo willing to help you. Fact is Jilo like you, more than she ever thought she could care for a Taylor. But don't you never think Jilo loyalty don't lie with her own blood."

"Except when it's to your own benefit to betray them. Oliver told me what happened after Grace died. I know you lied about your sister, and that Ginny gave you the source for the power you've been using. You took advantage of the situation with Grace to get something for yourself."

Jilo's face lit up with amusement. "You done caught Jilo, ain't you," she said, but then her smile flitted away. "'Sides, my Grace was gone. There nothing Jilo could do about it."

"But you didn't kill your sister. She isn't buried at your crossroads."

"Jilo got three sisters. Two alive and one who died in Detroit five years back. Jilo wouldn't harm a hair on they heads."

"But you encouraged me to kill my sister!"

"Jilo just wanted to see if you capable of it. And for a short spell, you considered it. That why you got all sick and stumbled away from Jilo."

I considered her words. I searched my heart, disgusted by the thought that she might be right. No, I realized, this was another one of her games; she was trying to throw me off. "No, Jilo. We both know that the thought never crossed my mind. But here's something you should consider. What if I left here and went out to your crossroads? Dug up the crystal Ginny gave you and crushed it into dust?"

Anger flashed through Jilo's eyes, but then she nearly doubled over with laughter. "Jilo lied about where the power from," she gasped out. "But she done told you the truth when she said it almost spent. You go ahead and dig. You ain't gonna find much there anymore. That why Jilo brought you here, 'cause she got a proposition for you."

"I have no desire to make deals with you."

"You just wait and hear Jilo out." The old woman leaned forward on her seat and waved a warning finger at me. "You got power today. You feel it. You taste it. But we both know tomorrow it gonna be gone. You help Jilo, though, and she can set us both up with a source of power that will last longer than either of us will in this world."

I knew I should stop her—I had come to break the deal I'd made with this devil, not to go into business with her. But I held back, I listened. The allure of having unlimited access to power was too hard to resist.

"Old Candler, here," Jilo said, "it full of energy. You touched it, Jilo know. Jilo can smell it on you."

"It's full of misery. Someone should do something."

"Someone done did something. Yo' grandfather hisself the one who made the spell holding the energies in here."

"But why would he have wanted to trap all this pain at Candler?"

"To keep it from wandering the streets of our fair city," Jilo said and smiled like a cobra, her lips pulled back tightly, her eyes hard, dark, and hypnotic. "Oh, don't you worry, missy. His motives were pure. After they closed the hospital, folk around town up and started disappearing. Little ones who'd be in they beds at sundown would be gone come sunrise. Your granddaddy tracked the things down to their home in Candler. When they closed the place, the shadows had gotten hungry and started hunting farther afield than they ever had before. Yo' grandfather, he wove his net and walked away, never considering that he had built a pressure cooker without a safety valve. And Jilo tell you that it gonna blow, and it gonna blow soon. We be doing this town a favor by releasing the pressure little by little. Keep it from exploding and ripping the whole of Savannah clean apart."

"Why do you need me? Why don't you take all the energy for yourself?"

"They others who have tried, and Jilo learned from their mistakes. You think it by chance that the big tower built no more than a couple of blocks from Candler? They set up the tower where it is so that Candler's energies could be broadcast throughout the whole damn world. But they still couldn't get to the power, 'cause it locked by Taylor magic. It gonna take a real witch to unlock it. After all, Jilo ain't no witch. I thought we done covered that."

I remembered the spanking I had received after just thinking about undoing the spell. "I already tried," I said, and Jilo's face turned into a mask of pure panic.

"You what, you stupid girl?"

"I wanted to free the spirits trapped there, but I couldn't. The magic is booby-trapped or something."

Jilo calmed herself. "They no way you, armed with yo' day pass to magic could even knock a chink into your grandfather's wall. But your sister, when she get home, you get her to unlock it, just a little. You show her that keeping it locked up tight is dangerous, that it need to blow out a little of its steam. You get her to create the valve, and Jilo handle the rest. She will show you how to tap into the energy like a tree setting its roots into the ground. They will be plenty of power for the both of us. Jilo and you both set for life."

I had come here to force her to break the spell she had placed on me, but now I had a bargaining tool. Of course I'd never let the old woman profit from the misery of the trapped souls inside Candler. I'd talk to Maisie all right, but only to get her to rectify the situation our grandfather had inadvertently created. Jilo didn't have to know that.

"Break the spell. The one you placed on me, and I'll talk to Maisie when she gets back."

"Oh, my girl, breaking a love spell is no easy thing," she said. "It better if we wait until Jilo has full access to her power again before she try."

"You're lying," I said. "I could break it myself if I took a bit of your blood and mixed it with mine."

Jilo rose up like an injured lioness, her head held high, her teeth exposed. "Take Jilo blood? You think you can just take Jilo blood?" She stepped away from her throne, spanning the distance between us until we stood practically nose to nose. "Oh, you is a Taylor all right. The second you get tanked up on yo' uncle's sweet juice you come pushing your way in, threatening Jilo. But you remember one thing, my girl. Tomorrow, this power of yours will be gone, and Jilo will be in charge again. So you stop and you consider real good before you start talking about taking anything off of Jilo."

Deep down, I knew she was right. I had come here with the intention of using Oliver's power to force my way if Jilo refused to cooperate. The real Mercy, the one I would have to wake up to tomorrow, knew it was wrong. I looked deep into Jilo's eyes and said, "I'm sorry. And not because you're going to have the upper hand again tomorrow. I'm sorry for threatening you, for even thinking about making you do something against your will, just because for the moment I have the power to do so."

Jilo looked back at me as if she couldn't believe what she was hearing. She took a few backward steps away from me. "God help this old woman, but Jilo do like you far more than she know she ought to." She held her right hand up in the air, and a knife with a long and menacingly sharp blade appeared in front of it. "You understand what Jilo doing, she doin' for your own good." She swung the knife down quickly yet deftly, making a gash in her left palm. Then she pointed the knife, handle first, at me. "Go on, it your turn now."

I reached out for the handle, bringing the blade against my own left palm. It hovered there; I was unable to bring its sharp edge to my skin. "You said you needed to mix yo' blood with Jilo's. You brave enough to face Jilo, you shouldn't be scared of a little cut." I lowered the blade, slicing it into my palm. The pain was fiery and fierce, causing me to wince, but it soon faded, and I held out my palm to Jilo. She grasped it tightly in her own, and our blood mingled, falling in heavy droplets to the earth. "Go on then, break the spell."

I looked down at my heart, where I could still see the mottled green and red aura. I willed the spell to end, but nothing changed. The colors continued to envelop my heart—if anything, they seemed to glow even brighter. I pulled her hand nearer, placing our conjoined hands against my chest, staining my shirt and moistening the pendant with our combined blood.

Trust my instincts, Ellen had told me. And I was trusting them. I held our hands over my heart and visualized the colors fading, the spell losing its hold and evaporating. But though I sensed that I was doing the right thing, the colors stayed as vibrant as ever. I wondered if there were words I should say, a verbal spell to enhance my efforts. Jilo stood patiently still, not saying a word. My shirt was irrevocably stained, and I sensed that the cuts on our hands were coagulating, closing off.

"I don't understand," I finally said. "I sense that this should work. I should have been able to break the spell by mixing the blood of the one who set the spell with the blood of the one who requested it."

Jilo calmly removed her hand from mine, and made a soft fist. When she opened it again, the wound was gone. "And that why Jilo let you try, 'cause she knew you never gonna believe her unless you try yo'self."

"Believe what?" I asked, still feeling the pulse of pain in my own hand.

"Weeks before you showed up at Jilo's crossroad, they was another who came to her in Colonial. That redheaded boy of yours."

"Peter?" I asked.

"Yes. He came to Jilo. He said he was losing his pretty miss, and he was willing to do anything it took to keep that from happening. The spell was done before you ever set foot on Normandy Street, before you ever even had the idea of coming to Jilo."

I stood there, feeling like the knife had gone straight through my heart instead of into the crease of my palm. Jilo moved closer and placed her hand over my heart and closed her eyes, her lips moving wordlessly, as if in some silent prayer. As I looked on, the colors flooded away from me and into her hand. She closed her fingers around them, and when she opened her hand the spell was gone just as surely as the cut on her hand had vanished. "There, it revoked," she said and moved heavily back toward her haint blue throne.

I should have thanked Jilo, but when my mouth opened, the words, "He betrayed me" spilled out. He had made love to me, knowing that Jilo's spell was what brought me to his bed. I had been able to accept Jilo's intervention when I'd thought the spell was my choice. Knowing that he had arranged for it made me feel violated.

"Open yo' eyes, child! It ain't just your man who betrayed you. Everyone, and I do mean every last one, of the folk you love, the ones you think love you, they all done betrayed you in one way or t'other. Truth is Jilo just might be the only one in this world you can trust."

"I can't believe that," I said.

"Believe it, don't believe it. It ain't no never mind to Jilo. But sooner or later, you gonna come to believe it, and when you do, you gonna be wishing you had power of your own, if only to protect yo'self. You be smart. When yo' sister get back to Savannah, when she all nice and settled in, you talk to her, and then you leave the rest up to Jilo."

I said nothing. I simply clasped my hand around my necklace as if it were a magical life preserver. The power began to surge through with renewed force, gaining strength as my hunger for it grew, and although my anger remained, the pain I felt over what Peter had done instantly dulled. He was, after all, only a human.

TWENTY-FIVE

As I crossed the dark bridge that connected Jilo's world to Candler, the living shadows began to press in around me, their touch like cold silk, seductive and terrifying in equal measure. I sensed that they were unrelated to the child killing demon my grandfather had trapped within the hospital's earthly boundaries, but these entities were undoubtedly just as nasty. I could tell that the scent of blood was what made them hungry. I kept moving, certain that if I stopped for even a moment, I would lose myself to them. They stopped abruptly as a ray of true sunshine pierced the gloom from above. I forced myself to carry on at an unhurried pace, fearing that if I gave sudden flight, it—they—might risk the sun's rays and give chase.

Finally, I found myself standing in the narrow shaft of light that illuminated the tunnel's entrance. I climbed the steps and found myself standing near the old hospital once again. With a wave of my hand, I moved the heavy sheet of metal back into place, sealing off the tunnel. Witch markings, invisible to the human eye, were etched across the cover. Perhaps these too were made by my grandfather, but some sixth sense told me that they had existed long before he'd walked the earth.

Time had moved differently in Jilo's world. The light that had led me out of the darkness was the last ray that could have managed to find its way down there. Another half an hour more, and I might have been lost. A chill ran down my spine, but I shook it off. I turned to find Connor directly behind me.

"You hurt yourself?" he asked, his eyes appraising the blood on my shirt. I almost tore into him for stalking me, but there was real concern in his voice, a genuine caring that my human ears had never been able to pick up on. I looked at him for the first time through a witch's eyes. Instead of the bloviating and disapproving dictator I had always known him to be, I just saw a man. A man who'd been quite handsome in his youth—I'd seen the pictures—and had cut a dashing figure sixty or so pounds ago. A man who looked tired and defeated. A man who had never quite been able to achieve what he wanted most.

"No, I'm fine," I said. "It's nothing."

"It doesn't look like nothing from here," he said and reached out to take the injured hand. I pulled it violently away from him, but I was a touch too slow. He caught hold of my hand and turned it palm up so that he could assess the wound. "Well, I'm not Ellen," he said, sighing, "but I think I can handle this."

He traced the length of the wound with more gentleness than I'd thought him capable of, and I watched as the cut healed beneath his touch. I was impressed. I was excruciatingly familiar with the tracking tricks he did with his pendulum, and he was pretty good with moving small items with telekinesis, but I'd never seen him do anything like this before. The effort seemed to have tired him. He was sweating and looked a little gray. "There, now. Care to tell me what you've been up to?"

"No, not really," I said, but with none of the rancor that my heart usually held for him. "Thank you for healing my hand."

"You probably could have done it yourself today," he said. "The golem told me that you're all juiced up on Oliver's magic." He paused and looked at me, weighing his words.

"You've obviously got something to say, so out with it."

He grimaced. "I do. I have something very important to say. Actually a lot of important things to say, but I'm trying to figure out how to say them without pissing you off." He started to speak again, but hesitated. His shoulders drooped forward, and he shook his head. "You always see me as the enemy, Mercy, but I'm not your enemy. So hear me out for a few minutes, okay?"

Part of me would have preferred spending more time with the living shadows in the tunnel than listening to my uncle's lectures, but I nodded anyway.

"Good," he said, adding "thank you" in an uncharacteristic show of good manners. "Regular hospitals aren't equipped to handle witch births. You two were born at home, and you came early. Only Iris and Ellen were home when your mama started labor. I wasn't there when you girls were born," he said. "I was out of town. But Iris told me that Maisie came out shining with life and power. We all thought your mama was only carrying one child. You weren't even expected. Emily picked the name Maisie out for your sister as soon as she was sure the baby was a girl." Connor stopped speaking for a moment and chuckled to himself. "She said there were too many damned witches named Sarah and Dianna in the world. You were a surprise to us all. When you came out, you were scrawny and blue—you'd practically starved to death in your mother's womb.

"Your mama, she was dying," he said, and a large tear dropped down his cheek. He brushed it away without seeming to notice that he had shed it. "Ellen was a gifted witch back before Ginny docked her powers, but even she had her limits. Nature only lets her get away with so much. A choice had to be made, and your mama made it. She refused Ellen's help, using the last of her strength to beg Ellen to save her baby. To save you."

Tears formed in my own eyes, tears too large and numerous to ignore. Connor waved his hand like a stage magician and produced a handkerchief. He held it out to me, and I took it.

"Ellen held you tightly in her arms and breathed her own breath into your little lungs. It took a while, but she got your body to warm up. By the time you had some color in your cheeks, your mama had already passed on. Ellen named you Mercy then and there, 'cause she thought a poor child like you was going to need some mercy. I, on the other hand, took a different tack. Once we determined for sure that you were powerless, I took it upon myself to personally knock you down every time the opportunity presented itself. I bullied you. I said bad things about you. I rubbed your nose in your failures every chance I got. And I did it all because I love you. I wanted you to be tough enough to face the rest of the witches who were saying much worse about you behind your back. I wanted you to be tough enough to face—"

"To face Ginny," I interrupted him. He nodded his head yes, and to my surprise tried to pull me into a hug. I resisted, and even used a bit of the witch power I'd borrowed from Oliver to escape his grasp. I wasn't ready to forgive a lifetime of hurt, at least not yet. I saw the pain of my rejection flicker through his eyes.

"She had it out for you from the beginning," he said. "She blamed you for your mama's death. And then, when she realized you had no powers, she started calling you 'The Disappointment' behind your back." The words cut through my heart. "So I started calling you the same thing to your face to make you stronger. But you gotta know, Mercy, you were never a disappointment to me. Not to any of us, other than Ginny."

He circled around me to block me from leaving. It was only then that I realized I had been moving away, trying to evade the pain his candor was causing me. "Listen," he said. "I kind of know what it's like. Ginny looked down on me too. She thought that Iris had made a mistake in marrying me, and that I didn't carry enough power to be a good match. The old bag cut me off at the knees and embarrassed me about my limits every chance she got. I know that she joked about me with the extended family. But you," he said, and the expression on his face told me that he had never fully understood what he was about to relate, "she hated you, Mercy. I'm sorry to say it, but we all knew it was true."

"I always knew it too," I said. "But why did she bother putting up protective charms for me if she hated me so much?"

"Pride," Connor said. "The old bitch wasn't going to let you be the weak link in her armor. If someone had harmed you, it would have been an affront to her dignity." He reached out for me again, placing his hand on my shoulder. I let him, and then he surprised me by tilting my chin up so that I was looking him in the eyes. "There are things I want to share with you. Some that I've only recently figured out, and some that I've known all along and should have told you about years ago. But I can't just tell you. I have to show you. I need you to come with me," he said, his eyes pleading.

"Where?" I asked, knowing the answer before he even replied.

"To Ginny's," he said, confirming my suspicion. "If you'll go with me, I'll be able to explain everything."

"I'll go," I said, hoping that the show would be worth the price of admission. I had intended never to set foot in Ginny's house again.

"Thank you," he said again, relief flooding his face. "But first, let's get you cleaned up a bit." He pointed at my ruined shirtfront. He started to work his magic, but I held up a hand to stop him. I ran my right hand down the front of my shirt, and the dried blood that would have been impossible to remove by any other means instantly erased itself. That being done, we crossed over Drayton and walked into Forsyth Park, taking the center path past the Confederate Monument with its four rebel angels. Darkness was taking hold, and I watched as the last of the wholesome families evacuated Forsyth, their departure acknowledging that at nighttime the park belonged to the drug dealers and thugs that never seemed to get mentioned in the visitors' bureau's brochures.

As we drew near Park Avenue, the park's lower boundary, my attention was captured by the monument memorializing those who had fought in the Spanish American War. I stopped dead in my tracks when I looked at the southern-oriented soldier's face. I'd seen it a million times or more, but today, with the way the dying light was caressing it, I recognized an unmistakable resemblance to Jackson. My feelings for him washed over me like a tidal wave, aggravating my anger at Peter and my guilt for whatever role I had played in crushing Maisie's dreams of a happy marriage. The temptation to run away with Jackson was strong, but I knew that if I gave in we'd both someday regret it.

"You okay?" Connor asked. I said nothing; I simply nodded and crossed the street. We turned left onto Barnard Street and then carried on to Duffy. Sooner than I would have liked, Ginny's house stood before us. The house had stood vacant since the murder, and that's more than likely how it would remain, a museum to the life and death of one Virginia Francis Taylor. I knew Connor and Iris had spent a lot of time there lately, sorting through Ginny's belongings, which were few, and cataloging her magics, which were much more numerous. I started to ask him whether or not he had found anything interesting, but he raised his hand to stop me. "Inside," he said and held the door open for me.

The first thing I noticed was that Connor must have removed the battery from Ginny's clock—its annoying strumming had stopped. I let my witch senses kick in, trying to pry any secrets they could from my surroundings.

Connor seemed to understand what I was doing. "There's nothing down here," he said. "Ginny kept the important stuff upstairs." He left me at the foot of the stairs and slowly made his way to the upper story.

I was filled with a giddy uncertainty. Ginny had never allowed me on the second floor. Never. I put my foot on the first step, applying gentle pressure as if I expected it to be booby-trapped. It took my weight without any objections, and the next step beckoned me. Each step I took felt like an act of retribution against the old woman who had done her best to alienate me from my family because I didn't share their gifts.

A door stood open at the end of the hall. Sensing that it had been Ginny's room, I crossed the threshold, running my hands over her dressing table, bed, and nightstand, trying to pick up any remaining vibrations. All I felt was Ginny's absence. Emboldened, I flipped on the light, only to see pictures of Maisie at various stages in her development staring back at me. One of them had originally been a photo of the two of us, but Ginny had cut the picture in half and used thick matting to hide the part of my presence that couldn't be easily excised. I tried to convince myself that it didn't hurt, that it didn't matter. Ginny was gone. Truth was, it hurt like hell.

Connor's voice called to me from another room, so I extinguished the light and went down the hall. He was standing in the doorway of a pink and girly room that was obviously Maisie's home away from home. He stepped aside to let me enter.

One full wall was taken up by a built-in bookcase, filled from one end to the other with modern journals and ancient texts. I opened one of the newest looking ones to find notes Maisie had made during a lesson she had received at Ginny's feet. The idea of

Ginny happily training my sister while forcing me to wait downstairs staring at a blank wall angered me. I threw the notebook to the floor and pulled another one out at random. The handwriting in this one was more mature, the spells more complex. Diagrams I couldn't even begin to understand were traced along the margins, composed of geometric shapes that seemed to defy Euclid's wildest imaginings and strange symbols that I had never seen before, some of them seemingly astrological. I almost returned it to its shelf, but instead tossed it to the floor in another gust of temper.

Connor sat on the foot of Maisie's bed, and with a casual gesture of his hand, the chair from her dresser pulled up next to me. "I think you'll want to sit for the next part," he said, his voice breaking nervously. I complied without protest. "These books, the knowledge in them, I never wanted to hide any of it from you. Not really. But as long as Ginny had her hands on the reins, none of us dared to defy her, not even Maisie. Now that Ginny's gone, I'm glad that the families support your education. I never wanted to keep you in the dark. Do you believe me? Do you believe everything I've been telling you?" His desire for me to say yes buzzed around him as brightly as a pawnshop's neon sign.

"Yes, I guess I do at that," I said, wondering why it mattered to him so much.

He smiled at me again, and seemed to be struggling with how to express what he wanted to say. "I've made a lot of mistakes in my life, Mercy. A lot of mistakes with you for sure, but a lot of mistakes in general." He hesitated for a moment, then just dove in. "I married your Aunt Iris for my parents' sake. I never loved her," he said, scanning my face for a reaction. I didn't give him one, but I felt betrayed, not only on Iris's behalf, but on my own as well. That he could have implicated us all in his lie made my blood boil. I stayed silent, and after a few moments he continued.

"My parents were proud that a Taylor woman would have me. They were proud that I was marrying above my station. Iris was beautiful and wealthy and a much more powerful witch than I'd ever be. And she loved me. I thought it would be enough."

He got up from the bed and began pacing the small room, filling it up with his bulk. "Your Aunt Ellen had just become a teenager when Iris and I married. Your mother was still only a redheaded pipsqueak, skinny as a string bean and as willful as a . . ." He hesitated and faced me. "Well, as an I don't know what."

He returned to the foot of the bed. "You know that Iris and I lived away from Savannah the better part of a decade. We visited often enough, but I never really connected with your grandparents or Iris's siblings. It was only after Iris's last miscarriage that your grandparents insisted we come back to Savannah. Iris had almost died in our last attempt to have a baby, and, well, your grandparents decided they wanted their girl home. They held the power, and Iris held the purse strings, so home we came."

I watched his hand as it alternately worried and smoothed the pink bedspread. "By then your mama was all grown up, and the truth of the matter was that she was more educated about the world than I was in a lot of ways. She knew that I was unfulfilled. She had joined a kind of club here in Savannah," he said.

My stomach started churning as I anticipated his next words. I wanted to stop him from speaking, but all I could do was listen.

"You see, it was Emily who first started up with Tillandsia, and she brought me into it, with Iris's acceptance, if that matters to you. After that last miscarriage, Iris wasn't much interested in marital relations anymore. But I was a normal man, in the prime of life. I had a normal man's needs, and Iris accepted that." He patted his stomach. "I know you can't see it now, but a couple of decades ago, there were plenty of women who wanted to be with me."

"I don't care," I spat out. I was embarrassed beyond belief. The very last thing I wanted to think of was Connor as a sexual being, and I definitely didn't want to think about him getting his thrills as my mother watched on.

"I'm sorry," he said. "I should stick to what's important."

"And what is important?" I asked, my patience wearing thin.

"What is important is that I loved your mother. I loved Emily. Completely and with all my soul."

"I see," I said. "And do you think she loved you?"

"She gave her life to have my children," he said and the earth stopped moving in the heavens.

My whole body went ice cold, but I began to sweat in the same instant. His words had knocked the wind out of me. "She *what*?" I asked when I found my breath.

"You girls. You and Maisie. You're my daughters," he said.

"Oh, no. That is not possible." I held out my hand as a warning that he should not try to approach me. "It is not true," I said, just so I could hear the words and try to believe them.

"Look at me, Mercy. Right now, you have a witch's power. If you look at me, you can tell whether I'm lying to you."

I studied him intently, every slight wrinkle on his face, every black mark on his soul, and as much as I loathed the idea, I knew beyond a shadow of any doubt that he was not lying. He was my father, our father. The idea struck me as hilarious, and laughing like a maniac, I stood with such force that I knocked over the chair where I'd been sitting.

"Your aunts made me promise to wait until you turned twenty-one to tell you, so you would be adult enough to handle the truth. I know I'm rushing things by a few hours, but I couldn't wait another minute," he said. "I needed you to know that I wasn't lying. Without Oliver's power to confirm the truth, a part of you would always doubt me. Hell, I could walk up to you with a DNA test and a signed birth certificate and you still wouldn't want to believe me."

"Does Maisie know?" I asked. I felt like screaming and crying. Now it was abundantly clear why Iris would be worried that I'd turn out like my mother, with a taste for other women's men.

"No," he responded. "At least I don't think so, but with all of the power she can access, who knows what she's learned? I was hoping to tell you both together. At the same time. I never anticipated Ginny's murder."

"I don't think any of us did," I said, moving toward the door.

Connor's arm shot out and grabbed mine. "I think you're wrong there. I think one of us did."

"Okay, I'm listening," I said. Releasing my arm, he reached into his pocket and unfolded an oversized sheet of paper. The paper was enchanted, and the creases smoothed themselves out instantly. "I found this among Ginny's affairs."

I took the paper from him and scanned it. Without my borrowed magic, the page would have appeared blank, but when I focused on it with a witch's gaze, words appeared—words so ancient that I would by no honest rights have the ability to understand them. But somehow I did. "It's a dissolution spell," I said, turning the paper into the light. At the moment I had no patience for deciphering the scrawls, so I folded the spell and put it into my pocket so that I could examine it more closely later.

"She was going to do it," Connor said. "Ginny was going to do away with Wren once and for all, and we both know Ellen would never allow that to happen."

"Ellen would never have killed Ginny!"

"You so sure about that?" he asked. "I'm not. We both know that she's been holding on by a thread for a decade now. If it weren't for the whiskey and Wren, she would have quit trying long ago."

I wondered if he could possibly be right. The pieces all added up, but I wouldn't let them fit together. Having Connor for a father was bad enough . . . I wouldn't believe that my sweet aunt was capable of murder. "No. You're wrong. I won't believe it."

"Don't believe it if you don't want to," he said. "Frankly, I think Ellen did us all a big favor. I sure ain't going to turn her in to the families. As long as she managed to cover her tracks okay, I'm fine with what she did."

Connor had revealed more to me tonight than I'd be able to process in a hundred years. "All right," I said. "You've told me what you wanted to. I'm ready to leave now."

"You can't go yet," he said. "I brought you here for a reason. There's one more thing I have to share with you, but I need to do it here." He turned and walked over to the bookcase, pulling down one of the newer journals. He held it out to me, and I could see Maisie's name scrawled across the front. The childishness of her signature clued me in to the fact that it was older than it looked. "I've tried to take it from the house, but I can't. It won't let me. I had to bring you here to show it to you." He handed it over.

My hands struggled against the binding, but I couldn't open it, try as I might. It had been magically locked. I brushed my hand across the cover, and even though it wouldn't open, some information leaked through the seal. I could tell that the journal contained information far more valuable than all of the Witchcraft 101 manuals on the bookshelf combined. It was sealed because it contained the secrets of the line. Even in my ignorance I was aware that Ginny should never ever have shared these secrets with Maisie; they were only to be passed from one anchor to another.

"You know what's in there, don't you? You can sense it," Connor asked, delight spreading across his face. "I knew the second I touched it."

"It's about the line. This journal is full of its secrets—things only an anchor should know."

"The families would have bound Ginny if they'd known she was telling Maisie these things."

"Look at the writing on the cover! Maisie was far too young to know what she was getting into."

"Sure, that's how we see it, and the families would most likely have agreed. But Ginny, though, that's a different matter. They would've shown the old gal no mercy. She would have been bound and deposited far, far away from any place she could access the line."

"Okay," I said. "But she's dead, and Maisie is going to be the anchor. What's the point of showing me this?"

He righted the chair that I'd knocked over then sat in it himself. "The point is that this is our chance to learn how to tap into the mainline, yours and mine. You've tasted Oliver's power. Are you telling me you wouldn't like your own? And not just a touch of it either, but a connection to the source itself? 'Cause I sure do, Mercy. I'm tired of living in your family's shadow, with just enough of my own magic for parlor tricks. I want more."

"Then take it. Why share it with me?"

"For two reasons," he said. "First, you are my beautiful daughter. I want you to have all the power you've ever wanted. I've watched you since you were little. You've always done your best not to be jealous of Maisie, but I know that deep down, a small part of you can't help but covet her abilities."

"And the second reason?" I asked, sensing that it would be the true reason he was taking me along on his joyride.

"The book. I can't take it from the house, and . . ." he hesitated. "I can't open it."

I laughed out loud and fanned myself with the journal. "And you think I can?"

"No," he said cautiously, sounding like he was worried that he'd moved too quickly and put me off. "Not normally, that is. But I am hoping that maybe, what with you being Maisie's twin—"

"Fraternal," I interjected, to remind him of that fact.

"Okay, but you're still her twin. And you're full of Oliver's magic right now. Maybe the combination of those two things will be enough for you to convince the book to open for you. And you have to remember, Maisie wasn't the one who was chosen as the anchor by the lots—you were."

"You said it was a mistake."

"I thought so at the time, but now I'm not so sure. Just try to open it while we still have the chance." His hands were clenched so tightly that his knuckles were turning white. His eyes pinned me in place like a butterfly to cardboard. I could tell how badly he wanted this to work.

"And when it's open?"

"We'll copy all of its secrets. And when Oliver's power leaves you in the morning, you'll have a bottomless well of your own to draw from."

"No, Connor. It is tempting. It is so tempting, but it's too dangerous. I don't care what Ginny's reasons were for sharing this with Maisie. We aren't anchors, and we should not be tampering with the line. God only knows what damage we might unintentionally do."

"Then you're willing to let the power go? Or do you think Jilo will honor the little pact you made with her today? Yeah, I know who hides out in that tunnel you snuck out of. The two of you made some kind of blood pact, but I can tell you from personal experience that Jilo does not live up to the promises she makes."

"I made no pact with Jilo," I said, trying to sound calm.

"Then take this chance with me! Help yourself! Help your father! Just try. Your mother believed in you. She wanted you to live up to your full potential. Don't let her death have been in vain. Just try. I beg of you."

The room fell silent for a moment, and Connor stunned me by falling to his knees in tears. I couldn't say if I was moved by his display or simply embarrassed. But I had to try, if only to get him up off the floor. I knew it was wrong. I knew it was dangerous. Deep down, though, I never believed it would work. "Know me," I commanded, and a jolt traveled from my fingers into the journal's cover. It sprung open, and I stood there with my mouth gaping in amazement. I swiveled to look at Connor, who had rebounded to his feet and turned back to the book. But before I could even read the first sentence, Connor simultaneously ripped the book from my hands and the necklace from my neck. The power failed me the second the hemp cord snapped.

A serpent's smile curved on his lips; he held my amulet up before my eyes and magically dissolved it into dust. "You always were the simple one," he said, and with a wave of his now free hand, he sent me flying backward into the wall. My head hit the plaster, and for a while there was only darkness.

TWENTY-SIX

Light returned to me in painful bursts. I was still propped up against the wall like a doll, exactly where I'd fallen. I was unable to move, but I knew it wasn't due to magic. The snap I'd heard upon hitting the wall had been one of my vertebrae.

Connor sensed that I'd returned to consciousness. "I really am your father," he said, never taking his eyes off the book, copying it as quickly as his hand could move in a shorthand that no human eye would ever unravel. "But truth is, you have been a terrible, terrible disappointment. The thought that Emily gave her precious life in exchange for yours is one of the greatest tragedies this world has ever witnessed. Oh, and I am including all of the wars, pestilence, and famine in history. At least those served the purpose of thinning out the herd. Rest assured, if I had been at the house the day you pulled your worthless self into this world, your mother would still be alive, and you'd have long since rotted to nothingness in a shoebox in Bonaventure."

"You were the one who killed Ginny." I managed to gasp out the words.

"No, my dear. I most emphatically did not. I am merely profiting from the actions of another. Isn't that right, Wren?"

After everything that had happened that day, I should have lost the capacity to be surprised, but I was still shocked when Connor said Wren's name and the boy materialized directly in front of me. He had evidently been standing there all along.

"She was going to kill me," Wren calmly explained. "I couldn't let her hurt me."

"But we've got a deal now, haven't we, Wren?" Connor asked cheerfully as he carried on with his note taking.

"I'm sorry, Mercy, but Connor has promised me not to tell anyone about Ginny if I help him."

"Help him do what?" I tried moving again, but couldn't even squirm.

Connor looked up from his work and smiled at me. "In one hour, I am going to be having drinks with the crème de la crème of Savannah at a charity auction. I will be photographed repeatedly with my beautiful wife Iris on my arm. In one hour and fifteen minutes, Wren will crack your skull in, just like he did Ginny's. I'll find your body here in a few days, after it's much too late for Iris to pull any impressions from the scene."

He turned back to the journal and continued copying. "I took photos of all of this with my cell phone's camera," he said. "But you know how magic can interfere with technology. Just a few more pages, and I'll leave you two to the rest of your evening."

I couldn't find the wind or the will to say another word. Connor carried on, occasionally repeating a phrase to himself or double checking the accuracy of one of the traces he'd made. His satisfaction seemed to increase with every conquered line until he turned to the last page, and shut the book with a satisfied sigh.

Suddenly the journal burst into hot and sticky flames. Cries began tearing from Connor that spoke of something deeper than terror and more pointed than pain. The flames clung to his fingers even after he had cast the journal aside. It must have been booby-trapped to prevent its secrets from ever leaving this house.

After a moment, Connor fell to the floor wailing. Between screams, he ordered the flames to stop, but they continued to pour from the open journal and rush across the floor to engulf him. He managed to climb onto his knees, and he turned to face me, his hands extended as if I were capable of helping him. What remained of his face was contorted with fear and pain, his eyes reflecting the knowledge that the fire would not abate, that it would consume him. Still unable to move, I could only watch as his hair smoldered and caught fire and his skin blackened. He rose and tried to take a step toward me, a living candle, but then fell back to the floor. As his body jerked up and down, the flames began to spread, and what was left of Connor became the epicenter of a fire that was expanding in every direction. I could feel the heat of the conflagration on my face but was helpless to escape it.

Desperately hoping that I might still be able to access some of Oliver's power, I tried to will the burning to stop, but it continued on unabated, racing faster and faster to the furniture and up the bookcase, melting the books' bindings before the books themselves burst into flame. The room was thick with smoke, and the only reason I could see what was going on around me was because my head was so close to the floor.

"I'm sorry, Mercy," I heard Wren's voice call out to me as the door to the room slammed shut. The fire licked at it almost instantly, defying me to try to touch the now glowing knob. I could hear sirens in the distance, but I knew they would never arrive in time. The flames enveloped the wood of the door then seemed to collect and regroup themselves. Suddenly the fire began advancing on me with full force.

It stopped abruptly, close enough to redden my skin with its heat and choke my lungs with its residue, but not to do any real damage. The flames were like none I'd ever seen. Even without a witch's vision, I could see their true form. Hundreds of small, salamander-like creatures. Suddenly I realized that they weren't from an actual fire at all—they were fire elementals. A chorus of razor-sharp voices exploded around me, angry and confused, and then there was a single unified gasp. The creatures circled me, each shooting out a tongue to lick at my foot. To my surprise, the contact left me cool and unharmed. A wave of murmurs poured out from each of creatures in a language that had long since faded from this world.

The flames joined together and covered me. I was certain that my life was over, but instead of burning me, they enveloped me and lifted me gently to my feet. I felt sensation return to my body in a rush, and my limbs finally started obeying my commands again. The united flames floated me upward and out a window that had shattered upon my approach. Below, I could see the fire trucks, their hoses aimed not at the fire itself but at the other houses surrounding the charred and twisting remains of Ginny's house. I was carried unseen above it all, then the flames released me a street or two over, beyond the smell of smoke and the red and white lights of the emergency vehicles. I landed on my feet as surely as a cat, and the fire elementals burrowed themselves deep into the earth, leaving behind no trace of their existence.

TWENTY-SEVEN

Peter was on me the second I entered my house. A look of relief flooded his face, and I realized that whatever anger I'd felt toward him earlier had taken a backseat to the rage and terror that were pulsing through me. I pushed past him, right into Ellen's arms.

"Thank God you're here. Thank God you're all right," she repeated over and over again, rocking me.

Oliver came up behind me and planted a kiss on top of my head. "You smell of smoke," he said. "You were at Ginny's?"

"You know about the fire?" I asked and then realized that they would have been alerted by the fire department.

"What happened?" Peter answered my question with one of his own.

I looked him directly in his eyes and said, "You shouldn't be here."

"But I'm worried about you, honey," he said, trying to pull me away from Ellen and into his arms. "I want to give you my support."

"You shouldn't be here," I repeated.

Oliver sensed something in my voice that he didn't understand, but knew enough not to like. "Leave," he commanded, and Peter instantly withdrew and headed out the door.

I extricated myself from Ellen's embrace. "Connor's dead," I said and watched for her reaction.

"We know, sweetheart," she said.

"But how could you know?" I asked, my fear leading me to wonder if she had learned it from Wren. There was no way the fire department would have had the opportunity to look for remains yet, and given that the fire had had a supernatural cause, I strongly suspected that there wouldn't be any.

Ellen didn't respond—she just took my hand and led me into the library. As we approached, I could hear Ray Charles playing on the ancient stereo turntable that Connor had insisted on keeping, even though its boxy wooden sarcophagus took up valuable space. He had always claimed that vinyl records had a warmth and depth to them that other recordings lacked.

Ellen reached down and opened the door. I stepped in to find Iris floating in the center of the room, lifted by a controlled gust of air. The gown she had intended to wear to the charity auction fluttered angelically around her. I had never known that Aunt Iris could fly or that she could control the wind, but there she was. She normally kept her hair pinned close to her head, but tonight it hung loose, and the wind that kept her aloft teased it wildly in every direction. It was a strangely beautiful sight. Tears streamed backward along her cheeks, but she stayed perfectly silent. The only sign that she was still with us was when she restarted Ray after the record player's needle came to the end of the recording's groove.

Oliver had followed us into the library. "She was sitting in the kitchen having tea with me. Everything was fine," he said. "Then she stood up and started wailing. She kept saying something about Connor and a fire, then she told me that he was dead. She came in here, and she's been floating and playing that record over and over again for the past half hour."

"We got a call from the fire department," Ellen added, "saying that Ginny's house had gone up in flames. The fire was too hot for them to do anything but contain it. They aren't sure what caused it, but they said it looks electrical."

I struggled to find the words to tell them what had actually happened. "He tried to kill me," I finally managed to say, as if the words were the punch line to the world's funniest joke. Rage suddenly ripped through me, and I advanced on the turntable, tearing the needle from the record before shattering it against the opposite wall. "I said he tried to kill me!" Iris landed on her feet with a thump, and a stunned silence filled the room.

"There was a book Connor wanted," I continued, even though no one had asked. "He tricked me into opening it for him. And then he stole my necklace. He was going to kill me," I repeated as another pump of adrenaline shot through my system. "He was going to have Wren kill me," I said, on some level pleased by the sickened shock that spread over Ellen's face. I knew then that she'd had nothing to do with Wren's crimes.

"Wren killed my husband?" Iris asked, almost willfully misunderstanding me.

"No, Iris. The book, or whatever was in it, set fire to your husband. And it kept your husband from killing me. But Wren killed Ginny," I said, turning to look at Ellen again. "She had decided to dissolve him, and she might have even tried to do it by herself. She had the spell; it felt really old and powerful. But she failed, and Wren killed her instead. Connor found the spell and figured it out. He promised Wren that he'd keep quiet if Wren killed me tonight while he and Iris were at the auction. When the fire started to spread, Wren left me there to burn. But it wasn't a normal fire. The flames were alive."

"Elementals?" Oliver asked.

"Yes. They didn't burn me, and they carried me out of the fire. Connor had hurt me. Bad. They healed me."

"But why would Connor have wanted to hurt you?" Iris asked.

"I'm sorry, Aunt Iris," I said. "I don't want you to feel any worse than you already do. I know you're in pain. But you have to believe me. It was the book he wanted—Maisie's journal. Ginny shared things with Maisie that she shouldn't have, and her journal contained the secrets of the line. Connor wasn't satisfied with the power he had, and he thought he could get more by reading it." My words tumbled out, not lining up the way they should have, but I knew that my family understood.

"And he knew you'd tell us what he was up to if he let you live," Oliver finished for me.

"But he helped raise you," Iris said, struggling. The look of resignation on her face told me that she didn't doubt me. She was just shocked that she could have been so blind to Connor's true nature for so long. "He was a father to you."

"No, Iris," I said, a sense of calm descending over me, courtesy of Oliver no doubt. "He *was* my father. He told me so himself."

Iris exchanged a quick look with Ellen. They knew the truth too. The shock on Oliver's face could not be counterfeit. "Oh, come on!" he said, shaking his head in disbelief.

Ellen sighed and then said, "They're both gone now, no reason to hide the truth anymore."

"Then tell her," Iris responded, her voice resigned. "I can't find the words, not after everything that happened tonight."

Ellen reached over and took my hand. "Connor was not your father," she said softly, and I felt a wave of cool relief wash over me. "But he thought he was. We always let him believe it."

"Why?" I asked, genuinely puzzled.

"Because you girls needed a father. And I wanted to hold onto my husband," Iris said. "I let him believe he was your dad so that he'd stick around and help raise you . . . but I also wanted to give him a reason to stay."

Sharp words began to line up on my tongue, but Ellen spoke before I could speak them. "But there's another reason. A more important reason," she said. She and Iris locked eyes again before she continued.

"We were afraid of what Ginny might do if she knew the truth about you two," she said. "The truth about your parentage."

She hesitated for a moment too long. "Spit it out," Oliver commanded, his face flushed and covered with worry lines I'd never seen before.

"I told you, Mercy," she began. "I told you how Ginny prevented me from saving Paul, because of the prophecy that foretold that the bloodlines that gave birth to him would give rise to a great witch who would reunite all thirteen families."

"Yes, and you said that Ginny was dead set against that reunion," I said.

"We had Paul before Ginny discovered the prophecy. Afterward, she prevented us from having any more children. Just as she limited my healing powers, she tampered with my ability to conceive another child. She didn't let me save Paul because she didn't want him to grow up and father children. I honestly think she might have killed him outright herself if the witch in the prophecy hadn't been female."

"Maisie," I said, the pieces coming together.

"I knew that she was Erik's girl the second I laid hands on her. That you both were," Iris said. I wondered why it had never occurred to me that her psychometric powers would have told her who our father was, even if my mother hadn't.

"Yes," Ellen said. "My husband Erik fathered you and Maisie. We couldn't let Ginny find out. We just couldn't."

"My God, you must hate us," I said in amazement.

229

"Oh, no, my darling girl," Ellen said, beaming at me with nothing but love in her eyes. Her expression was tender as she said, "I could never hate you. You are the daughters Ginny denied me."

"And the daughters I could never have," Iris added, approaching us almost shyly. She and Ellen joined together and took me into their arms.

"We forgave your mother years ago," Ellen said. "She was a weak and willful woman. She went after both of our husbands, if only to show us she could take them away. But in the end, she gave us you and Maisie." It hurt me terribly to realize again all the harm my mother had done, and I promised myself then and there that I would never be like her.

"And now," Iris said, her voice catching, "you girls are all I have left." She hesitated a moment and looked at me through eyes that were filled with tears. "I am sorry Connor died the way he did." The wind began to creep up around her again, lifting the three of us who'd embraced an inch or so off the ground. "Because I wish I could have killed the son of a bitch myself."

She let go of Ellen and me, and we landed lightly on our feet. She held up her hand, and a piece of paper flitted into it from the desk. Letters and lines began to fill the once empty page, and as soon as it was full, she turned it to face us. I couldn't make out the words, but I recognized Connor's sprawling signature at the bottom. Iris had written him a suicide note.

"Oliver," Iris said, "you should call Detective Cook. I just found a letter from Connor. He said he couldn't live a moment longer with the guilt of what he did to Ginny."

"And now we need to deal with Wren," Ellen said, the resolve in her voice a sure sign that all of the fondness she'd felt for the charming illusion had faded forever.

"Let's slow down a bit and unwind all of this first," Emmet said, appearing from nowhere. "Your family always falls victim to its passions. You act on the spur of the moment without thinking."

Without thinking, I crossed over and slapped the smug look right off his face. "You show up when you think it's time to criticize, but where the hell were you when I needed you?" All nine parts of him were taken aback. "Shut up!" I warned him when he started to move his lips again.

Iris's face was set as hard as concrete. "Call Cook," she repeated to Oliver.

TWENTY-EIGHT

I was sent upstairs to wash off the smell of smoke before the police could arrive. Emmet stood guard for me outside the bathroom door in case Wren showed up. I blow-dried my hair so that Cook wouldn't have any reason to notice that I'd been busy washing away what he would have deemed as evidence. While I showered, Oliver and Ellen searched the house and garden, but neither of them could pick up an impression of Wren. He had gone into hiding.

It was a little after midnight when Detective Cook left our house, Connor's suicide note carefully preserved in a plastic evidence bag. The tears Iris had shed before the detective were real, although she was grieving the death of her good impression of Connor rather than the man himself. When Cook passed me on his way out, his eyes locked with mine, and his expression shifted in a blink from an "I told you so" to an "I'm sorry for your loss" without ever pressing the clutch.

With Cook gone, it was time to deal with Wren. Iris, Oliver, Ellen, and I gathered in the library, waiting wordlessly for Emmet to corner Wren and bring him to us. It was odd because until tonight I had never suspected that Wren was capable of existing apart from our family. It had never occurred to me that he could leave our house and go out into the world at large.

Ellen sat next to Iris and wrapped her arm around her elder sister's shoulders. Iris stared straight ahead, her expression revealing her determination to be strong no matter what. Ellen's face was a jumble of emotions: guilt, sadness, anger, and then more guilt.

Oliver broke the silence. "Mercy, honey, I know it has been one hell of a night," he said, "but is there any chance that you remember anything about the dissolution spell? It's just that I'm not sure what we should do. Wren came from my six-year-old psyche. I can barely even remember being six, let alone what I was feeling when he was created."

"And even if you could," Ellen said. "You'd never be able to re-create it."

"Maybe we could just agree to tune him out, starve him off slowly," Iris proposed, and I knew she was just trying to protect Ellen from the pain of being part of his dissolution.

Ellen understood her motives as well as I did. "No," she said. "We have to deal with it tonight. We can't allow him to carry on as he has been. Besides, we're not even sure that he's been getting his energy from us."

"But I thought it was you," I said, shocked. "I thought you were feeding him the energy."

"No," Ellen said. "I've been expecting him to fade away for years. Listen, I know . . ." She paused and swallowed hard. "I know I've been using Wren as a crutch to help me deal with Paul's death. But he was never a substitute; no one could replace my boy."

"Regardless of where he's been getting his energy, we need to put him down," Oliver said. "Can you remember anything at all?" he asked me.

Suddenly I remembered that I hadn't returned the spell to Connor. I'd tucked it into the pocket of my shorts, the ones I'd just tossed into the hamper. "I have it!" I said. "Connor gave me the spell, and I put it in my pocket. It must still be in there."

I ran to the upstairs bathroom and riffled through the hamper, pulling out the smoky smelling clothes I had been wearing at Ginny's. I shoved my hand into the right pocket—nothing—then the left. There it was. Heaving a sigh of relief, I pulled the paper out, and even though it smelled as badly of smoke as my clothing did, the paper unfolded itself with a single shake of the hand, the creases disappearing instantly. Now that I no longer had a witch's vision, it looked like an empty page, but I knew that my aunts and uncle would be able to read it. Together they could use it to send Wren back into the ether where he'd been formed.

I stepped out of the bathroom and into the hall, surprised to see the pool-like aquamarine light from Jilo's secret world spilling out onto the walls. The door to the linen closet, the room Jilo had connected with her own chamber, stood wide open, and I walked toward it, keeping my steps as silent as the creaking old floorboards would allow me. I crept up to the door and peeked around it. Jilo sat there on her throne in her haint blue room, her eyes filled with terror. A knife was pressed to her throat. Wren was invisible, but I knew he was the one holding the weapon. It threw me to see someone I'd once thought of as so unassailable looking so old and fragile. Somehow Wren had surprised her, made it past her defenses. I knew about her haint blue room, and how it was connected to my house. But she had *wanted* me to know. She had invited me there. I had a suspicion of how Wren had found his way here. She must have invited him there at some point too. Part of me considered just walking away. Taking the spell down to my aunts and uncle and washing my hands of it all. But I couldn't bear the thought of witnessing more violence tonight. I stepped through the entrance, and the door slammed shut behind me, shattering my hopes for assistance.

"Drop the knife, Wren," I said calmly.

"Do as she says," Jilo squeaked out, only to have her neck pulled further back, the length of her throat even more exposed to the sharp blade.

Wren's form materialized behind her. He floated in the air at her back, one hand laced through her hair, the other clutching the blade. "That spell Connor gave you will kill me, Mercy," his child's voice said pleadingly. "I don't want to die." His eyes looked big and were welling up with tears.

"And neither did Ginny," I started.

"I was only protecting myself. She was going to hurt me," Wren sobbed, defending himself like a six-year-old who was explaining why he'd punched his sister.

I wanted to tear into him, but I kept my cool for Jilo's sake. "But I never did anything to hurt you, and you were ready to kill me all the same."

"I didn't have a choice. Connor made me promise," he responded.

"But you have a choice now. Jilo's never done anything to you. You've got no reason to hurt her."

"I came to her for help," he said, "but she wouldn't give me any. I've been watching your family for her for years, telling her everything she wanted to know, but she won't help me anymore now that you know what I did to Ginny."

"She's the one who's been feeding you?"

"Yeah," was all the boy said.

Jilo had used Wren to spy on my family. I quickly considered the implications of that and decided that although she deserved a good ass-kicking, spying was not a capital offense. "You let Jilo go," I said, "and I'll give you the spell. You can destroy it."

"It's too late. You'll tell everyone what I did to Ginny," he said.

"No," I lied. "I'll never say a word, and neither will Jilo. Isn't that right, Jilo?"

"Yes," she breathed out cautiously.

"No one has to know. We can go back to the way things were. Ellen's worried about you. She was asking me if I'd seen you. If you let Jilo go, I'll give you the spell." I held the paper out to him. "We'll have a do over," I said.

He looked at me warily. "Promise?" he asked.

"I promise," I said and drew closer to them, holding the spell in an outstretched hand, but keeping it far enough from him that he couldn't snatch it away. "Just hand me the knife, and I'll give you the paper. He silently nodded, and I could see the hope return to his eyes. "One," I said, stepping within reach. "Two," I said, holding my left hand out for the knife. "Three," I said, handing him the paper.

The knife's handle fell into my waiting palm, and I watched as his face turned bright with joy. He stood beaming up at me, the spell clutched in his little hand. Without hesitating, I swung the knife through the air, slicing a deep cut into my right palm. I reached out, and in one movement, smeared my blood across Wren's forehead and shoved him backward.

Immediately catching on, Jilo staggered up from her chair and opened a gateway to the realm of hungry shadows that lay somewhere between where we were and Candler. Both of us knew that the human blood combined with Wren's fear would make him an irresistible target. Wren stumbled, almost caught his balance, and then tripped backward, falling into the world of the living shades. I saw his face for only an instant, and then a blackness swooped in on him, lifting him up and away. We heard his screams for only a moment, then the sickening crunching sound of mastication. Jilo slammed the portal shut.

"Well how in the hell did you think Jilo knew all yo' family's secrets?" I could tell that her feistiness was her means of defense. She had expected me to come out swinging at her, but I felt nothing but relief.

"You, I will deal with later," I said, happier than I ever would have imagined that she was safe, that we both were. "Now, open the door and let me go home."

Jilo leaned forward on her chair and looked at me. "You just saw Jilo feed that little one to the night. You trust Jilo that the door she open is the one to yo' home?"

"Actually I'm the one who fed him to the shadows. Besides," I said, "I am starting to think you really are the only one I can trust."

TWENTY-NINE

Hours had passed in our world by the time I returned home. The house was in upheaval, and my family was tearing it apart both physically and psychically in search of any evidence of what had happened to me. I saw Oliver first. He was standing on the other side of the linen closet door, a marker in his hand. Symbols and lines like the ones I'd seen in Maisie's notebooks had been written all up and down the hall. Strangely, my first thought was how much primer it would take to cover the marks.

He dropped his marker and pulled me into his arms. "My God, Mercy! What happened to you?"

"It's a long story," I said. "Let's find Iris and Ellen, and I'll tell you all about it."

And I did. Oliver, Iris, Ellen, and Emmet, who had insisted on joining us, all clustered around the kitchen table, and I started at the beginning and told them everything. I spoke of my feelings for Jackson. I confessed about my visit to Jilo's crossroads, telling them about the love spell I'd wanted and the love spell Peter had bought, which Jilo had, in the end, broken. I told them about the damaged souls at Candler and the living night that existed somewhere in a realm not so far from our own. For the benefit of their understanding, I relived Connor's manipulations and my own

238

foolish actions. I told them about how Wren had spied for Jilo and what his fate had been. They all sat silently listening to me. The stillest of all was Emmet, who was too reticent to speak and nine times too smart to judge.

It was a little before six when I stood and left them. No one objected to my departure, and no one asked me where I was going. There were all too busy processing everything I had told them.

I stepped out into the garden, then crossed over to my faithful bicycle, which was leaning against the garage. The air had changed in Savannah; it felt charged but fresh, as if a storm had passed through in the night. I hopped onto my bike and pedaled up Abercorn and around Lafayette Square. St. John's loomed across from me, its spires reaching up to heaven. I directed my own eyes upward, thanking whomever was in charge for getting me through the night and asking for the strength to make it through the coming day.

I dismounted and walked the last few steps through the park, crossing the brick street to Jackson's GTO, which he had parked directly in front of the church. Jackson was leaning against the hood of the car, drinking a cup of drive-through coffee. He was staring westward, as if he intended to keep to his word about not seeing another sunrise in Savannah. I took one last long look at him before he caught sight of me, knowing all too well that I might never lay eyes on him again. The light of the eastern horizon had already begun to glow in his golden curls, but his face remained shaded. He turned to face me as if he felt the power of my gaze. There were dark circles under his eyes, and I could tell he had been out all night, probably fighting, certainly drinking. He raised his cup to me in a salute.

As I got closer to him, I noticed that there was a vicious cut along his right cheek, and a bruise on his temple. He reached up and touched it. "Last night out. I shared my reasons for getting out of this little piss-hole of a town, and the natives didn't take too kindly to my opinion."

"I'm not going with you," I said, ignoring him. "At least not today. And you can't leave today either."

"Naw," he said after a moment, still rubbing a finger over the bruise. My heart almost melted at the sight of his swollen face. "It's time for me to be moving on. I'm all packed up, and I quit the docks yesterday. There's nothing to hold me here."

"You can't leave Maisie without facing her. You need to stay and talk to her. Explain things."

"Yeah, and let her turn me into a frog," he said, trying to make it sound like a joke, but I could tell that he was terrified of facing Maisie.

"She won't do that. She'll scream at you. Heck, maybe even throw something at you. But you're breaking her heart, you deserve to face a little screaming. You've got to stay here and face up to her. And if there is ever going to be something between us, you have to let me take the time to face up to her too."

"She'll hate you," Jackson said.

"We're sisters, a big part of her already hates me," I said and smiled. "But a big part of her loves me. I couldn't just run off with you behind her back. We could never be happy together that way."

"I've told you, Mercy. I can't stay here. Not even for you. I can't live with your family's weirdness, with this crazy magic crap. I need a normal life." He paused. "I was hoping that it could be with you, but I guess that wasn't meant to be."

He threw his cup to the ground, the last of his coffee bleeding out onto the bricks. He gave me one last look, got into his car, fired up the engine, and headed west as quickly as the wheels would carry him.

I watched the taillights of his car buzz down Harris Street and lost sight of them a little after he crossed Bull. I knew I could never love a man who would desert my sister without even saying good-bye, and I could certainly never love a man who was a coward. I picked up the spent cup, Jackson's last insult to Savannah, and threw it away in a trash can in the park. I walked my bike home and spent a lot of time wondering how much of what I'd loved about Jackson had been real, and how much I'd invented myself. The Jackson I'd grown to love was not the man who had just left. He was in all probability a creation of my own mind, no more a real man than Wren had been a real child.

I arrived home and leaned my bike back up against the garage. Sunrise met me in our garden, and with a jolt I realized that it was my birthday. Our birthday, I corrected myself, as I sent a wave of love out to Maisie. I hoped that in time she'd be able to forgive me for everything that had happened with Jackson. I hoped that her vision of him would grow as clear as my own suddenly had.

I was glad that no one had locked the kitchen door after I'd left. When I stepped inside, Ellen was waiting for me at the table all by herself. "Hey, you," she said. "Get in here and let me see your hand."

For the second time in twenty-four hours, someone took my hand and erased an injury. It seemed like a lifetime had passed since Connor had been the one to cure me. "I know you're tired, but sit with me for a while," Ellen said.

"I'm sorry," I replied. "I just want to get to bed. You could use some sleep too, I'm sure."

Her face was drawn, and she looked much older in the golden light coming through the window than she ever had before. "No," she said firmly. "I need to tell you a few things first, and then we can both get some sleep."

"All right," I capitulated and sat down next to her.

"First of all," Ellen said. "Happy birthday." She smiled at me. "No, I didn't forget. None of us did, but I doubt that we'll get around to much celebrating today."

"It's all right," I said and yawned, hoping that Ellen would take it as the signal it was intended to be.

Ellen reached out and took my hand. "I also want to be sure," she said, "that you know that I will always be there for you. I loved Erik, your father, and in spite of what happened between him and Emily, I believe that he loved me too. I know he loved you girls. He once told me that not claiming you as his own was the hardest thing he'd ever done. But he agreed that it was better if Ginny never learned that he was your dad."

"But how could you overlook the fact that he had children with your sister?" I asked.

She took a moment to consider her response. "He was a special man," she finally said. "I loved him more than life itself, and he was my son's father. Somehow I managed to forgive him. He deserved children, and Ginny kept me from having any more after Paul was born. I am glad that you were born. When Erik rebelled against his family, they disowned him. You, me, Maisie, and Paul were all he had in this world. I think that made it easier for me to get over his fling with Emily."

She reached down and uncovered an old photograph she had been shielding from my sight. "I don't have a lot of things to share with you from his life before we were married, but I do have this. It's a picture of Erik's grandmother, your great-grandmother. Her name was Maria."

She had clear and perfectly spaced eyes, arched eyebrows, and heart-shaped lips. The photo was black and white, but I was sure that the woman's beautiful long hair must have been the same shade as Maisie's honey blond locks. "She looks exactly like

Maisie," I said, taking the picture into my hands to investigate it more closely.

"Yes, she does," Ellen replied. "But even though you look more like your mother, I can still see a bit of Maria in you."

"May I keep this?" I asked, growing almost enchanted by the face staring back at me from the photo.

"Of course. It's yours," Ellen replied.

"Thanks," I said, starting to stand, but Ellen reached out and stopped me.

"Sweetie, there is one more thing."

"Okay," I said, her tone worrying me.

"Last night after you came home from the fire, I sensed something when I hugged you. Things were too wild last night for me to try to verify it, but I'd like to do that right now, if that's okay."

"Aunt Ellen, you're kind of scaring me."

"I'm sorry," she said, standing up and leaning over me. "It's nothing to be frightened about." She lowered her hand to my stomach. "Sweetheart, it's just as I thought. You're pregnant."

THIRTY

Just shy of three weeks had passed since my last Liar's Tour. I was sure that my pack of suburban dads had already pretty much forgotten about me, wrapped up as they were in soccer matches and sales meetings and reporting deadlines. Since I'd dropped them off at the Pirate's House, they had fought with their wives, made up, mowed their lawns, and played a few rounds of golf. I'd probably never cross their minds again. But I was sure I'd never forget them, because the hours I'd spent with them had marked the end of my normal life. From the moment I saw Jilo in Colonial Park Cemetery and got it in my head to pay her a visit, my world had gone mad.

Ginny's murder and the drawing of lots. Maisie's jealous rage and disappearance, even if only temporary, from my life. Jilo's spells pulling me into her dark world then sending me running into Peter's arms. Grace's revenge and my borrowing Oliver's power. Connor and Wren. The fire and dark spirits that had fed on them. Jackson, and Jackson's departure. The microscopic infant in my womb.

I found myself sitting on the base of the Waving Girl statue at the riverfront, staring out at the water and wishing for a return of the simple life I'd always known. All of a sudden I understood

Florence, and why she'd come out here for forty years waving her apron. She wasn't waiting for a man, she was hoping for the return of the girl she'd been before her life had been turned upside down. I wasn't sure I'd ever have the heart to lie about her again.

I was going to have a boy, Ellen told me, provided that I chose to have it. It, he, would be healthy, she assured me, if I decided to carry him to term. The embryo was only a few days old, and it would take hardly any witch magic at all to undo the union of sperm and egg. If that's what I wanted, it could all simply go away, like it had never happened.

I watched the light gleaming on the river, and my hand fell instinctively over my stomach, protecting the blooming life I knew was there, even though it would be days before there were any non-magical signs of its existence. I'd never judge another woman for doing away with an unexpected pregnancy, but abortion was not for me. There were no two ways about it. I would have this child, even if it meant risking my life like my mama had done. And that meant that I would forever be linked with Peter. I'd have to find a way to forgive him, because my baby was not going to grow up without his father. That didn't mean I'd ever be his wife. I wasn't sure I trusted him, and I could never marry a man unless I trusted him. To be fair, I wasn't so sure I trusted anyone anymore.

A group of tourists arrived, snapping pictures of themselves next to the Waving Girl. I didn't want to be the shadow in their photos, so I slid off the statue's base and headed up River Street, replaying the tours I'd done over the years in my mind. *Mind the cobblestones and never mind the cobbled together lies. The bars lie dead ahead! Don't forget to tip your guide.*

I had to talk to Peter, and the sooner the better. I needed to get everything settled before the next rush of insanity arrived. It was less than a week before the investment ceremony, when the anchor energy would be linked to Maisie for her lifetime, and soon the Taylor house would be filled to the brim with representatives from each of the nine other families who would be there to participate. I found a new appreciation for Emmet, since he was a much more manageable way of housing nine guests at once.

Maisie would be back the day before the ceremony. I wondered how much I'd have to tell her about what had happened and how much she already knew. It was hard to believe that she'd only been gone for a week.

The story about the fire at Ginny's house and Connor's suicide had headlined the newspapers gracing half the doorsteps in Savannah and had also been on all the local television stations. I turned up East Broad, doing my best to evade anyone I might recognize. They'd want to talk about what had happened, and I was in no mood. Let the people of Savannah think what they wanted, but for God's sake, let them keep it to themselves.

I fished my cell phone out of my backpack while I walked, and turned it on. Thirty texts, mostly from Peter. A couple of voice mails from Ellen and Oliver. I opened Peter's last message and without even reading it, responded "Meet me at home."

He was waiting for me outside in his truck when I got there. He started to get out, but I climbed in to the passenger's side instead. "I know you went to Jilo," I said. "I know you had her put a spell on me."

Shame turned his face a deeper red than his hair. "Mercy," he started.

"And then you took me to bed," I interrupted him. "Knowing that I was under the influence of Jilo's magic."

He slammed his fist into the steering wheel, and tears started streaming down his face. The guilt he felt wouldn't let him look at me. "I thought I was going to lose you. I thought I was going to lose you to him."

"Yeah, well 'he' is gone, and I'm still here. But you done lost me anyway," I said, feeling more resigned than angry.

Peter buried his face in his hands, his broad shoulders heaving up and down in the rhythm of his heavy sobs. "I am so sorry, Mercy. I am so sorry." He lifted his face from his hands and looked at me. "I won't ask you to forgive me. I know I don't deserve that. Just know that if I could take it back, I would. I even tried. I went back to Jilo a couple of days after I sought her out. She told me it was too late to take it back. I hoped that she'd fail, you being who you are."

"And who am I?" I asked. Was he holding back more secrets? Had he, along with the rest of the western world, known who my father was all along? Irrational questions, maybe, but I was fresh out of trust.

"Well, a Taylor," he said flustered. "I thought maybe—"

"You should have told me what you did," I said.

"I know I should've, but I was so afraid," he said. "It's no excuse, I was a coward."

"Damn right you were," I said and glared at him. "You were the one person in my life I could count on to simply be what you said you were. No tricks. No lies. No magic. And what do you do? You use magic on me." Hearing myself say the words, I realized that this was the real reason I felt betrayed. It wasn't because Peter had had a love spell set on me. It was because I'd always believed that magic was the one weapon that he would never—could never—use against me. But then he had gone and done it.

On the other hand, there was no circumventing the fact that I too had gone to Jilo asking for the self same spell. I had been willing to use her magic to deceive myself, and by extension, Peter. My attempts at righteous indignation started to feel a little bit less righteous.

"All I can say is that I am sorry," he said. "I'll always love you, Mercy. And I will go to my grave regretting what I did." He took in a ragged breath and slumped back in his seat. "I'll understand if you don't want me to be a part of your life anymore."

Seeing the regret written across his face, a face that had been a part of my world since I spent my days dressing like a tomboy and climbing trees, convinced me that even though I might never marry him, I'd always want him around. Dishonesty didn't come naturally to Peter. "Well, it's a little too late for all that, seeing as how we are having a baby."

"I'm sorry," he said. "What?"

"We're having a baby, Peter. Ellen felt it in me, and she's never wrong about these things."

His face morphed from the red mask of guilt I'd been looking at a moment ago to the ashen white of fear and then settled into a glow of joy. "Oh, Mercy. I don't deserve this," he said reaching out to me, trying to pull me to him for a kiss.

I slapped his hand away, and his eyes went wide with fear and regret. "We're having a baby together," I said firmly. "That doesn't mean that we're together, or that we're going to be."

"I'm sorry," he said and retreated to the far side of the truck's cab.

"I haven't forgiven you yet," I said. "I will. I must. My child will not grow up without his father. Ellen says it's a boy by the way. We'll name him Colin after your dad, and we'll celebrate every holiday and birthday together. But," I concluded, "that does not mean I am going to be your wife. You hear me?"

"Yes, I hear you," he said meekly. "It's more than I have the right to ask for."

My piece had been spoken, and whatever anger I was holding had been spent. I looked over at his sweet face. "It's going to take time for me to move past this, but I'll try. For Colin's sake."

"Okay," was all he said, relief written all over his face.

"That's enough about us for now," I said. "We have family business to attend to."

"I should get out of here then and leave you to it," he said and tried to smile.

"Sorry there, buddy," I responded as I climbed out of the truck. "You are most definitely family now. Get on in here."

When we entered the house, we found Ellen in the library, busy boxing up Connor's phonograph albums. "Charity truck is coming for all of this tomorrow. Kind of a shame," she said. "For a total prick, he had good taste in music."

"We're doing this so fast?" I asked.

"It's what Iris wants." She turned away from her task and took a seat on the love seat. "So you two have spoken."

"Yes, ma'am," Peter replied.

Before risking a faux pas, Ellen gave me a lingering look to make sure that I'd really told Peter about the child. I nodded my head. "Good," she said. "And may I ask what you've decided to do about the baby?"

"We're going to have it," I responded, and Ellen jumped up and took me in her arms, spinning me around.

"Oh, I'm so happy," she said. "It has been far too long since this house has had a child, a real child in it," she said, thinking of Wren. "With all the death that's struck our family lately, it will be wonderful to have a birth to look forward to."

For the first time, I let myself feel the joy of having a child growing in me. "Yes. This is going to be good for all of us," I said. I motioned for Peter to take a seat as Ellen and I settled onto the love seat. "Ever since you told me I was pregnant, I haven't been able to focus on anything else but now I need to know, how is Iris doing?"

Ellen licked her lips and looked at the floor, and I could tell that she was trying to work out what she needed to say. "Iris is devastated," she finally began. "She has been forced to see that the man she loved, and God only knows why she loved him, was a monster, a murderer. She has a black, black anger against him, and she wants him to pay for what he tried to do to you. But Connor—or, rather, the man she *thought* Connor was—was the only man in the world for her. And while she's angry at what he did to you, she hasn't even begun to get angry over all the things he did to her. She has a lot to reconcile, a lot to move past."

"Should I go tell her about the baby?" I asked.

"Sweetie, she is going to be so happy to learn about the baby. He may be the only thing that helps pull her through this mess. But she isn't here now. She and Oliver are down at the police station."

"Why?" I asked.

"They had to go answer some questions. You see, Iris served as Connor's alibi for the day of the murder. When she handed over that forged suicide letter, Cook wanted to know why she'd lied for her husband."

"They aren't going to charge her with anything?" Peter asked.

Ellen practically snorted. "Please, Oliver went with her to make sure that wouldn't happen. He'll get her off the hook and probably find some way to get himself laid in the process. But I'm afraid I do have some vexing news. We got word today that some of the families are sending their representatives for Maisie's investment ceremony early. They've heard about what happened with Connor and Wren—the truth, not the nonsense we've fed the police—and they've decided that they should come early to 'help us out' with the preparations due to our 'bereavement.'"

"Which means we have to shift into high gear to prepare for their arrival," I said, standing.

"You got it," Ellen replied. "And Iris wants all of Connor's belongings out of here before they arrive. You could help me by packing up his clothes and other effects from their room before Iris gets back," she said and paused. "'Effects,'" she repeated. "An interesting choice of words when talking about a man like Connor." She shook her head. "Well, you know what I mean."

"Yes, I do," I said. It would take a long time to soothe the ripples Connor had set loose in our lives.

"And you, Peter, can carry these heavy boxes of records out to the garage. The less that reminds Iris of Connor around here, the better."

"Don't get me wrong," Peter said. "I'm glad to help out in any way I can, but couldn't you . . ." He hesitated. "Well, couldn't you do some kind of spell to handle all of this?"

Ellen laughed. "Yes. I could. But I need something tangible to focus on right now. Besides, I'm told that doing things the non-magical way builds character."

"Okay," Peter said. He turned to me. "Don't you go lifting anything heavy."

"Oh, and so it begins," Ellen said and smiled.

I took a couple of empty boxes up to the room that Iris and Connor had shared for longer than I'd been alive. I opened his closet and pulled out his rack of ties and his three suits—two dark ones and the tan one he wore during Savannah's hottest months. Those went into the first box. Next, I swept his shirts up in my arms, leaving them on their hangers. As I shuffled over to lay them on the bed, his scent rose up around me like a shroud. I tossed the shirts down and started removing the hangers. Folding them up as fast as I could, I stacked them into another open box. There was a lot more of Connor in this room than I'd be able to cart out in two cardboard containers. A sense of heaviness began to overwhelm me, and I left off to go grab a few more boxes from the library.

Ellen and Peter were nowhere in sight when I returned, so I grabbed some of the still flattened containers and headed back

251

upstairs. The door to the room had swung shut behind me, so I had to fumble with the doorknob, the boxes awkwardly tucked under my arm. When I stepped into the room, I felt all hope abandon me. I sat on the side of the bed, put my head in my hands, nearly crushed by the weight of my sorrow. I felt more than saw a movement, and lifting my head, I caught a glimpse of Connor in the mirror. The misery I was feeling was radiating from him. I knew then that Savannah had refused to grant him peace or pardon him for his sins.

THIRTY-ONE

Three of the witches arrived early to prepare the house and grounds for the investment. The ceremony would take place outside, so I sought sanctuary from their activities in one of the library's wingback chairs. But in spite of my best efforts, I found myself at least momentarily in the thick of it. Rivkah Levi, a tornado from New York, swept past me, Emmet in tow. The two were meticulously searching the house for energy leaks or ingresses. It was important for all of the psychic energies to be balanced and accounted for before the anchor energy was settled on Maisie. "It's worse than cleaning for *Pesach*," Rivkah said to me cheerfully as she dragged Emmet away.

Bodaway Jones, who was loaded down with enough silver and turquoise to fill a jewelry store, drifted by me, chanting and fanning a smudge stick with a feather. He nodded an acknowledgment of my presence without stopping his chant. His intent was to drive all of the negative presences from the house. I wondered if I should warn him about Connor, but I didn't have the heart to tear another layer of skin off Iris. If he was doing his job correctly, he might catch Connor up in his net without Iris ever having to know.

Ekala Maringar had arrived with the other two, but she'd disappeared into a guest room soon afterward and hadn't come out for food, water, or anything since. I occasionally caught snatches of her voice from behind the closed door. Ekala was living in dreamtime, working with her ancestors to weave the silver cord that would bind the line to Maisie, or at least that's what Bodaway had told me. It was of the utmost importance for no one to disturb her, so I gave her room a wide berth when I could.

The truth of the matter was that the whole process struck me as absurd. In the end, the whole event would probably hold all the charm and allure of a justice of the peace wedding, but they were all building it up to be a full-fledged coronation. I'd never had the taste for pomp and circumstance, so I wasn't in the least bit hurt when they sat me down and explained that only those born of the power could be present for the ceremony. Rivkah had very diplomatically requested that I find some other place to be while it was taking place, and I was more than happy to oblige. "We'll skip all this, won't we, buddy?" I asked my child, not sure if there was a soul in there yet to respond to me. Even if there wasn't, something about knowing that Colin was growing inside of me made me feel at peace.

"Who are you talking to?" Oliver asked, stopping to place a kiss on my forehead.

"I am talking to Colin," I said proudly. "And we both think we should get out of the way of all of these witches for a while."

"Well, Mr. Colin," Oliver said. "I figure that you are about the luckiest soon-to-be-in-the-world boy for having such a beautiful and understanding mother. I hate that you are being chased out of here," he said, meeting my eyes. "But you saw what happened at the drawing of the lots. We like to pretend that everything is cut-and-dried, but things can easily go wrong when you have ten strong personalities playing volleyball with a nuclear bomb."

"How can this be safe for Maisie?" I asked. "She was sent off for less than two weeks of training, and now she's expected to come back and anchor our end of the line."

Oliver smiled. "Gingersnap, this may seem like a strange concept to you, but even though she's only been gone for a few days on our timeline, she's been gone for years on her timeline. She's had plenty of training, and the training has been with *the* anchor. Maisie has received very special treatment. Gudrun does not make herself available to just anyone."

I wasn't in the mood to get into how well acquainted I was with time's capriciousness. Suddenly I realized that the loud ticking of Ginny's discount store clock had served some purpose for her. The incessant and repetitive noise must have been like a subconscious metronome that had helped her keep the line in sync with our dimension. I wondered if Maisie would find such a tool useful, and whether I should get one for her. Or maybe the other anchors would include one in her welcome basket. Congratulations on your investment and good luck with taking on the weight of the world!

"Will this Gudrun be part of the investment ceremony?" I asked instead.

"No, she no longer exists on our plane," Oliver said. I could tell that there was a lot he wasn't saying.

"I saw her once," I said.

Oliver's face turned gray. "That can't be," he said.

"No, I did. I saw her and Maisie through the mirror when I was borrowing your power."

"Did she see you?" Oliver asked, his usually smooth forehead crinkling.

"Yes, but only for a moment. She waved her hand and broke the connection."

"I see," he said. "Listen, Mercy, it would be best if you didn't even think about Gudrun again."

"Yeah, yeah," I said unimpressed. "Ellen already warned me. Force of nature and all that."

"No, sweetheart, you need to listen. Don't do anything to draw Gudrun's attention." He ran his hand through his hair. "Listen, Gudrun is not where she is by choice but as punishment. She won't be a part of the investment because she isn't allowed back into our world. Working with Maisie was less of a goodwill gesture than it was an act of penance on her part. And," he added, "a warning on Maisie's part. For your sake, for Colin's sake, leave this one alone."

"Okay," I said, appropriately chastened. "I won't pull any more loose strings."

"Good," he said, relief transforming his face back into a youthful mask. "And while we're on the subject of people you should stay away from, I don't want to hear about you hanging out with Jilo again." He pointed upstairs. "We've broken her link to the linen closet. You should have never kept it secret from us."

"I know," I said. "I'm sorry."

He looked at me through narrowed eyes. "Nothing about her is real, you know? It's all a show," he said. "And I don't just mean that she has to borrow her power. I knew her granddaughter, remember, and I know things about her. She might go around acting like some backwoods Hoodoo priestess who can't use a personal pronoun or conjugate a verb, but it's all an act. It's good for business. It's what people expect. Truth is, the woman's a graduate of Spelman College. She holds a degree in chemistry. If she'd been born twenty years later, she would have most likely ended up a medical doctor, not a root doctor." He read the surprise on my face. "That's right, nothing's real about Jilo other than the trouble she can land you in if you don't keep clear of her."

"I'll stay away," I said, somehow knowing it was a lie. I was connected to the old woman now. Even if everything about her was a lie, there was some ineffable link between us, and I wasn't sure I'd ever be able to shake it off. I wasn't sure I wanted to.

"Good," he responded, too distracted to read me as he usually might. "Your sister comes home in a few hours. You ready for that?"

"Yeah, I think so."

"She's going to want to talk to you, but I'm afraid you two won't have much time together. The representatives from the rest of the families will be arriving just before she does, and they're going to keep her busy."

"Does she know about Connor?" I asked.

"Yes, she's aware of what he did. She knows about Wren as well. I know she's desperate to lay eyes on you, to see for herself that you're okay." He paused. "We haven't mentioned the baby. We figured you'd want to tell her yourself."

"And Jackson?"

"She knows he's gone," Oliver said. "Remember, Gingersnap, from her perspective, she's been gone for a very long time. She's had time to grieve for Connor, in whatever form that grieving might have taken. And she's had time to get over Jackson too. I think that both of you girls have realized that although he came in a very nice package, there wasn't much substance there. If there had been, he would have at least waited to tell Maisie good-bye face-to-face."

I just nodded my head in agreement. "Okay, my girl. I have to get back to business," he said and started to walk away. Suddenly he stopped in his tracks, and swiveled around. "Wait!" he said. "I have a surprise for you first." I looked at him warily, and he laughed. "No, this one is good. Your aunts and I made a reservation for you at the Mansion tomorrow. While we're dealing with the families, you'll spend the day at the spa and then enjoy a night in your very own park view suite," he said, doing his best imitation of a game show host.

"That sounds wonderful," I said. "Thank you."

He winked at me. "Anything for my favorite niece," he said blithely. He paused for a long moment, and when he finally spoke, his voice had taken on a more serious tone. "And I want you to know that I mean that. Maisie has always been the apple of everyone's eye, and don't get me wrong, I love that girl to bits, but you're my little Gingersnap, you hear me?"

He was the black sheep, and I was the dud. Deep down I'd always known I was his favorite, but it felt good to hear it anyway. I smiled. "Yeah, I hear you," I said. "Now get out of here before we both start crying like little girls." He laughed and left the room. I followed him out a few minutes later and went outside to sit on the side porch. The past few weeks had caught up to me all at once, and I felt a thousand years older than the age on my driver's license. I sat quietly, focusing on controlling my breath. The cicadas did a wonderful job of drowning out the sounds coming from inside the house, and the warmth of the sun lulled me into a mercifully dreamless sleep.

I awoke to the sensation of a soft hand pushing my hair back from my forehead. "Hey, you," Maisie's voice instantly wrested me from sleep. Before I had the chance to remember our horrifying last encounter, before I could feel the guilt of helping to drive Jackson from her life, I felt a surge of love—the kind of love that could only be understood by those born a twin. The person I'd come into this world with had been returned to me, and I pulled her close. Nothing mattered beyond the comfort of her presence.

I loosened my hold after a moment so that I could get a good look at her. She was my sister, all right, but she had changed. She had an air of serenity and maturity about her that I'd never sensed before.

"I need to apologize to you, Mercy," she said.

"No, I should apologize to you!" I replied.

"For what? For Jackson?" she said and laughed. "I know it's still fresh for you, but I've had a long time to get over what happened with Jackson."

"He's gone," I said, hearing the detachment in her voice but not emotionally capable of comprehending it.

"For now, but I'm certain we haven't seen the last of him. He ran away, but once he's had time to think things through, he'll come back to me."

I didn't know how to respond. I couldn't bring myself to tell her about his last request—that I go with him. All I could do was hope that for her sake he was well and truly gone and that someone better would come along to take his place.

"They're going to be looking for me soon," Maisie said. "And I won't have time to talk to you again until after the investment, so please listen to me." I met her eyes to let her know that she had my full attention. "I need to apologize to you for how I behaved on the night of the drawing. I must have been out of my mind to treat you that way. When you ran from me, I realized how much I must have scared and hurt you. I wanted to call you back, but . . ."

"It's all right," I said.

"No, it *isn't*. You are my sister. My best friend. Sometimes I think my only real friend. The way I treated you, the way I treated the entire family, was unforgiveable."

"I can't speak for the rest of the family, but as far as I'm concerned, you're forgiven."

"You sure do live up to your name, don't you," she said, leaning in to kiss my cheek. "You have no idea what your forgiveness means to me." She paused. "You know, some of the family felt that the line had chosen you as anchor and I was stealing its power from you."

I laughed. "I am pretty darned sure that the line never intended me to be anchor. And frankly, even if it did, both of us know that you're the better choice. I know Ginny shared things with you that she shouldn't have, but maybe it's for the best. You've been training for this your whole life, and you're going to be the best anchor the line has ever known."

"So you're saying that you wouldn't object to the power falling to me even if you were the one who was selected? I don't care what the others think, but I need to know that you don't feel that I'm stealing from you."

"You," I said, "are stealing nothing from me. Anybody who thinks otherwise will see how wrong they are after you've had time to settle in as anchor. You are going to be wonderful."

"Thank you," Maisie said and kissed me once more. "I can feel the others tugging at me," she said. "I need to go join them, but when all of this is over, I want the two of us to take a couple of days to talk about what happened with Connor," she said and held up her hand to fend off any protest I might make. "You need to be able to tell someone exactly how much you hate him for what he did, and Iris is not going to be up for that. And given Wren's involvement in the whole thing, we should spare Ellen and Oliver as well. They created and nurtured a murderer. They may be acting like they don't feel horrible about that fact, but they're just trying to shield you from any further pain. Now, I've got to go."

"Wait!" I said, reaching out and grabbing her skirt like a little kid. She looked down at me with an amused expression on her face. "There's something important I need to tell you."

"Okay, but make it fast."

"No," I said, letting go of her. "You go on, it can wait." I smiled at her, and she shimmered and disappeared right before my eyes.

Soon the investment would be over, and we'd have the rest of our lives to catch up. "We can wait to tell her about you, can't we, buddy?" I asked, placing my hand over my stomach. "You are well worth waiting for."

THIRTY-TWO

The drawing of the lots had taken place thirteen days after Ginny's death, and the investment ceremony would take place today, thirteen days later. Oliver's prediction had been spot on—other than the few minutes I'd shared with Maisie upon her arrival, the families had kept her pretty much sequestered. What she'd told me had surprised me. I couldn't believe that some of our family members truly believed that the line had truly chosen me as anchor. I chuckled to myself as I finished packing an overnight bag for my stay at the Mansion, not my ratty old backpack, but one of Ellen's fancy, honest-to-God overnight bags. She had blanched when I'd told her I was planning on taking my backpack and had practically flung the thing at me. And even though we only lived about ten blocks from the hotel, Oliver had arranged for a town car to pick me up.

There was a rap at my door. "Your coach awaits, Cinderella," Oliver's voice called out to me.

"Tell the driver I'll be right down." My own reflection caught me by surprise as I grabbed my bag and headed for the door. The woman I saw in the mirror looked happy. In spite of everything that had happened over the past several days, I honestly felt like it would all turn out okay. Once the investment was over, I'd spend time with Maisie. We'd catch up and finish working things out. And then I'd get Iris away from here for a while. My first installment from the trust had hit my checking account on my birthday, and I was astounded by the size of it. There was plenty enough to take us to Paris, or maybe Florence. It would do us both good.

Uncle Oliver had decided to relocate his business to Savannah. He was staying home for good this time. That would be good for all of us, especially Ellen. Oliver might be a tad self-centered, but he would look out for her until she was back on an even keel. Peter, well, we'd work things out. Whether or not we got back together, we'd raise our boy right. Colin Taylor Tierney would be a blessing to this family—he'd be the new start that we all so badly needed. I smiled at my reflection and went down to meet the car. I gave Oliver a quick peck on the cheek on my way out, then winked at the driver as he took the bag from my hand and opened the door for me.

"It's only a few blocks," I said. "It feels downright decadent."

"Nothing wrong with a little decadence now and again. Enjoy it, ma'am." After closing the door behind me and stowing my bag in the trunk, he got into the driver's seat and pulled out onto the street, showing much more care than the casual driver. "Scenic route?" he called back to me, glancing at me in his rearview mirror.

"Please," I said. He turned the car in the opposite direction of the Mansion and zigzagged around so that he could circle the six closest squares.

As we neared Pulaski Square, he looked at me in the mirror again. "Oh, I almost forgot," he said, handing me a small but beautifully wrapped package over the seat. "Your sister asked me to give this to you."

"Thank you," I said and took it from him. The box was covered in velvety midnight blue paper and tied with a single silver bow.

I undid the bow and tugged open the box. On top was a note from Maisie. I unfolded it and read. "Even if you can't be here with me, I'll be able to feel your presence if you wear this."

"Everything all right back there?" the driver asked.

"Yes. Everything is perfect," I smiled up at him then took the necklace out from the box, kissing the beautiful stone that I recognized as azurite. Rounded and polished, it looked like a small globe of the world. As I slipped the chain around my neck, I closed my eyes and held the stone tightly in my hand, thinking of Maisie and sending her all my love.

When I opened my eyes, the driver was still looking at me in the rearview mirror, but his brown eyes had changed to a sapphire blue. The face beneath the driver's cap had morphed into a completely different one. I'd know those eyes anywhere. That face. "Jackson?" I said, gasping.

"She told you I'd be back," he said, throwing me a grin over his shoulder. His eyes were gleeful, crazed, and full of hate. I reached over to try the door, but it was locked.

"I don't understand," I said. He turned the car onto Barnard and sped across Liberty Street with the gas pressed to the floor. I screamed as he pulled into oncoming traffic.

He laughed as the vehicles passed right through our car—and us—without so much as a tickle. "Well, I'll be glad to explain a few things to you. Starting with how we're just a little out of sync with the world you're used to right now. Those charms your buddy the golem set up for you ain't gonna work here. And you can try and run away from me if you'd like, but you'll never get home without me. See, I kind of like it here. We can see and hear what's going on in the other world, but nothing and no one there can touch us. Unless that someone happens to be wearing the mate of that necklace you just put around your pretty little neck. Care to guess who that might be?"

"Maisie," I said, once again astounded by my own stupidity, my willingness to be deceived.

"That's right, my girl," he said, continuing to drive. The familiar landmarks we were passing surprised me—we were heading back in the direction we'd come from. "Your sister set you up."

"But why?" I asked.

"That's a bit of a long story, but I guess we got the time for it. Unless you'd rather I smear blood on your head and toss you to the shadows like you and Jilo did to me?" He looked back over his shoulder at me again.

"All I ever did was love you, Jackson. That's what we did to Wren, not you . . . we had to stop him, " I said.

"You just don't get it, do you, girl?" he asked. "I *am* Wren."

"You're Wren?" I asked, completely thrown.

"That's right," he chirped in Wren's falsetto, before his voice broke back into Jackson's range. "And thanks to your sister, I was finally able to break out of that way too small shell. Maisie helped me grow." He winked at me. "Of course that's what any good woman should help her man do, but in this case, I mean it literally."

As I sat back in wonder, we pulled up in front of my house. It looked fairly quiet from the front, but I knew a world of activity was going on inside. He stopped the car and got out. "Shall we go back in and say hello to the family?" he asked. Flinging my door open, he yanked me out roughly, doing his best to hurt me. I didn't resist; I let myself coast on his energy, going with the flow instead of fighting.

We walked straight through the door without stopping to open it. I found myself wishing that I'd never told my family that Jilo had linked her realm to the linen closet. If the portal had still existed, I might have been able to use it to escape. The thought of escaping to Jilo's realm instead of from it struck me as funny, and in spite of my fear, or maybe because of it, I began to laugh.

Jackson shook me like I was a rag doll. "You think this is funny, do you? Well, you'll stop laughing when you see what we have planned for you."

My laughter dried up under his hateful gaze. Iris and Oliver passed in front of us, so close that I could have reached out and touched them. I started to call out to them, but the strength of Jackson's grip made me think twice. It was his turn to laugh. "Go ahead," he said, shoving me aside. "Scream! Nobody's going to hear you."

He jumped right in front of Oliver's face. "Hey, faggot! Can your niece get a little help here?" Oliver passed directly through him, and Jackson doubled over with laughter. "I guess we'll have to take that as a no." He pushed me into the library through the foyer wall, and I landed at the foot of the love seat. "Interesting, isn't it? You can walk right through walls, but the floor is still holding you up. That, Mercy, is because you are working magic. You're so sure that the floor is going to support you that it does. Your magic is what's holding you up." He reached down and tugged me up. "Have a seat if you want. I'm sure your magic will let you, and you'll look a little less ridiculous than you do right now."

I bent my knees until I could feel the material of the love seat underneath me. It felt tangible and real, and it held my weight. "You're wrong," I said, despite all evidence to the contrary. "I have no power. I can't do magic."

"Oh, spare me the sad tale," he bellowed. "And let me tell you a little story of my own." He dragged a chair in front me and straddled it, putting us nearly nose to nose. The eyes looking out of his face weren't human, the blue in them cold flames.

"Once upon a time," he began, "there was a very wicked witch named Ginny and a whore named Emily. Now the whore slept with a whole bunch of men. But only one of them was special to her. Problem was, this man already belonged to her sister. Now I know this might sound familiar to you, but you just hang in there with me." He winked at me. "The whore knew that her sister's husband wanted children, and for some reason her sister had only managed to give him one. Of course you and I both know that the wicked witch had put an end to the babies, because she was afraid that the children born from of the combination of these particular bloodlines could overpower her, reuniting the thirteen families and turning her back into the nothing she knew herself to be. When the wicked witch learned that the whore had gotten herself knocked up, she bided her time. She pretended to believe that the father of the bastard children was the husband of the whore's other sister, but she knew the truth all along.

"She knew that the boy born from the legitimate union was powerful but that he posed no real threat. The one who'd been foreseen was a girl. All sugar and spice and sweet and pink as you please. Well, when the witch realized that the whore was going to give birth to two girls, she started to pay a lot of attention. She sensed that the first one wasn't going to be much of a problem. She had power, all right, but not nearly enough to rock the boat. The second one, though, well, she was something special, even for a Taylor witch. Ginny knew that this was the one whose coming had been foretold, and she was not about to let her live to see the light of day.

"She did all she could to end the pregnancies, but that second little one, she was just too strong. She kept both herself and her sister alive and unharmed. And Ginny could feel the little one's power increasing with each passing day. So she hijacked the power. She had to do it in steps; first she started feeding it from the strong sister to the weaker one and then, once she'd managed to get the energy flowing away from its owner, she sent it away. She grounded it in another dimension, close enough that she could access it herself, but far enough away that it could pass right through a Taylor witch without him or her ever noticing. As a matter of fact, it's all around us right now. This was where Ginny sent your power. She did her best to starve you to death, and it might have worked if your Aunt Ellen hadn't given you the boost you needed to survive delivery."

Ginny had stolen my power and tried to kill me. No wonder my mother didn't survive our birth. I had a whole new pack of reasons to grieve, but the knowledge that I wasn't responsible for my mama's death was like a wave of absolution, freeing me of the guilt that I had carried for as long as I could remember. Oddly, this was one of the happiest moments of my life.

Suddenly the proportions of the room shifted, and Maisie was standing directly in front of me. Jackson was several yards away, hanging at an angle that should have been impossible but wasn't.

"She kept me under her thumb," Maisie continued Jackson's narrative seamlessly. "Not because I was some kind of prodigy, but because she saw me as a time bomb. Picture my surprise last year when I stumbled across her old journals. She kept such careful notes about me. She should have shown more care in keeping them hidden. Breaking the charms on them was child's play. She couldn't undo the siphon of power she'd set up between us. She couldn't just take what she had been pumping into me and shift it somewhere else. She had inadvertently turned me into an anchor for your power. If the power started flowing back to you, the whole dam would have eventually burst, and she was prepared to stop at nothing to keep that from happening. You would be astounded to know just how much she hated you. She wrote about trying to find a way to bend time. To go back and prevent your ever having been conceived."

"She was crazy. She had to be, but Maisie, how can you be doing this to me? You have got to stop this. You've got to let me go."

"No, actually, I don't. You see, this is how I'm going to finally get my revenge against Ginny. And you."

"Against me? But for what?"

"For stealing my life! Ginny trained your power into me. She turned me into a freak."

"At least she loved you," I said, not even knowing anymore if that was true. Could Ginny have really loved Maisie and used her as she had?

"As a reflection of her own twisted self, maybe, but not for any other reason. She didn't let me out of her sight, and there you were, roaming free, making friends, meeting boys, finding love." She grimaced at me. "I got to watch as you won the heart of the only man I could ever love."

I started to protest that Jackson wasn't even actually real, just a twisted, grown-up version of Wren when the dots suddenly connected. "Peter," I said.

"Yes, Peter!" Maisie replied, anger spilling over in her voice. "Haven't you noticed, Mercy? Most regular men won't even come near us. And even witches are afraid of me because of this thing Ginny turned me into. I could never figure out why, but Peter is completely unfazed by the magic. It flows right over him, and he doesn't even care. He could have loved me . . . and he would have if you weren't around. I tried to take him from you, and the damnedest thing is that he never even noticed I was trying. I didn't want to be alone anymore."

"So you took Wren and started transforming him into Jackson."

"Yes," Maisie admitted, shaking her head. "I did, but it took a lot more energy than I possessed. It took *your* kind of power. A

part of you recognized your own energy in him, and you inter-
preted those feelings as love."

"Now that's ironic, isn't it?" Jackson asked. The distance between us had dissolved, and he was standing right by my side. He
leaned in and kissed my cheek, then forced his lips on mine.
Repulsed, I pulled back.

"Everything was going great for a while, but Ginny realized
what I had done," Maisie said. "She couldn't tell the family, so she
decided to dissolve Wren on her own."

"She summoned me there, thinking she could control me."
Jackson said. "But she couldn't. I really enjoyed killing her."

"But what do you get from all this?" I asked Jackson.

"I get to live. I get to live in your world, and that's all I have
ever wanted."

"When the anchor energy settles on me—the same power you
told me just yesterday that you'd give me of your own free will—
I'll finally be strong enough to undo what Ginny has done. I'll
unground the power that she stole from you, and with it, I'll help
Jackson fully and finally actualize in our world. And then I won't
just anchor the line, I'll take control of it. I'll bring the thirteen
families back together, all right, but they'll be under my thumb.
And when I'm firmly in control of our reality, I'll make Peter love
me too."

"But if you unground my power, what's to keep it from coming back to me?" I asked and was chilled by the look on my sister's
face. She was astounded.

"You don't get it do you? When I unground your power, there
won't be a *you* for it to flow back into." I was too stunned to speak.
"I'm out of time here," she said, addressing Jackson. "Get her
ready and make sure she's in the correct position."

As far as I could tell, I didn't move an inch, but I was suddenly
naked and tied to one of the trees that grew in the garden of my

own home. My hands were pulled up and tied above my head, a second band of coarse hemp secured me tightly by the waist, and a third was above my knees. The bark of the tree was rough and it dug into the skin of my back. Worse than that was the coarseness of the rope that held me in place.

Jackson stood beside me, smiling beatifically at me. "What a beautiful martyr you'll make," he said.

Witches milled around us, walked right through Jackson without even noticing that we were there. Mere yards away I could see Emmet talking to Ellen. Maisie walked over to join them, and Ellen leaned in and whispered something in her ear. An expression of surprised anger flitted across Maisie's face, but she hid it quickly, smiling and hugging our aunt.

Jackson leered at me as he used his pointer finger to draw symbols and designs on my body with a warm, sticky liquid. Even if I'd been blind, its scent would have told me that it was blood, and I found myself saying a prayer for the spirit of whatever poor creature had been sacrificed. "Your sister is something else, ain't she?" he asked. "It was pretty amazing the way she handled Connor. He came close to cocking up the whole works when he figured out that Ginny had been sharing her secrets. Maisie managed to deal with him from another dimension without anyone being one bit the wiser."

"The fire," I said.

"That's right," Jackson beamed at me. "Had to be fire, 'cause we knew it would take him out without harming you. We needed to keep you alive for the ceremony today."

"But how could you know that the fire elementals wouldn't harm me?" I asked.

"The protective charms the golem set for you included protection from fire, natural or magical. But in my opinion, the charm was unnecessary. If anyone, including you, had the slightest idea of who you really are, or what you're really made of, they would have realized there was no need to protect you from flames. Suffice it to say, the fire recognized you as its own. From the looks of things, it healed you up nicer than even Ellen could have. The way you were laid out on that floor, I figured your walking days were over."

"I can't believe she's doing this." I was talking to myself, but he answered me all the same.

"Oh, believe it," he said. "But don't you worry, she isn't going to get quite the outcome she's expecting, so you'll get the last laugh in the end. Well, on second thought, you won't, 'cause I'll have to kill you before you can have that laugh, but you've been such a good girl, and I'm feeling generous.

"When it comes right down to it, lies are pretty simple. It's the truth that's complicated. It's like an onion, and there's always another layer if you keep peeling." He chuckled to himself as he continued making marks on my body. He stopped suddenly. "Well what have we here?" he asked after a moment. "Looks like I'm going to get two for one this time."

I knew he had sensed Colin, and I felt a deep sense of mourning for my child, who'd never even be born. Tears started streaming down my face, and Jackson wiped them away with his bloody fingers.

"Oh, there, there," Jackson said. "You won't live to give birth to this one, but through your death, you'll become the mother of thousands. You've seen your children, Mercy—my brothers and sisters—when you passed through their world on your way to visit Jilo."

"You're . . . you're one of the shadows," I managed through my tears.

"Yes," he said, then placed a gentle kiss on my lips. "Imagine how it felt to almost be destroyed by my own kind. The sweet blood you wiped on me. It excited them, confused them. If they hadn't been so starved and I so well fed, they might have ripped me apart before they knew what they were doing. See, you are much smarter than that sister of yours. She never even questioned that I might be something other than a little fellow your uncle dreamed up." He gave me a thumbs-up and a beaming smile that revealed his straight white teeth. "I have to tell you, we've been waiting for this day for millennia. Your birth, Ginny's intervention. It was nothing less than miraculous. We want so badly to live in your world, Mercy. But there's only enough power for a few of us to get out at a time. When the witches activated the line, we got trapped between worlds, neither entirely in the world the witches created, nor wholly in the one they left behind. When the tunnels near Candler Hospital were dug, they filled up with such sweet despair and misery that we were drawn to them, but even feeding off all of that exquisite agony didn't allow us to draw a fraction of the power we needed to pierce the veil. There were too many of us, and the line was too strong.

"So we've bided our time. Only a few of us could break free at once, and even then only for a little while. We learned that we could draw strength from the dreams of sleeping humans, and eventually we began to meet magic workers who would assist us in return for performing small favors for them. They'd give us skins that we could use to walk in your world, but the skins never lasted for long."

"The shadows are boo hags?" I asked, every bit as surprised as if he'd told me they were leprechauns.

"Yes, that's what we've come to be called in the low country, but we've had a lot of different names. Heck, you couldn't even pronounce our real name if I told you. There, finished," he said, then stuck his finger back into the blood and licked it. He tossed the container to the ground. "I got real lucky one day when I met an up-and-coming root doctor named Mother Jilo Wills. She promised me that if I kept an eye on you Taylors and reported back to her, she'd teach me how to weave my own flesh. She'd find a way to feed me enough energy so that I'd never have to go back to the world between.

"Her plan started with tricking the Taylor child named Oliver into believing that I was his special friend. After that, his desire to keep me around would be enough to hold me in your world. Oh, how proud your grandparents were of Wren. They took me as proof positive that their Oliver was the brightest and most powerful little witch ever. I could draw enough energy off the little bastard to live quite well for a while," he said, standing back to admire the drawings he had made on my body.

"But all little ones must grow up, and soon Oliver lost interest in me. With Jilo's help, I managed to hang on through the dry spell, but it was like living off grass after years of feeding on cow. Things started looking up when your cousin Paul was born, and then when your mother gave birth to you. Ginny did her best to ground your energy here, but she did a rather sloppy job of it, leaving a bit leaking off here, a little leaking off there. Feeding off your power, I was able to grow strong. You see, ever since you came into the world, you're the one who has made my existence possible. You should be proud, for I am every bit as much your child as that clot in your womb. Soon your other children are going to burst free from their prison too. And it is truly all thanks to you and your fantastically screwed up family."

He held up a dagger before my eyes. "This is the blade that will end your life. Don't worry, it's sharp, and I promise to make it as quick and painless as I can. Your death is the grand finale to your sister's plan, you see. As soon as the investment ceremony takes place and the anchor energy settles into her, she will signal me, and I will drive this blade into your heart. At that very moment she'll free your magic, and it will unite itself with the closest match to your living blood. In the end, it always comes down to blood, doesn't it?" he asked.

"Maisie thinks that she'll be the closest match, but . . . well, now we've reached the part of my plan that is probably going to be the most unpleasant for you." He took the dagger and sunk the tip of its blade just above my breast. I screamed out from pain, and then from revulsion, as he pressed his lips to the wound, sucking the blood from my flesh.

"I need to do this at each one of these points," he said, touching a few of the places he had marked on my body. Then he made a quick swipe of the blade at each of them, pressing his mouth to the wounds and drawing in deeply. He moaned in pleasure. "Oh, girl, you do taste good," he said, his teeth red behind his bloody lips. "Your blood burns in me," he said, growing intoxicated. His lips sought out the wounds over and over again, and my vision began to blur from the pain and blood loss. And then he suddenly pulled away.

The sounds I could hear from the other dimension weren't fully audible and were out of sync with the visual images I could perceive, but even though my strength was sapped and my senses were weakened, I could tell that the investment ceremony had started. I felt the sharp blade of Jackson's dagger poise itself directly above my heart.

I heard Maisie's voice scream the word "stop" once, twice, and then a third time. Then everything turned to fire.

I felt the power of the line reject Maisie. The ground in both worlds quaked as its energy reverberated around her, causing her image to shimmer like a mirage. Then, in the blink of an eye, she was gone.

The witches who had formed the circle around her looked shocked and horrified, but they held to their discipline, keeping their hands linked together. From the middle of the circle rose up the most beautiful ball of light I had ever seen. It turned at an angle that wasn't possible in a world with only three dimensions and removed itself from their reality. The ball brushed against Emmet's side as it disappeared from the witches' world and entered into mine, growing ever larger and shining ever brighter.

I could still feel the point of Jackson's blade pressed into my flesh, and with one last desperate move, he tried to stab me. But the orb expanded around us, burning into the shadow that had masqueraded as Jackson. A roar of flames drowned out his cries of rage and anguish and vexation as he disappeared into ash. The dagger he had been holding fell to the ground before me, landing blade first in the earth.

There was a brilliant flash of light, an effulgence that took over my body, and I felt the power of the line enter me, but before it could entirely settle in me, before I could even acknowledge the rapture pulsing inside, a second wave hit me—my own power. I was drowned by a feeling that lay somewhere between ecstasy and coming home.

When the light faded, when the elation subsided, I was no longer tied to the tree. I was in the center of the circle of thunderstruck witches, on a patch of burned earth that would never again grow a blade of grass.

THIRTY-THREE

"I ran into Peter this morning," Ellen said as she unloaded a bag of organic fruit and vegetables from the farmer's market onto the kitchen table. "He was walking on cloud nine. He's ecstatic that you're letting him take you in for the baby's first sonogram."

"He's Colin's father. Of course he's going to be there," I said.

Iris entered the kitchen with another bag of groceries and set it on the counter. "Well, call me old-fashioned, but if you're going to marry the boy, I sure wish you'd do it before little Colin is born. It would be nice if both of his parents had the same last name on the birth certificate."

"Stop pressuring her," Oliver said, coming in on Iris's heels. "The other nine families pester her plenty enough about taking over anchor duties. She doesn't need any pressure from us."

"Thank you, Uncle Oliver," I said and with a snap of my fingers, I put away the groceries they'd carried in.

"Now you are just showing off," Iris said, barely able to suppress a smile.

"Emmet says it's good practice to start with the little things first," I responded, crossing my arms and sticking out my tongue.

"You keep practicing like that, and it'll be your butt growing, not your abilities," Iris said and made a playful swipe at me with a dish towel.

"About Emmet," Oliver said in a serious tone. "Are you sure you're okay with spending time alone with him? I mean, aren't you a little weirded out by him?"

When the power of the line had brushed past Emmet on its way to me, it had broken the nine intelligences he'd embodied off from their sources and had somehow melded them together into a single consciousness. Emmet was no longer a mere golem. He might not exactly be a real man, but for all intents and purposes he was close enough. I wasn't sure if he had what you might call a soul, but who was I to judge?

"No," I replied. "I was a little weirded out by him before, but now he seems *right* to me. And he's the best teacher I could have hoped for," I said. After all, he had maintained the knowledge of each of his nine creators.

After the investment, my aunts, uncle, and I had made a pact: no more lies or secrets, even if they were well-intentioned. I decided that the present would be as good a time as any to live up to my side of the bargain. "Listen, y'all. I've been thinking about something. Well, more than thinking about it . . . I've been working with Emmet on it."

"And what might this 'it' be?" Iris asked, folding her arms and leaning back against the sink.

"I want to find Maisie," I managed to say before the others piled up on me.

"The families will never allow it," Ellen said, as if that should be the end of it.

"To hell with the families," I responded. "I mean it. To hell with what they want and with what they'll allow."

"Gingersnap," Oliver said, "you have to think about what's best for you and your baby. We all loved Maisie, but you have to realize she's probably dead. And even if she isn't, I'm not sure you'd recognize what's left of her as Maisie."

"It's out of the question," Iris said. "She was going to sacrifice you. She lost her place in this family and her right to be in this world."

"You said she tried to stop the investment at the last minute," I said. "I heard her ask you all to stop it. I don't believe she was capable of going through with her plans. You said something to her, Ellen. Right before. Something that changed her mind. What was it?"

Ellen looked at me, the corner of her mouth twitching as she spoke. "I told her that you and Peter were having a baby."

"From what you've told us, Mercy," Oliver said, "she may not have tried to stop the ceremony to save you. Maybe she just had second thoughts about harming Peter's child."

"I see," I said, pushing my chair away from the table. "If you will all excuse me for a moment, I think I could use a little time alone."

"You go on, sugar," Iris said. "If you need anything, you call out, okay? I'll be right there for you."

Oliver had dedicated himself full time to clearing, cleaning, and painting the room across the hall from mine, getting it ready to serve as Colin's nursery. Toys—some old, some new—lined a shelf that Peter had mounted the previous weekend. Peter's old fire engine had pride of place, and I found myself unable to resist the urge to add something of my own to sit by its side.

I crossed the hall to my room and dug out the box of toys I'd been saving ever since I'd outgrown them myself. As I rifled through it, the old Ball jar Maisie had given me for our birthday pressed itself into my hand. I pulled it free. Inside danced the flames of the nineteen memories that Maisie had captured for me before the drawing of the lots, back when I had still believed she loved me in spite of my selfish heart. I opened the lid and watched as they flew out. With trepidation I reached out and touched the closest. I found myself sitting in this very same room at an incredibly small table. Maisie and I were having a tea party for the new dolls Aunt Ellen and "Uncle" Erik had brought us from their vacation in Europe. The memory faded.

I reached out again, this time with more determination, and touched a spark that seemed to be trying to escape me. Warmth flooded through me, and I relived the experience of my first dance recital with my sister. Our performances were laughable, but we were both certain that we were destined to be ballerinas when we grew up. It was written in the stars. And then it was over.

I looked at the remaining flames and gasped. It took a moment for me to realize that it wasn't just my imagination—they had lined up in a single row and were moving away from me. No, they weren't just moving away from me, they were trying to lead me to Maisie. As the realization hit me, the flames flew back to me and danced around me. "All right," I said. "But for now, I need to wait." The flames obediently returned to the jar. I closed the lid on them and returned the jar to the box of toys, burying it deep inside the closet.

I would go to her, and I would find a way to bring her back. I didn't know how we had gone so wrong, but in spite of everything I still loved her, and somehow I'd find a way to set things right. But first I needed to learn how to control not only my own powers, but those of the line. If I was going to go find my sister, I was sure that I'd have to go through the nine other families, and maybe even my own as well.

THIRTY-FOUR

"Jilo been wonderin' when you were goin' to come for her," the old woman said when she spotted me entering Bonaventure.

"And when I came for you, you figured I'd be bringing flowers," I said, lifting the bouquet I'd brought with me up so that she could see it. I dismounted my bike and began to walk it.

"No, Jilo reckon as not," she said, falling in step next to me. I slowed my pace so that she could keep up with me comfortably. After a few steps she took a breath and said. "I didn't know what your sister was up to. I thought that Jackson was for real. Jilo didn't know he had anything to do with that worthless boo hag."

"I know that," I said and kept walking.

"And I didn't know that the power Ginny gave me in that stone was yours. I didn't know that I was stealing from anybody, especially you."

"And if you had known, would you have accepted it anyway?" I asked.

"Damn girl, you know I would have," she said, and we both stopped dead in our tracks and laughed. Her laugh dissolved into a hacking cough, and it took a few moments for her to compose herself. "I don't have much time left here in this world, Mercy. Don't make me spend what I got left watching over my shoulder for you. You want to get even with this old woman, you do it here. You do it now."

I pulled a rose from the bouquet and handed it to her. "I got no need for revenge. I figure there has been more than enough hurt hanging around me lately."

"Well, you tell me, girl. You tell me what I can do to make it right to you."

"All right," I said. "First of all, leave those poor souls at Candler alone. I just heard that it's been bought for use as a law school. I'm going to do my best to free the spirits before that tragedy befalls them."

"All right, I'll do that for you, even though it means you are leaving Mother Jilo dry."

"Well, we can't have that," I said, and I held out my hand, palm facing up. A pearl of energy began to form in my hand, and I let it grow to the size of a golf ball before handing it to her. "A little gift for your crossroads," I said, but then snapped it back from her quivering reach. "This one comes with a couple of conditions though."

She grimaced and gave me a sour look but concluded, "Okay, name them."

"One," I said as I dropped the ball into her outstretched palm. "No killing."

"Okay, there goes half my business, but you've got me between a rock and hard place. What's the second?"

"Two, if someone comes back to you and tells you they've changed their mind, you had better let them, you hear me?"

"I hear you," she responded, her eyes gleaming as she stared at the luminous ball in her hand.

"Good, now get on out of here and leave me and my family alone," I said, trying to hide a smile as she turned from me and hobbled off toward the cemetery's gate.

"Come on, Martell," I heard her addressing what appeared to be thin air. "Now Granny gone be able to make it so folk can see you again."

I turned away and carried on toward the river. Section K was where my people were buried, just on the far side of Evergreen Circle. I curved off Bonaventure Way and followed down Tattnall, taking in the live oaks and blocking out the sound of the lawnmowers that were busy growling from one grave to another.

I wasn't even sure what had brought me here today, but I had an overpowering desire to introduce my as yet unborn son to his great-grandparents, whom I myself had never met. Even more than that, though, I wanted to be near my own mother. Regardless of her faults or her sins, I wanted—no, needed—to be near her grave and to tell her about Maisie, ask her advice about Peter, and give her a chance to say hello to Colin. Part of me felt like I was being foolish. I'd never felt her spirit lingering, and I knew that she was one of the souls Savannah had let escape her grasp.

I found my way to their graves and leaned my bike on its kickstand. I split the bouquet into three separate bundles, a few for my grandfather, a few for my grandmother, and the lion's share for my mama.

"Mama," I said, taking a seat on the ground above her grave. "I'd like you to meet your grandson Colin." I smiled as I put my hand over my stomach. "He isn't very big yet, but he's starting to show a little." I paused to watch the play of light and shadow as the wind blew through the live oaks, and unconsciously I crossed my arms, hugging myself, hugging my child.

"I don't know quite how I'm going to do it, Mama, but I'm going to make this world a better place for him," I said. "Peter and I will work something out, somehow. He's a good man. I know it. He made one monumentally poor decision, but I will learn to look past it. I'll forgive him and forget." I smiled at her headstone.

"He's your grandbaby's father, so I've got to find some way to do it."

I took advantage of my unhurried solitude to probe my feelings for Peter once again. And that was where I found my answer. "It does help that I love him," I said. An unexpected happiness rushed up through me. "Colin deserves to have his father, and I don't think I could ever see myself settling down with anyone besides Peter anyway." The truth spoken, I pulled my knees up to my chest, and sat there enjoying the moment of peace that this revelation had brought me.

Then I remembered Maisie. I leaned over and placed my hand on my mother's marker. All my life, this had been the only physical contact I could have with her. This time the gesture was a hug, a childish tug at her skirt, and a scream at waking from a bad dream all rolled into one. The nightmare was over, all except for the cleanup. "I am going to find some way to fix this entire mess, Mama. I'll find Maisie." My voice failed me as I said her name. "I promise you that," I said more firmly. "And I will take care of her. I know things have gone badly between us," I said and then laughed. "Well I guess you know that is a bit of an understatement. But don't you worry. I will fix things."

The smell of the river was carried over to me on a breeze, and my thoughts turned from Maisie toward the rest of my family. "I will look after Iris too. And Ellen." The two of them had been doing their best to hide their pain from me, pouring all of their energies into preparing for Colin's arrival. "They've both lost the people they loved most on this earth. I don't know what I can do for them yet, but I'll figure something out to get them back on track. Uncle Oliver too. He may not show it, but he's as lost as the rest of them."

Somehow I was going to do all of this and still find a way to work with the other witch families who had been hounding me

284

since the moment the line's energy had taken me. "I am almost ready to take over as anchor. It's time for me to grow up, I guess. No more Liar's Tours," I said. "No more lies at all. I'll make you proud of me, Mama. That's not to say I'm just going to do as I'm told. I'm going to do things my own way. I have to believe that the line chose me because it wants something different going forward. If it had wanted more of the same, it had plenty of that to choose from. I'm not just going to pick up where Ginny left off."

The thought of my great-aunt stirred up a whole brew of conflicting emotions, most of them bad. Anger, a desire for revenge. I did not deny that the feelings were there; I acknowledged their presence, but I would not give in to them. Yes, I had been wronged, but I was never going to find happiness for my family or myself if I focused my energies on that. I knew what that meant, even if I didn't like it.

"I'm going to forgive Ginny too," I said. I knew from what had happened with Maisie that forgiveness was not a one-time act. It was a decision to move on and focus on a person's good features each time the hurt over what they've done crept back up on you. Ginny hadn't left me much to work with. "It's going to take me a while, but I will not let her poison live on in me," I assured my mama. "Somehow, I will move past what she did to me, what she did to us," I said and then realized out loud, "and I guess today is as good of a day to start as any."

I stood and brushed the earth from my skirt. "I'm going to say good-bye for now, Mama, but I'll be back real soon," I said. I reached down and removed a single rose from the flowers I had put on my mother's grave. "I'm gonna go and spend a little time with Ginny now. She always did love roses." Flower in hand, I hopped back on my bike. I pedaled farther down toward the river, where I turned left and headed up to Greenwich Cemetery.

ACKNOWLEDGMENTS

I would like to thank my agent, Susan Finesman of Fine Literary, as well as the amazing team at 47North, especially David Pomerico and Angela Polidoro. Thanks also to my literary midwife, Kristen Weber, and to my niece, Tara Rockey, who helped me by reading way too many versions of this story. Finally, much love to my three furry co-authors: Quentin Comfort, Duke, and Sugar.

ABOUT THE AUTHOR

J.D. Horn was raised in rural Tennessee, and has since carried a bit of its red clay with him while travelling the world, from Hollywood to Paris to Tokyo. He studied comparative literature as an undergrad, focusing on French and Russian in particular. He also holds an MBA in international business and worked as a financial analyst before becoming a novelist. When not writing he is likely running, and he has race bibs from two full marathons and about thirty half marathons. He and his spouse, Rich (proud father of Rebecca and Madeline), and their three pets split their time between Portland, Oregon, and San Francisco, California.